PETER STAMM was born in 1963, in Sche[...] the author of the novels *Agnes, On a D[...]scape, Seven Years* and the collection *In Strange Gardens and Other Stories*, as well as numerous short stories and radio plays. He lives in Winterthur. This collection was shortlisted for the Frank O'Connor International Short Story Award 2012.

MICHAEL HOFMANN has translated the works of many writers, including Franz Kafka, Joseph Roth and Hans Fallada. He teaches at the University of Florida in Gainesville.

'The problem with this bleak but brilliant story collection is that it's too hard to put down . . . Stamm's ability to explore dark secrets and lead them towards the light of reason may be cool, even clinical, but it is never completely heartless and is always unforgettable'
Irish Times

'These stories hint at emotion beneath the page with a compelling, regular insistence. Distinct craft is at work. Stamm's prose (in Michael Hofmann's fine translation) is unadorned and riveting'
Literary Review

'[A] superb, imaginatively challenging collection'
Times Literary Supplement

'Stamm has a style perfectly adapted to short stories, with abrupt dialogue and an endless supply of eye-catching opening lines. He's clinical but not aloof from the complexity of human emotions'
Metro

'Stamm's sharp observation and ability engage the reader immediately . . . [*We're Flying* leaves] a trailing vapour of wondering long after the book has been put back on the shelf' *Scotsman*

'[Stamm] is one of those rare writers whose words haunt his readers long after you put his books down'
Yiyun Li, author of *A Thousand Years of Good Prayers*

'His language cannot be faulted and his characters root in the mind. This thoughtful and thought-provoking collection deserves to be widely read'
Hampshire Chronicle

'Sharp and unadorned . . . It is a testament to Stamm's use of the short story medium and Hofmann's capacities as a translator that two elements – the psychological drama of everyday life and broad philosophical themes of the European tradition – are seamlessly held together . . . Excellent' *Full Stop*

'[These] tautly constructed stories, with echoes of Patricia Highsmith and Anton Chekhov, take root in the psyche and will not let go' *Library Journal*

'Precise, disquieting, and high-impact, Stamm's new collection slices away surface tissue to reveal the downright messiness of human life . . . Fascinating'
Three Percent Review

'Skilful and refined . . . Stamm's name deserves to be up there with great masters of the genre'
Wiltshire Society

'A master storyteller, Stamm succeeds in stripping away layers of superficiality to uncover the complicated daily psychological struggle of the average person. Michael Hofmann deserves credit for his emotionally taut translation . . . Simultaneously haunting and uplifting'
World Literature Today

WE'RE FLYING

— Stories —

PETER STAMM

Translated from the German by MICHAEL HOFMANN

GRANTA

Granta Publications, 12 Addison Avenue, London W11 4QR

First published in Great Britain as an ebook by Granta Books 2012
Hardback edition published 2013
This paperback edition published 2015

Published by arrangement with Other Press, New York, USA

The first part of this work was originally published in German as *Wir Fliegen*
by S. Fischer Verlag, Frankfurt am Main, 2008.
The second part was originally published in German as *Seerücken* by S. Fischer Verlag,
Frankfurt am Main, 2011.

The translator would like to thank the Canton of Wallis/Valais for the award of
residency in Raron, where this translation was completed.

Several stories in this collection have previously appeared elsewhere: "The Suitcase"
in *Subtropics* 14, Spring/Summer 2012; "Sweet Dreams" in *The New Yorker*, May 14, 2012;
"Expectations" in *Guernica*, May 15, 2012; and "We're Flying" in *A Public Space* 16, June
2012.

Biblical quotations in "Children of God" and "Holy Sacrament" have been adapted
from the Authorized King James Version.

A CIP catalogue record for this book is available from the British Library.

1 3 5 7 9 10 8 6 4 2

ISBN 978 1 84708 768 3

This book was set in 12.25 pt Filosofia by Alpha Design & Composition of Pittsfield, NH.

Offset by Avon DataSet Limited, Bidford on Avon, Warwickshire

Printed and bound by CPI Group (UK) Ltd, Croydon, CR0 4YY

CONTENTS

WE'RE FLYING

Expectations *3*

A Foreign Body *21*

Three Sisters *36*

The Hurt *60*

The Result *81*

We're Flying *93*

Videocity *106*

Men and Boys *116*

The Letter *124*

Years Later *140*

Children of God *150*

Go Out into the Fields . . . *178*

THE RIDGE

Summer Folk *195*

The Natural Way of Things *215*

Holy Sacrament *233*

In the Forest *241*

Ice Moon *272*

Seven Sleepers *289*

The Last Romantic *315*

The Suitcase *330*

Sweet Dreams *343*

Coney Island *368*

WE'RE FLYING

Expectations

THINK IT'S FUNNY the way I can pick out a sound, even when there's a lot of noise and it's not a big sound, just because I'm waiting to hear it. I bet the others haven't heard it. They don't recognize the sound, the quiet creak of a floorboard in the apartment upstairs. They carry on talking, as though nothing had happened. They chat and laugh and drink my wine and eat the food I cooked for them, without anyone saying thank you or this is delicious. Presumably they think they're doing me a favor by visiting. Statistically, most women meet their eventual partners at work. But our work revolves around five- and six-year-old children. And their parents—either couples or single mothers. Karin and Pim hooked up when they were Scouts, Janneke and Stefan met on holiday in Australia. They must have told the story a hundred times. Two Dutch people meeting in Australia—it had to happen. They can't get over it. And now they're talking about their New Year's resolutions. Lift the seat, says Karin to Pim. Do you not do that? asks Janneke, making a face. She says she trained Stefan to pee sitting down. Karin says men have different notions of hygiene. What about women who chuck their used tampons in the wastepaper basket? asks Pim. That's the way they always talk. Not a pleasant or sensible word all evening.

Is there coffee? Stefan asks, as if I was the waitress. No, I say. At first they didn't even hear. I have to say it again, loud and clear. I'm tired. I'd like you to go now, please. They just laugh and say, Well, we'll just have to have our coffee somewhere else. As they file out, Janneke asks me if I'm all right. She makes a sympathetic face, as if I was one of the kids that had fallen down and scraped a knee. You would think she was on the verge of tears herself, but she's not even listening when I reply, Yes I'm fine, I just want to be alone. I don't think they will stop off anywhere on the way home. I don't think they'll talk about me. There's nothing to say, and that suits me.

I go back quietly into the living room and listen. There's a long silence, and then I hear the creak again. It sounds like someone creeping around on tiptoe, trying not to make a noise. I follow the footsteps from the door to the window and then back to the middle of the room. A chair or some piece of furniture is pushed, and then there's another sound I can't identify. It sounds as though something had fallen down, something heavy but soft.

I've never met Mrs. de Groot, I only know her name from the doorbell. Even so, I have a feeling I know her better than anyone else in the world. I've heard her radio and her vacuum and the dinnerware, so loud it's as though someone was washing up in my kitchen. I've heard her get up at night and shuffle around, heard her run a bath, flush the toilet, open a window. Sometimes water dripped onto my balcony when she watered her flowers, but when I leaned out and looked up, I couldn't see anyone there. I don't think she's ever left her apartment. I liked the sounds. They gave me the sense of living with a sort of ghost, a benign presence watching over me. Then a couple of weeks ago, everything went quiet. I heard nothing since. And now the creaking again.

My first thought was: it's a break-in. While I'm undressing and going to the bathroom, I wonder whether I should call the police or the super. I'm in my nightgown when I decide to go up there myself. I'm surprisingly fearless. But then I'm not really afraid of anything ever.

You've got to learn that, as a single woman. I pull on my robe and slip into some shoes. It's eleven o'clock.

I have to ring twice, and then I can see the light come on through the peephole, and a young man, much younger than me, opens the door and says in a very friendly voice, Good evening. I'm thinking it was a mistake to go upstairs, and why do I always have to get involved in other people's affairs, instead of looking after my own. But then you keep reading about people dying, and their bodies left to rot in their apartments for weeks without anyone noticing. The boy is wearing black jeans and a black T-shirt with IRON MAIDEN on it, which I think is the name of a rock band. He isn't wearing any shoes, and his socks are holey.

I tell him I live downstairs, and that I heard footsteps. And because Mrs. de Groot has clearly moved out, I thought it might be a break-in. The boy laughs and says it's brave of me to come up and look all by myself. If it was him, he'd have called the police. What made me think a woman lived there? He has a point. All it says on the bell is P. de Groot. For some reason I was convinced that that had to be a woman, an elderly woman living by herself. I tell him I've never seen anyone, just heard the noises. He asks if women sound any different than men. First I think he's making fun of me, but then he seems to mean it as a serious question. I don't know, I say. He looks at me with

this rather boyish look, a mixture of timid and curious.
I apologize, and say I've just got out of bed. I have no idea
why I'm lying. He has this way of making me say things
I didn't want to say, and that from the very first moment.
We look at each other in silence, and I think I ought to be
going. Then he asks if I'd like a coffee with him. I say yes
right away, even though I never drink coffee at night, and
I'm in my robe. I follow him inside. When he locks the
door, it occurs to me in a flash that he might be a burglar
after all, and has asked me in to silence me. He is quite
pale and slimly built, but he's about a head taller than
me, and has muscly arms. I imagine him grabbing me
and throwing me down on the floor, then he sits on my
belly and holds my arms in a painful grip, while he jams
something in my mouth to keep me from screaming.
But instead he goes to the kitchen, fills a pan with water,
turns on the stove. Then he flings open, it seems, every
one of the kitchen cupboards. Coffee pot, coffee, filters,
he mutters to himself as if it was a spell he'd learned by
heart—sugar, sweetener, milk. When he can't find the
coffee, I suggest getting some from my place. No, he says,
so firmly that it makes me jump. He thinks for a moment.
We could always have tea instead, he says.

The apartment looks exactly the way I imagined it would
as an old woman's apartment. A TV magazine on the coffee

table, knitting on the sofa, crocheted rugs and coasters, various knickknacks and passe-partouts with pictures of ugly-looking people in old-fashioned clothes. We sit down, me on the sofa, him on a great big armchair. On the arm-rest is a little box with a couple of buttons. He presses one of them, and a footrest slowly comes up from the bottom of the chair. With a switch he tilts back and then forward again. For a while he's busy pressing the buttons, like a kid showing off a new toy. We haven't introduced ourselves, he suddenly says, and he jumps up and thrusts out his hand. I'm Daphne, I say, and he laughs again, and says, I see. Oh. Patrick. Funny we've never met before. The whole time he's holding my hand in his. He asks me if I live alone. He asks about my life, my job, my family. He asks me so many questions, I don't get a chance to ask him anything back. I'm not used to people taking an interest in me. I expect I tell him way too much. I talk about my childhood and my little brother who died four years ago in a motorcycle ac-cident, and my parents and my job in the kindergarten. It's not exactly thrilling, but he listens carefully. He has shin-ing eyes, like the children when I tell them a story.

We finish the tea, and Patrick gets up and opens a side-board. He finds a dusty bottle of Grand Marnier that's al-most full. He sets a couple of small glasses on the table, fills them, and raises one.

Here's to unexpected visitors.

I empty my glass, even though I don't really like liqueur. He makes a face when he drinks as well, as though he's not used to it. I had company earlier, I say, a couple of colleagues from work and their husbands. We always get together on the first Friday of the month. I don't know why I'm telling him this. There's nothing more to say about it. He says January is his favorite month. His birthday's in January, in a couple of weeks' time. He likes the cold.

Which is your favorite month?

I've never thought about it. I know I hate November.

He has a favorite month, a favorite season, a favorite flower, a favorite animal, a favorite novel, and so on. That's all he has to say for himself. I think he has nothing else. He's just like my kids at kindergarten. When I ask them what they did on their vacation, they say, Played. He really is like a child, cheerful and helpless and sometimes a bit shy. He seems to be perpetually surprised. And he laughs a lot. He asks me if I like children. Sure, I reply, it's my job.

That doesn't have to mean anything. You can be a butcher and still love animals.

But I do like them. That's why I work in a kindergarten.

He looks alarmed and apologizes, as though he'd said something terrible. He pours us another. None for me, I say, but then I drink it anyway.

I guess I shouldn't be so nosy.

No, I guess you shouldn't.

I must sound just like an old kindergarten biddy, but the fact is I'm already hooked on his curiosity, his questioning look that gives significance to the most banal things. Sometimes he doesn't say anything for a long time, and just looks at me and smiles. When he asks me if I have a boyfriend, I get cross. I've heard the question too many times. Anyway, it's none of his business. Just because I don't live with a man doesn't mean . . . He looks at me with big, staring eyes. I don't know what to say, and my uncertainty makes me even angrier.

Now you're angry with me.

No I'm not.

And so it goes on. We drink and talk about everything under the sun and about me, only not about him. I find him provocative, but I don't think he means to be. He's staring at my legs until I see that my robe has fallen open, and he can see my thighs. I must get my legs waxed again. But who really cares. I pull the robe together, and Patrick stares at me as if I'd caught him doing something forbidden. I'm quite drunk at this point. I'm thinking he could do anything to me, and then straightaway I'm ashamed of the thought. He's so young I could be his mother. I'd like to run my hand through his hair, press myself against him, protect him in some way. I want him to hug me the way the kids do, I want him to lay his head in my lap and go to sleep in my arms. He yawns, and I look at my watch. It's three a.m.

I really better go.

It's Saturday tomorrow.

Even so.

Then he sits beside me on the sofa. He asks if he can give me a good night kiss, and before I can say anything, he's taken my hand and kissed it. I'm so astonished, I pull it away. He jumps up and crosses to the window, as if he was afraid I'm going to punish him.

I'm sorry.

You don't have to be.

Then he says something peculiar. I respect you, he says. After that neither of us says anything for a long time. Finally he says, Look, it's raining. Now the snow's going to melt. I say I don't like snow, and all at once I'm not sure if I mean that or not. I don't like snow, because the kids come bundled up in lots of clothes, so it takes you half an hour to get them changed, and they dirty the place with their shoes. But when I was a kid, I used to love snow. There were lots of things I used to love then. It feels to me like I've spent the whole evening moaning and griping. He talked about things he liked; I talked about things I didn't like. He must think I'm a negative person, an embittered old maid. Maybe that is what I am. At least in the city, I say. I don't like it because they go and grit the streets, and then everything . . . I picture us going for a sleigh ride. Patrick's sitting behind me, and his inner thighs are pressing against me, making me warm. He's snuggled his face into my hair, and I can feel his breath on my neck. He whispers in my ear. Completely out of the blue, he says what a wonderful woman I am, and he was so happy he'd met me. Well, I certainly didn't see that coming.

Can I see you tomorrow?

I always visit my parents on Saturday.

I say he can come to supper on Sunday if he'd like that. It doesn't matter to me whether I cook for one or two. I like cooking, I manage to add. There's something at least that I like to do. When we say good night, he kisses my hand again.

I can't sleep. I listen to him walking around upstairs and washing up and going to the bathroom. He is kind and attentive and terribly polite, but he's a little bit scary too when he smiles. It's too bad we always distrust people when they're nice.

In the morning I wake up with a splitting headache and a bitter taste in my mouth. Over breakfast already

I've started looking through my cookbooks for ideas. I said I would make something really simple, but now I feel like impressing him. There's not much in the way of interesting vegetables in the stores this time of year. Most of it has come a long way and doesn't taste of much. Green beans from Kenya, I mean, come on. I'd rather buy frozen. That night I get in a stupid argument with my father.

On Sunday I spend the whole afternoon in the kitchen, preparing dinner. I can't hear anything upstairs. Maybe Patrick's gone out. But punctually at six o'clock the bell rings. He's bought me an enormous bunch of flowers, and he kisses my hand again. I hope that's not his thing he does with everyone. I don't own a big enough vase, and I have to put the flowers in a plastic bucket in the bathtub to start off with. I don't get flowers often—never, really—and I don't buy them myself either. Lots of them are supplied from the third world, and the men who pick them get sterile because of the spray they treat them with. Now I'm being all negative again, instead of thanking him for the lovely flowers.

Over dinner, he keeps on telling me how delicious everything is, until I can't stand to hear him say it anymore. Although, it has to be said, dinner is good. Cooking is one thing I can do. You can cook too, he says. I must be

perfect. I almost laughed in his face. I can't bring myself
to take his compliments seriously. It always sounds as
though he's parroting something he heard some grownups say. I really do seem to impress him, I can't imagine
why. Each time I open my mouth to speak, he stops eating and stares at me with big round eyes. And it seems
he remembers everything I say to him. Already he knows
so much about me, and I don't know the first thing about
him.

When we're sitting on the sofa later, he clumsily knocks
over his glass. I almost gave him a smack, the way I do
with the little ones, when they do something naughty.
Luckily I manage to restrain myself at the last moment.
I go to the kitchen for salt and mineral water. I picture
laying Patrick over my knee, pulling his pants down, and
smacking his naughty bottom.

Of course I can't remove the stain. I'll never get rid of
it. What a stupid idea anyway, buying a white sofa. But I
liked it, I like my white sofa. I bought it after my brother
died, and somehow it's something to do with him. Patrick is standing next to me vaguely, watching me scrub
away at the stain. He apologizes profusely and says he'll
buy me a new sofa cover. But I'm still annoyed and shortly
after I say I need to go to bed, tomorrow is Monday. He
gets up. In the doorway he shoots me a tragic glance, and

apologizes one more time. Never mind, I say, what's done is done. We don't arrange to meet. He doesn't say anything, and I'm still a bit pissed at him.

I wonder if he can hear me as clearly as I can hear him. When I'm taking a shower, I suddenly feel naked. When I go to the toilet, I lock the door and sometimes don't flush, so that he doesn't hear. I need to drink plenty of water for my kidneys: I seem to spend half my life peeing. In fact I'm only just starting to realize how much noise I make. That I keep my street shoes on in the apartment, turn up the radio when vacuuming, sometimes scold or sing to myself. I'd better stop all that right away. I buy a pair of soft-soled slippers. When I drop a glass and it shatters, I listen for minutes for some sound from upstairs. But nothing—silence.

I can't stand it that he's so near, doing God knows what, and listening to me. I start to go out a lot. Then I sit in a cafe, or go for a walk, even though it's gotten cold again, and I need to be careful not to catch anything. Last year I had a bladder infection that simply refused to go away. I had to take antibiotics and was off work for days. Afterward, Janneke and Karin made snide remarks. A bladder infection. To them, that could mean only one thing.

Three days later, Patrick rings the bell, right after I've got home from work. He must have been waiting for me.

He's got a new sofa cover, and a gift-wrapped box. He helps me cover the sofa. Our hands touch. Inside the box is a fish kettle. Just because that time I made dinner, I said I wished I owned a fish kettle. Now he goes and buys me one. They're not cheap.

You're crazy. You didn't have to do that.

Because of the trouble I put you to.

He smiles. We kiss for the first time. It just happens, I couldn't say who started it. There's something greedy about his kisses, he drapes his lips over mine, and shuts them and opens them and shuts them as though to gobble me up. The whole time he holds me firmly in his arms, and I feel how strong he is. I can hardly move. When I tell him he's crushing me, he lets go right away and apologizes. He does like an apology. He seems embarrassed about having kissed me. I imagine him undressing me and sleeping with me on the newly slip-covered sofa. Sperm stains are tricky, by the way. Why do I keep thinking of all this nonsense. He's just looking at me.

Now he's upstairs again. I keep having to think of him though. I don't know anything about him, not if the things in the apartment are his, not if he lives there, or is only staying for a while. I don't know his middle initial, or his age, or what his job is. He seems not to be short of money for generous presents. I imagine what Janneke and Karin would say if they saw us together: Oh, she's lost it now. Or: She's beyond good and evil anyway. Or: She must be paying him, he's exploiting her. And all the time I feel I'm exploiting him.

From now on we see each other every two or three days. Sometimes he comes down, sometimes I go up to him. We always know when the other is home. Sometimes we talk on the phone for hours. Then after a while I'm not sure if I'm hearing his voice through the phone or through the ceiling.

When we eat dinner together, we drink a lot, but he doesn't seem to get drunk. We chat like old friends. We only kiss good-bye. It's almost become a habit. I started the French kissing. I started stroking him. Then he does it too, but only with his fingertips, my hips and the small of my back where I feel pain sometimes. When I put his hand on my breast, he leaves it there for a moment inertly and then takes it away again. He needs time, I think. But I don't have the time. Of course I don't say so. I've gotten to be careful about what I say and don't say. I keep an eye on him. I listen.

Some nights he doesn't come home. I don't sleep on those nights, and stay up and listen and in the morning I'm dog-tired. I hate myself for it, but I can't help it. The next time we see each other, he tells me straight out where he was, with his parents or some friends or other that he hasn't mentioned to me before. He must have sensed my distrust.

At work, Janneke asks me how I'm doing, and whether I'm sick again. She says I'm looking tired. I'm not sleeping properly, that's all I say. I've lost weight. What can I do if I don't have any appetite? Janneke says she wants to leave Stefan, that was one of her New Year's resolutions she hadn't yet told him about. We talk about her problems. Everyone comes to cry on my shoulder, but when I give them good advice, they don't take it, they just say things aren't that simple. Karin is in a bad mood, she doesn't know why. She's unbearable sometimes, even with the kids. Until one of them starts to cry. Then she cries too.

Patrick says he really likes me, and I'm much too good for him. Then he kisses me again, but he keeps me at a distance. I've already asked myself whether perhaps physically there isn't something wrong with him. He looks fit enough, but that can be deceptive. There are more men all the time who can't get it up, or who can't be bothered with sex. The quality of sperm is falling off a cliff. It has to do with female hormones that leach into the groundwater.

I've set myself a deadline. If he hasn't decided by the end of the month, then I'm putting an end to it. But now what do I mean by decided? I'm not exactly sure what I'm expecting from him. That he rips my clothes off and jumps me on the sofa? Certainly not. But that he opens himself to me. Entrusts himself. It's a matter of a few words.

When I get home the next day, I can hear *Hello* by Lionel Ritchie booming down from the top floor, much louder than the music he usually plays. It was a CD I played to Patrick once. He must have bought himself a copy. He's been waiting for me to come home, and this is his way of welcoming me. I'm expecting him to call, or come downstairs. I hear him leave his apartment. But he keeps going, and shortly after, the street door falls shut. It's after midnight when he gets back. I hear his footfall, the slow steps, the creaking of the floorboards. For a second, I think he's not alone, but that can't be. Then silence. Silence is the worst. I can't sleep. I haven't slept for days. I have the most ridiculous imaginings, horrible things that I feel ashamed to entertain.

On his birthday, he makes me dinner. He's gone to unbelievable trouble, he's even decorated the table with chocolate ladybirds. I manage to get a stain on my blouse and take it off to wash it out properly. Patrick has followed me into the kitchen, we're talking, he's looking at me. But he acts as though there's nothing the matter. I could strip naked in front of him, he wouldn't even notice. That can't be normal. I wonder what his game is. I go downstairs and put on a clean blouse. While I'm downstairs, I hear him go to the toilet, and flush twice. Ideally, I wouldn't go back upstairs. We're in closer touch when we're apart, when we only hear each other.

We drank a lot of wine with dinner, a whole bottle. When we kissed good-bye, he suddenly started whispering it's not fair, and he stopped. Now I'm lying in my bed, and I can't sleep. He's directly above me, just a few yards away. I spread my legs and imagine him on top of me, doing it to me. He's pinning my arms, the way he does when he kisses me. He's grabbing my hair, pulling it, slapping my face. I throw my legs around him. He's kissing me hungrily. We're sweating. There's silence, all I can hear is him breathing, his breath in my loosened hair. I stretch out my arms to him. Come, I whisper to him, come! Come! He's so close, I can almost feel him.

A Foreign Body

CHRISTOPH SWITCHED THE light off and the group fell silent. After a few seconds of darkness, there was disquiet, chairs creaked, someone cleared his throat, there were other sounds that were hard to trace. As the first whispers began, Christoph switched on the microphone, and the sudden element of amplification made the space appear still bigger and the darkness still more intense. If he'd been very concentrated and managed to focus his attention on the group, then surely it would be possible to get by without slides, and finally even without words, and just be in the dark and allow time to elapse for an hour or two.

For hundreds of thousands of years no light, no smell,

no life, no sounds but for the dripping of water, the plink-
ing and flowing of water penetrating through cracks in
the rock, collecting in trickles, widening cracks, form-
ing courses, small streams by now, one or ten or hundred
thousands of years later, a cavern or system of caverns.
Christoph switched the projector on, and the Water Dome
was there, a domed arch lit by several flashbeams, its
upper reaches lost in the darkness. The first image was
the most important, that had to captivate the audience
straightaway. He had chosen it carefully, and let it stand
for a long time, without saying a word. He felt it would be
a good evening.

After that first shot, there were others, less spectacular, the barred entrance to the cave, the first few hundred
yards, paved paths and wire balustrades, the odd stalactite
taken from somewhere on the inside and put out near the
entrance for the trippers to see. The group relaxed and listened as Christoph talked about the discovery of the cave,
the early expeditions into the interior, the technical difficulties of living under the earth's surface. One of the slides
showed a map of the passages that had been explored thus
far, a tangled web of lines in different colors.

Just over a hundred miles have been explored and
charted, but we have to assume that's just a fraction of
the whole.

The shot of a staircase going steeply down, and coming to a sudden unexpected stop in a pile of scree. The adventure is beginning, said Christoph, and showed pictures that needed no explaining. Difficult terrain, narrow couloirs, crevasses, meanders, faults. In some of the photos you could see cave explorers in dirty orange coveralls with carbide lamps on their foreheads crawling through narrow passageways or rappelling down seemingly bottomless gullies. Amazing the kind of places a man is able to slip through, Christoph commented.

Then there was a shot of the bivouac, and for the first time there was the whole group sitting over fondue and wine at camp tables. You could almost forget you were in a cave, said Christoph, but if you need to answer the call of nature, then you remember. If the torch fails, if the light goes out, then you lose orientation in a matter of seconds. He showed pictures of the group in sleeping bags on thick foam rubber mattresses encased in plastic sheeting. The faces looked dirty and tired, but there was a wild flash in the eyes as in people just awakened. And then a brief pause. You'll find my book on sale in the lobby, along with information on guided tours for a day or more. Christoph switched on the music and hurried out of the cave, to be the first at the book table.

A man of Christoph's age flicked desultorily through the desk copy of the book. Beside him was a slim woman who seemed a lot younger and had something elfin about her. Both were wearing fleece jackets. The man casually asked Christoph if he had ever been cave diving. Not bothering to wait for a reply, he volunteered that he'd been in cave complexes all over the world. His voice had an aggressive tone that Christoph had quite often heard among extreme sports aficionados. Sometimes he had the impression they only turned up at his talks to tell him about their experiences, and to measure themselves against him and challenge him. After the break he would show pictures from parts of the caves not open to the general public, Christoph said. He felt a little ashamed of the way he rose to the bait. The man didn't react, and carried on flicking through the book. He asked if Christoph had ever been to the caves at Gunung Mulu in Malaysia. An elderly gentleman stepped up to the table. He bought the book without looking at it, and asked Christoph to sign it for him with a personal dedication. The couple stepped aside.

Just before the end of the break, Christoph noticed them again. They were still by the table. The man was looking across at him and saying something to his girlfriend. There was a mocking expression on his face.

And now, said Christoph, a little hammily, let's explore Nirvana! This was a cave system that was hard to get to and that had only ever been seen by maybe a dozen or so people. He brought up the images from the darkness and slow-faded them, just the way they had flashed up in the cave and slowly faded on the retina: a candle stalagmite, a few needle-thin stalactites, gardens of karst that had grown up in the darkness since the last ice age, only to be seen in a single brief shock of light thousands of years later. Shades of brown, white, yellow, a mercury glimmer of damp-looking surfaces.

Each time Christoph saw the photographs, a shiver went through him. He felt the pressure of the masses of rock, the fear of the complete indifference of the mountain, that with a tiny movement could have squashed all life out of him. He had set up the flashes, loaded the camera, the practiced moves had something calming about them that dispelled his feeling of paralysis. But the fear remained. It would always be there.

There must be thousands of caves like these, said Christoph, where no man has ever set foot, where no man ever will set foot. There is a world beneath us in the rock, a world full of marvels and secrets. He stopped, he didn't know what else to say. Words weren't enough, pictures weren't enough either. You had to have been there yourself, and mapped out the senseless beauty. All that could be heard was the sound of the projector, the humming of the ventilator, and the clattering of the carousel that pushed one slide after the other in front of the beam.

When you go back outside, it's not the sun or the colors that overwhelm you, it's the smells of the forest, the smells of life, of things growing and rotting. The cave has no smell. The last shot brought the audience back to the surface, it showed a picturesque little forest lake that was fed from the inside of the mountain. Each year thousands of tons of water-soluble limestone are carried out, said Christoph, the water works day and night, hour after hour, enlarging the cave all the time. He switched off the projector and microphone and turned on the light. People applauded.

After the talk, a couple of the listeners went up to him and asked questions and inquired about the tours with shining eyes. When the last of them had gone, Christoph packed away the projector and the box of slides and put them on a cart, along with the unsold books. In the lobby he lit a cigarette. It had gotten cold.

Will you come for a drink with us?

Christoph gave a start when he saw the man standing a few yards away. He was standing in front of him, feet apart, it looked as though he was challenging him to a fight.

All right, he said out of politeness. But just one beer, I've got a long drive ahead of me.

The man went up to him and they shook hands. Clemens, he said, and that's Sabine. He pointed into the darkness, where Christoph could see the faint outline of the woman.

THEY'D BEEN SITTING in the bar for quite a while. The conversation was faltering. Clemens talked about expeditions he'd been on, an endless list of caves, all described with the same adjectives. He had taken thousands of pictures, he said. He'd be glad to show them to Christoph sometime. Maybe he could use them in his talks. Since being introduced, Sabine hadn't said a word. Christoph didn't say much either, just nodded from time to time and smiled, and pretended Clemens's stories were interesting. When, after a long description of a diving trip, there was a silence, Christoph asked Sabine if she'd ever been in a cave herself.

That's how we met, she said. And then—as though someone had pushed a button—she embarked on a list of caves she'd seen. She only listed their names and the years of the expeditions. Then she stopped, and Christoph wasn't sure whether she had spoken or not.

Why don't we go on a tour together, the three of us, suggested Clemens.

Christoph smiled vaguely, said, Well, one day, and OK, I'd better go, and waved the waiter over. For a moment there was silence, and then Clemens said, To Nirvana. He said it more quietly than he'd been speaking before, and at first Christoph wasn't sure he could trust his hearing, and then Clemens said it again: To Nirvana.

How do we get in there? he asked. There was something hungry in his look.

The waiter came with the check. Clemens said he'd have another beer. Will you have something else as well? His voice sounded beseeching, almost fearful. Christoph ordered an apple juice. He waited till the drinks came, then he began to speak. As he spoke, he had the sensation he was making the descent all over again.

He waded through a gallery deep in the interior of the mountain. The water was ice-cold and getting deeper, he was in it up to his belly, his chest, his chin. From the end of the grotto, where there were only a few inches between the ceiling and the water's surface, a passage led steeply up. It was so narrow that once Christoph had crept into it, he was unable to put his hands back. He pushed himself up with the tips of his toes, inch by inch, just behind the guide. They didn't speak, all that could be heard was the scraping of their boots and the occasional grunt or cough. He had long since lost all sense of time when the man in front of him stopped and said, We've reached the fault, it might take a while. Christoph was surprised by how close his voice sounded. Swearing, the guide pushed himself through the narrowest point. Christoph waited. The cold penetrated his neoprene suit and spread slowly through his body. He shut his eyes and pictured himself lying coffined in rock, a foreign body. We're buried alive, he thought, we'll never get out of here. Suddenly he became conscious that he was breathing fast. He forced himself not to think about where he was, tried to remember the words of children's songs, added up the royalties he would get for his pictures, pictured landscapes, a wide expanse of sky, passing clouds. Then the man in front of him was gone, and Christoph looked through the fault and laughed nervously. You want me to get through there? You can do it, he heard the voice of his companion, which seemed to come from nowhere but was still very close. We're halfway there. Christoph's body pushed itself forward, mindlessly as a machine.

Clemens had been listening with shining eyes. I've gotta get in there, he said, when Christoph stopped. Will you take me? Christoph said there were no tours to that part of the cave. You could put in a word for us, said Clemens. He said he was prepared to pay. Sabine looked into Christoph's eyes with a mixture of skepticism and adventure lust. It would be simplest for you, he said, you're slimly built. It's not dangerous, he said, the only danger is being afraid. Fear, he repeated, is the only danger.

Clemens went to the washroom. Christoph saw him exchange words with the waiter before disappearing downstairs. Even before he had returned, the waiter had brought a bottle of wine and three glasses.

How long have you two been together? Christoph asked.

Two years, said Sabine. He's crazy, she said. He does all kinds of things, freeclimbing, canyoning, off-track skiing. Once he smashed into a snow slab because he was in slack country. He's completely crazy.

YOU CAN STAY WITH US, Clemens had said, and ordered another bottle of wine, which he'd gone on to drink almost alone. They talked about the equipment, dry runs, and the best time for the expedition. Sabine hardly drank anything, and was as quiet as before. Christoph still disliked Clemens, but he allowed himself to be caught up in the excitement. It was like a game, a contest. It was all about—suddenly it dawned on him—who was going to get Sabine. They were fighting over this cool, childlike woman, who wasn't even paying attention. He felt he had blundered into a trap. When Clemens asked him to stay the night, he had no choice. The game had to be played to a finish.

Christoph felt the alcohol, but he wasn't drunk. Clemens staggered up the steps of the apartment complex. It took him forever to get the key in the lock. From the very first moment, Christoph felt ill at ease in the apartment, he didn't know why. His hosts seemed to have no sense of beautiful things. They had the bare necessities, and even so the apartment looked untidy. The furniture didn't match and was in the wrong places, jumbled together by chance, it seemed, as though it had been unloaded and left standing there.

Clemens had disappeared without a word. Sabine showed Christoph the guest room. He watched as she made the bed. She went out and came back with a towel. Clemens is asleep already, she said. He didn't even get undressed.

Christoph went to the bathroom. When he was finished, he found Sabine in the living room, leafing through a photo album. He sat down beside her, and she handed the album over to him and went to the bathroom herself. Gunung Mulu, Malaysia, he read at the top of the page. The pictures were not very good. You couldn't light a big cave with a single flash. On some of them you could see Clemens, on others there was a pretty blond woman, with a gamine expression. The last picture showed them standing together in dirty overalls, with tired smiles on their faces. Between them stood a native, about a head smaller, and with an alert expression. At the back of the album was a sheaf of photos that hadn't yet been stuck down. Christoph began going through the album from the front. Pictures from a different expedition. There was the blond woman again, this time in a diving costume.

That's his ex, said Sabine. She stood in front of him in leggings and an orange sleeveless T-shirt. She had narrow hips and a flat boyish chest. She asked him if he wanted a drink. What about a beer? A glass of water, said Christoph.

She brought it to him and sat back down. He went on leafing through the album, and they saw photos of beaches and old temples, and over and over again the blond gamine. They broke up over that business of the snow slab, Sabine said. It took Clemens a long time to get over her. Do you like her?

Her hands were folded in her lap. Christoph looked at her arms, which were anorexically thin, and covered with little black hairs. She gave off a smell—it took him a while to trace it—of camphor. It wasn't till she pointed out something in one of the pictures that he noticed her knotty hands. Sabine must be much older than he first thought, perhaps older than himself.

She laughed softly. He's crazy, she said, but I'm crazy too. And you must be as well? We're all crazy. Why do you think we want to go in that cave? Why do you want to go there? Nirvana. Because no one else has been there?

Christoph shrugged his shoulders and shut the album.

We want to fuck the planet, said Sabine. She stood up and held out her hand. We're going to fuck the planet.

SHE DIDN'T STOP WHISPERING. Never mind, she said. Her mouth was right up against Christoph's ear, he could feel her lips brushing against it. They had tried hard, but that hadn't helped. Christoph hadn't been able to shake from his mind the caves she'd listed in the bar, and he'd thought she was just out for one more conquest, another name on another list.

Never mind, Sabine said again, as if she wasn't quite convinced the first time. Her breath was coming and going in pants. Then she started fiddling with him again, with a silly giggle that got worse the longer

it went on. Stop that, he finally said. I don't feel like it.
Right away she stopped, and was quiet. He moved away
from her a little, he couldn't stand her nearness. But
she came after him, pressed herself against him. In the
end, he sat up on the side of the bed. It was dark in the
room, and he sat there and stared into the dark. What's
the matter? Sabine asked. Christoph still didn't speak.
Endure the dark, he thought, tolerate the silence. He
heard the rustle of the sheets. Sabine must have sat up
as well. She didn't touch him, but he could sense that
she was right behind him. It was completely dark. He
heard her voice coming out of the void, sounding very
calm and objective. You're not going to take us with you,
are you? You won't dream of it. The thought seemed to
amuse her, and she started her giggling again. Christoph turned his head half toward her, and said he didn't
think he would ever set foot in a cave again. Sabine laid
her hand on his bare back, as if to push him away. I can't
do it anymore, he said. And then, slowly and haltingly,
on the way down to Nirvana he had been more afraid
than he had ever been in his life. Previously, fear had
lent him wings, it was a source of tension that helped
him to concentrate. But there in that narrow crevasse,
he had felt lamed. It was as though all his strength had
deserted him. He had felt utterly helpless, his thoughts

spinning in his head. I don't remember how I got out. I can't remember the way back.

Sabine took her hand off his back and got up. He heard steps, a dull thump, and a stifled curse. Then the overhead light came on.

I've never been inside a cave since, he said and pulled himself upright. Christ, I don't even ride in elevators anymore. He laughed hoarsely. Sabine said she was going to bed. Her voice sounded dismissive. He said he would drive home, he felt perfectly sober. Sabine didn't reply. She watched him dress and followed him to the door. She held up her face to him, and he kissed her quickly on the mouth. She seemed offended. Clemens will be disappointed, she said. What about? Christoph asked. She looked at him with an absurdly serious, censorious expression.

The sky was clear, and the stars seemed to be burning in the cold air. Christoph felt the gratitude he felt after every expedition under the surface, the joy of having got back in one piece, and being able to breathe freely after days of being shut in. He walked through the silent village, got lost, and finally found himself in front of the village hall. He felt relieved, even strangely cheerful. Whatever sort of game it was, he had the feeling he'd won.

Three Sisters

HEIDI SKETCHED THE girl from memory. She drew the outline with swift strokes, the low, slightly heavy hips, narrow waist, and large breasts. She started to put detail on the sketch, worked on hands and hair, armpits and collarbone. Why isn't she wearing anything? asked Cyril. Heidi was working on the face, which was hard to do in its girlish simplicity. My turn now, said Cyril, who was standing next to her, watching. Heidi went on drawing. The shoulders were tricky, the transition to the arms, which the girl had extended behind her, like a swimmer on the starting blocks. Carefully Heidi selected colors, brown and red for the hair, pink and white and a pale yellow for the skin tone. Those are mine, cried Cyril, and he snatched away the box of colored pencils and tried to snatch away the paper as well. She kept him off, and went back to the face. She had to catch the expression, the pert look of a seventeen-year-old girl with oodles of knowledge and no understanding. Mama, wailed Cyril, and when she didn't react, he grabbed a red pencil and scribbled furiously across the drawing, until the point of the pencil broke off with a nasty click. Heidi tried to hold onto the drawing, the paper tore, and in a sudden surge of fury she pushed Cyril away from her so hard that he fell off his stool. He lay on the ground wailing, though not from pain, she knew his calculating cry, which was capable of driving her to white rage.

Heidi went and shut herself in her bedroom. She lay frozen on the bed, while Cyril pounded on the door with his fists. After a while he gave up, and she could only hear him whimpering. Slowly she recovered herself. She took a few deep breaths. She was sorry she had given the boy a shove. In the evening he would tell his father, and he would give her a concerned look but say nothing. He had been afraid from the very beginning that the boy would be too much for her. After all, he treated her like a child. The pregnancy had been uncomplicated and it had been an easy birth. Anyway she wasn't overburdened, she just had different views. He spoiled the child, and put up with all his nonsense, the way he tried to spoil her as well. Rainer is a pussy, Heidi's father had said once, and laughed. He got on better with him than she did.

Cyril whimpered quietly. Heidi opened the door, knelt down, and put her arms around him. No one likes me, he said. Of course I like you, she said, I'm sorry, I didn't mean to hurt you. Here, said Cyril, and she kissed the place. And here. You mustn't scribble on Mama's drawings.

CYRIL HAD GONE next door to play with Leah, who went to the same kindergarten. Heidi had carefully smoothed out her drawing and stuck it together with Scotch tape, and hidden it in the box at the top of the closet. Rainer mustn't see it, he wouldn't understand. Heidi went into town to buy something she had forgotten this morning. She stopped at the station and ran her eye down the train timetable. The train now ran a minute later than it had six years ago, now it was two minutes past midnight. She went through the underpass and sat down on one of the benches on the platform. The station was deserted, only from time to time a freight train clattered through at high speed, disappearing as quickly as it had come.

She had been all alone on the platform then as well. Her parents hadn't seen her onto the train, they had been dead set against the idea of her going to Vienna, now that she had learned a trade and had such good final grades. But then she and her father had stopped speaking months ago. If he hadn't been so concerned with what people might say, he would have thrown her out of the house.

Heidi packed her things at the last minute, she didn't need much, she would only be gone for three or four days. As she slipped into her shoes in the hall, her mother came out and watched her in perplexity. Then—Heidi was already in the doorway—she said wait, and went into the kitchen and came back with a bar of chocolate. Eat this before your exam, she said, it'll settle your nerves.

Heidi had got to the station much too early. She took a seat in the cafe garden opposite. The chestnuts formed a dense canopy, only a few dim strings of lights lit up the garden and made the night appear still darker. Only one table was in use—there was a group of men of whom she recognized none. Even so, the men greeted her exuberantly, perhaps to make fun of her. One of them was telling dirty jokes, one after the other. He kept his voice down, but in spite of that, or perhaps because of it, Heidi could hear every word. The men kept squinting across at her. She knew she looked younger than she was. When she went to the cinema, she had to show her ID, even now. The waitress came to her table, a girl not much older than herself, and said the cafe was closed. Last orders, she said, as she went by the men's table. She disappeared into the restaurant and came back a few moments later with a couple of bottles of beer. We're closed, she called to Heidi, who had remained sitting, and sat down with the men herself.

Heidi stood up to go. As she turned around once more, she saw that one of the men was gazing at her drunkenly. He got clumsily to his feet, and she was a little afraid he would come after her, but he went instead to the little outhouse where the lavatories were.

It was still warm. The foehn wind had been blowing for days, and even now at night the mountains seemed to loom unusually close. Heidi went over their names to calm herself, there was Helwang, Gaflei, the Three Sisters, the same peaks she could see out of her bedroom window. She remembered the story her teacher had told her at school. How instead of going to church on Assumption Day, the three sisters had gone up into the mountains to pick berries, and how the Virgin had appeared to them, and asked them for their berries. But the sisters hadn't wanted to give them up, and ever since they stood there, turned to stone. Heidi had always been on the side of the sisters, she didn't know why. She had sketched the forms many times and in all weathers, but she had never been up there herself. It was an exposed path, and she suffered from vertigo.

Two border guards with a German shepherd emerged from the underpass, and at the very back of the platform a railway worker in a luminous orange vest suddenly appeared. Then in the distance, Heidi saw the lights of her train.

She walked up and down, looking for her car. She was starting to worry the train would leave without her, so she finally asked a conductor who was standing in the open doorway of the sleeping car, smoking a cigarette. He pointed her the way and said she had better hurry, the train was leaving in three minutes. The border guards had already boarded, they were just changing the locomotive at the front. Heidi ran along the platform, watching the time on the big station clock. When the hands reached the vertical, she jumped in and went on down the narrow corridors until she got to her car. While she was looking for her compartment, the sleeping car attendant came by and asked her for her ticket and passport. A little reluctantly, she handed them over. He sensed her unease, and told her everything would be returned to her in the morning, when he woke her. Then, with a jolt, the train departed. Heidi almost fell over, but the conductor caught her by the shoulder, and then let her go again immediately, as if he'd done something wrong. He said good night and disappeared into his own compartment.

The train crossed the Rhine bridge. Now they were in Liechtenstein, and in a few minutes they would be in Austria. Heidi remained in the dimly lit corridor, gazing out into the darkness. Gradually her fear and tension began to melt away, and she began to look forward to the journey, and to Vienna, where she'd never been. The Academy of Fine Arts, she said the name over and over to herself, she was applying to the Academy of Fine Arts, she of all people, whom everyone treated like a little girl, and whose father even saw her going to Gymnasium as a waste of time, on her way to the Academy of Fine Arts. What makes you think you're any better than us, he had said, and got her the internship with the council. If she hadn't run into her old art teacher, it wouldn't have occurred to her that she might become a painter.

A couple of months before, Frau Brander had gone to the registry office, she had lost her purse or someone had stolen it, and she needed to get a new identity card. Are you still drawing? she asked, as Heidi filled in the form. Heidi nodded, and Frau Brander suggested she show her what she was working on.

So a couple of days later they met for lunch in a cafe, and Heidi showed Frau Brander some of her drawings.

The teacher looked at each one of them carefully, and then went on to the next. They're just things I tossed off, said Heidi. They're good, Frau Brander said, you have a nice clear line. Did you ever think of applying to art school? Heidi laughed and shook her head. You should think about it, said Frau Brander. Go to Vienna or Berlin. Don't go to Zurich.

Heidi had made inquiries without telling anyone. Might as well, she thought, it doesn't cost anything. The entrance exams were in September for Vienna and in October for Berlin, and it was only May. In the next few months, Heidi sketched more purposefully than before, and she went to the library and looked at art books and read the lives of artists she admired. And after some time it became clear that this was what she wanted to do, what she had secretly always wanted to do, to be an artist, as independent and confident as her teacher. When the boss called her into the office once to talk about her future, she said when she'd finished the internship she'd like to go to art school. He looked doubtful. What if they don't take you? he asked. He said he couldn't keep a job open for her. Heidi hadn't discussed her plans with her parents yet. The boss called her father, they were acquainted from way back, through the gymnastic club. Her father was devastated, what seemed to upset him most was the fact that Heidi hadn't taken him into her confidence. There was a short, vicious scene, Heidi called her father crude, and he called her crazy. And they'd stopped speaking to each other.

In August Heidi called Frau Brander, and said she was going to apply to Vienna. Frau Brander offered to help her put together a portfolio. Come by my apartment tomorrow night, she said, and bring everything you've ever done.

The following evening, Heidi packed all her drawings into a big cardboard box and cycled out to where Frau Brander lived, in an apartment complex at the edge of town. Heidi had never been to the area before. The building was old and run-down, but the apartment was nicely furnished. There were pictures on all the walls, little oil landscapes that showed the ugly warehouses of the transport companies, the freight station, and the silos. Go out on the balcony, said Frau Brander. Will you have a glass of wine? Heidi hesitated, then she said, Yes, please.

She stood by the railing and looked down at the enormous cornfield that began at the foot of the house and extended as far as the Three Sisters. In the distance you could hear the highway, a thrumming that alternately got louder and quieter. Frau Brander had stepped outside and was standing next to Heidi. She put her arm around her shoulder and squeezed her closer. I'm all excited, she said, it feels like it's me applying all over again. Heidi thought of the stories about Frau Brander, but they were such nonsense, it was just a friendly hug that didn't mean anything. That was the way artists were, easygoing and free from fear and prejudice.

Frau Brander had opened a bottle, and poured a couple of glasses. Call me Renate, she said, and they bumped glasses. Now let's see what you've brought.

They took hours making their selection. When it got too dark outside, they went into the living room and carried on there. They laid the remaining drawings on the wood floor. Renate was barefoot, and Heidi had taken her shoes off; suddenly she felt naked in this strange place. They walked up and down among the drawings, putting them in different piles, taking some out and putting in others. It was very warm in the apartment, and when Renate raised her hand to scratch her head in thought, Heidi noticed dark sweat stains rimming her sleeveless dress. They stood at opposite ends of the room, approached one another, stood silently side by side, squatted down in front of one sketch the better to take it in. Renate overbalanced, and caught herself laughing on Heidi's shoulder, and left her hand there after they had stood up again. Heidi could smell Renate's perfume, which didn't drown out the smell of her body, but blended with it to make a warm, summery scent of milk and grass.

In the end, there were only twenty pictures left, a few small portrait sketches, half a dozen landscapes, and a few recent things, colored-pencil drawings of strange organic shapes. Heidi felt confused when Renate had pulled the stack of them out of the box and asked what they were. She had shrugged her shoulders. This one looks like a vulva, Renate said, and this one too. She laughed, and looked Heidi straight in the eye. Heidi lowered her gaze, but not from shame. Do you have a boyfriend? Renate asked.

HEIDI HAD FOUND her compartment. There was just a dim emergency light on. She could hear someone breathing. She sat down on the lower bunk, opened her folder, and looked through the drawings once more. Hello, said a voice. Quickly Heidi shut the folder and looked up. A young woman was looking down at her. Where are we? she asked. We've just crossed the border, said Heidi. Oh, God, said the woman and she sat up and dangled her bare legs over the edge of her bunk. I can never sleep in these so-called sleeping cars. She climbed down the ladder and went off down the corridor. In a while she returned and stopped in front of the door to the compartment. She pulled down the window and lit a cigarette. Do you want one? she asked. She said that before boarding a night train, she always drank a beer to help her sleep. But in Zurich she had met some guys in a bar and had a few beers too many, and now she had to keep going to the bathroom. My name's Susa. What's yours? Heidi. Susa laughed. Is that your real name?

The conductor stepped into the corridor and said there was no smoking allowed. Asshole, muttered Susa, flicked the cigarette out the window, and went back inside the compartment. She said she was from Kiel. She had been bumming around Europe for the past couple of weeks. She had been to France, and Barcelona, and Italy, and Zurich. Now she was on her way to Austria and Hungary, and if there was time, the Czech Republic. What about yourself? Heidi said she was on her way to Vienna to apply to the Academy of Fine Arts. Are you an artist then? asked Susa. Heidi shook her head. I'm just applying, she said. I think your accent's cute, said Susa. Are those your pictures in there? Will you show me?

Heidi hesitated, but she did feel a bit proud as well, to have been taken for an artist. She opened the folder. Susa settled down next to her. Those are the Three Sisters, said Heidi, that's their name, they're mountains. That's

the Gonzen. That's the castle at Sargans, there's my mum,
and she's someone at work. And there's you, said Susa.
They're good. Yes, said Heidi. And that's a girlfriend of
mine. And what's that? That's just imaginary shapes,
said Heidi. Susa laughed and said it looked like a cunt.
Heidi stopped turning over pages. She could feel herself
blushing. Come on, said Susa, this is exciting. She pulled
the rest of the drawings out of the folder herself. Don't,
said Heidi, but Susa had already flicked on ahead. Just a
load of cunts, she said in disappointment. She said she
would try and sleep a bit now, so that she didn't look like
shit in the morning. She climbed back up the ladder.

Heidi gathered up her papers, returned them carefully
to the folder, and put the folder next to the small backpack with her things. Then she lay down, without undressing. She still felt ashamed. At the time she had done
the sketches, she had done them somehow automatically,
not even thinking about what she was doing. For the first
time, she had had the sense that she wasn't just copying
something, imitating, but making something original. It
had been effortless, a wonderful feeling, one line after
the next, as if the drawings were simply growing. Organic shapes, was the most she had thought, the organs
of some creature or other. Even now she couldn't see what
everybody else seemed to see. Maybe she was just naive.

She pictured herself standing in front of the selection committee, the experts looking on, and what they would make of it. She pictured herself standing naked in front of a group of old men, and one of them pointing at her pudenda, and saying that looks like a cunt, and the others cackling.

The train slowed down, and then picked up speed. It was warm in the compartment. Heidi got a water bottle out of her backpack and took a small swallow. She thought about Renate and the life she was leading. An art teacher in a small town, painting in her free time, and every couple of years or so getting a show of her work put on in some cafe room, or the staircase in an office building. Heidi had attended one of the openings, and even she had seen the full absurdity of the event. A local newspaperman had said a few garbled words about Renate's art, and a flushed-looking Renate had gone around pulling corks and filling glasses for the few people present, all of them outsiders like herself, and listened to them say how great they thought the pictures were. It was strange that Heidi had never had any doubts about Renate before, that she had never stopped to think whether her teacher's pictures were any good or not. Nor had she questioned Renate's judgment either. She thought about the works of the great masters she had looked at in the library. What, compared to them, were her pencil drawings, her child-ish sketches?

The train had entered a station, and a cold neon light came in through the cracks in the blinds of the compartment window. Heidi looked at her watch, it was twenty past two. Without stopping to think, she jumped up, grabbed her backpack and folder, and ran down the corridor. The sleeping car attendant was standing in the open doorway, talking to a railwayman. I want to get off, said Heidi. We're only in Innsbruck, said the conductor. I want to get off, Heidi repeated. The conductor muttered something that didn't sound pleased, and strolled back to his compartment. He seemed to be doing everything deliberately slowly, thumbing through the envelopes that contained the passports of the travelers. At last he produced Heidi's passport and ticket, and handed them to her. Outside, the whistle blew. Heidi jumped out of the car and the train pulled away. The railway employee was gone, there was no one in sight.

Heidi stood on the empty platform for ages. She was tired and confused and didn't know where to go. On the schedule she saw that a train back to Switzerland was due any minute, but she couldn't go home just yet. She picked up her things and left the station. She walked through the almost deserted city, which seemed very dark to her and rather frightening, with massive buildings and narrow lanes. There was the occasional light still on in a bar, and voices and laughter were audible, and sometimes music. But Heidi didn't feel like being with people, she couldn't have handled the nosy looks, the noise, and the drunken cheer of the night owls. On the banks of the Inn she sat down on a bench. She was cold, and put on her sweater.

That was the night that Heidi met Rainer. He was just going home with a few friends when he saw her sitting down by the river. He was worried she might do something silly, he said later, when she asked him why he had approached her. A woman by the river in the middle of the night, of course you thought of things like that. No, Heidi said, nothing like that had ever crossed her mind. Rainer's friends stayed behind, shouted to him a couple of times, and then went off without him.

Rainer had sat down on the bench next to Heidi, and she told him her story, but not what Susa and Renate had said about her sketches. He didn't seem at all interested in pictures. He took her home with him; after all, they couldn't sit out on the bench all night. He was very sweet, and then suddenly he put his arms around her and started touching her. She didn't fight him off for long, she had no strength and was tired and empty. Perhaps she even wanted it, the pain and the humiliation were apt

punishment for her cowardice, they set the seal on her
defeat. Heidi had to think about Renate, how different
she was, more confident but still cautious and sensitive.

Rainer stood by the window, and Heidi stared at his
hairy back and felt disgusted by him and by what he'd
done with her. He turned to her and asked how old she
was, and when she replied, Nineteen, he said, You're not
shitting me, are you? He was ten years older.

Heidi stayed at Rainer's for three days. He worked in
a sportswear shop, and left home every morning before
nine o'clock, and only returned after business hours.
Most of the time she spent in the flat, incapable of for-
mulating a clear thought. Once, she pulled out her drawing things, and she sat for an hour in front of the empty
sheet of paper without sketching a line. She sat in the
dusk, waiting for Rainer, dreading him but unable to
leave. She felt like a prisoner, even though he'd given her
a key to the apartment. Sometimes she stood behind the
front door without managing to open it. Once Rainer was
back, he didn't feel like going out. He had done the shopping, had bought bread and cheese and ham and wine,
and they ate and drank, and then Rainer stripped her
naked, and she let him. He was fit and strong and about
a head taller than her, and he turned and twisted her and
put her in positions that he liked, and demanded that she

do things that were difficult for her and shaming, but still she never had the feeling that it was personal, and that he was thinking of her. He seemed very detached and entirely wrapped up in himself and his pleasure, and that was some consolation to her. He used her, but perhaps she used him even more, because she felt nothing, not even pleasure. She viewed herself as from a distance, and was surprised at herself.

HEIDI HAD NO CLEAR RECOLLECTION of time after her return home. She withdrew to her room and didn't speak to anyone. She heard her father standing at the foot of her bed, and announcing in a loud voice, You can go back to the office now. He went away, he came back, stood there in silence and looked down at her. Her mother brought her meals, sat down on the side of the bed, talked to her or stroked her hair. Sometimes she cried. You can't lie here always, she said, you have to eat something, say something. At night Heidi stood in front of the window for hours, gazing out at the moonlit mountains, the stony sisters, that simultaneously drew her and frightened her. She got sick. The doctor was clueless, he performed all sorts of tests on her, and Heidi let it happen. She sat on the treatment table in her underwear. The doctor wrote something in her file, and then swiveled around on his much too low chair. Everything's fine, he said, making a face as though nothing was, except you're pregnant.

She asked him not to tell her parents, but after a while it was impossible to conceal the fact. Her mother was first to notice, and told her father. Her parents reacted with astonishing calm. They asked Heidi who the father was, and whether he knew. Oddly, it had never occurred to Heidi to let Rainer know. What did the child have to do with him? But on her parents' insistence, she called him. He came that weekend, and Heidi met him at the station. He was wearing good clothes, and she sensed that he had thought about everything and had a plan. They drank coffee in a place near the station, and Rainer cautiously tried to establish Heidi's view of everything, and whether she could imagine a life with him. By the time they moved on, to lunch at home with her parents, everything was decided.

Rainer got on well with Heidi's parents. He had a way of submitting to others immediately, and Heidi's father liked that. He helped Rainer get a job, and found them a little three-room apartment. From the balcony, Heidi could see the Three Sisters, and when the wind was in the right angle she could hear the trains, and even the platform announcements. On Sundays, Rainer and Heidi went to her parents', and they all acted as though the baby was already born and belonged to them. Heidi didn't say much, she sensed that it would pass, and that something different was in store for her, something she couldn't begin to predict. At the wedding, Heidi's father made a speech, poking fun at his daughter who had left home to become an artist, and had come back with a bun in the oven. Rainer looked sheepish, but Heidi smiled and raised the baby aloft, like a prize.

HEIDI WENT TO INNSBRUCK many times in the intervening years, but never once to Vienna. Rainer didn't care for Vienna, much less the Viennese. Anyway, he didn't want Heidi to get any stupid ideas, he said, otherwise she might start applying to the Academy again.

A train came in, and Heidi quickly stood up. She didn't want people to see her sitting there as though she had nothing better to do. She went to the supermarket, and then home. She stopped by the neighbor's. Cyril wasn't ready to go home yet, he wanted to go on playing with Leah. He can have supper with us, that's fine, said the neighbor. Not today, said Heidi. Cyril, she called out shrilly, and she stuck her head in at the door, past the neighbor. Cyril!

While she was making supper, she saw the teenagers hanging around the recycling containers. She knew one of the girls, who was a trainee at the bakery. At work she wore a shapeless apron, but on the street you only ever saw her in a miniskirt, with exposed navel and a push-up bra that made her breasts look even bigger than they were. She's just a kid, Rainer had said once, in a tone that made Heidi suspicious. He often made remarks like that about other women, he seemed to think of little else. In their years together Heidi had lost all respect for him. She refused to participate in his games, and kept to herself whenever she could. He suggested a course of therapy for her, came home with pamphlets for couples workshops. Never, said Heidi, I'll never do that, and I'll never talk about those things in front of other people either. She wouldn't even touch the pamphlets, that was how disgusted she was.

After some time Heidi had begun to draw again, in the mornings, when Rainer was out of the house and Cyril was in his kindergarten. Every evening she watched the trainee baker from her kitchen window, saw her parading back and forth in front of the boys, with her chest out and her bottom wiggling. Heidi wanted to ask her to model for her, but she didn't dare go down and talk to the girl. Instead, she drew her from memory, she imagined her in all sorts of poses, naked and clothed, from the back, from the front, squatting or kneeling, standing, face averted, with a hand in her hair.

Heidi stood naked in front of the mirror, and then drew the girl, based on her own body, a childlike figure resembling both parents without it being clear which features came from which parent. She hid the drawings in a cardboard box at the top of the closet in the bedroom. There must be hundreds of them by now.

Sometimes she wondered what would have happened if she'd stayed on the train and gone to Vienna, and submitted her portfolio. Most likely she wouldn't have been asked to take the exam. Or she would have failed the exam. Or she would have passed the exam and taken the course, and she would be an art teacher now in some little town or other. The only thing you could say for certain was that there would have been no Cyril, and she couldn't imagine a life without him, even if she did sometimes wish he had never been born, and she had remained free and independent and able to do whatever she wanted.

She would have liked to talk about all that with Renate, would have liked to show her the new drawings, but since her return she had avoided her former teacher. She thought of that night, the smell of Renate, and her bare feet and her hands, her tanned skin, her pale skin. She felt ashamed in front of her, and secretly she probably gave her some of the blame for what had happened. She never thanked Renate for the card and the soft toy that Renate had sent when Cyril was born. She had the feeling she was making fun of her in some way.

HEIDI WAS MAKING SUPPER. The news was on the radio. Cyril was in the living room, listening to a kids' tape. He had the volume on much too high, and his story was mixed in with items on the news, making an absurd collage. Outside, Carmen was showing off in front of her pals. In her mind, Heidi changed to the girl, parading up and down, confidently showing off her body, dolled up for no one except herself. Heidi knew by now that Carmen wasn't interested in the boys, she was just playing with them. She had talked to her, they had had coffee together, she had gone to buy clothes with her and underwear, which she only wore when Rainer wasn't at home. She had let Carmen put makeup on her and do her hair. And then they had taken pictures of themselves and each other, made little videos using Carmen's mobile phone camera, masquerades, games, whatever they felt like. Heidi had shown herself to the girl, she imagined her showing the little films to her friends with her cheeky laugh. Heidi was waiting for Carmen to look up at her, but she never did, probably she was just toying with her too.

Heidi imagined what would happen if Rainer found the drawings when she was no longer there. Sometime, looking for a reason, he would go through all her things, and open the box and find the sketches and the photographs. She's just a kid, he would say, and shake his head, and not get it.

The Hurt

A T THE AGE of forty, Lucia's mother had gone mad. I think that was the thing Lucia was most afraid of for herself. I asked her what had precipitated it. Just life, Lucia said, shrugging her shoulders. She married this man who loved her more than she loved him. I came along, she raised me, and eventually she couldn't take it anymore and she cut her wrists. When I found her she was unconscious. I was thirteen.

Lucia was two years younger than me. I met her one summer, when I was staying with my grandparents in the mountains. I'd finished school in the spring, and I was going to start college in the fall. I had been hoping to go walking with my grandfather, but he had fallen ill and was slow to recover, so I had a lot of time to myself. When it rained, I read to try and prepare for college, but when the sun shone I was outside all day, wandering around, swimming in the icy lake, and coming home late.

It was at the lake that I first met Lucia. We hit it off right away, and spent all our time together. We went walking in the mountains, lay in the grass for hours, and when the weather was bad we put on slickers and went out anyway. The meadows were springy underfoot, and when the sun came out the sky was blue like you wouldn't believe.

Often Lucia asked me to tell her stories. I'd hardly experienced anything in real life, but I always came up with something to tell her about. I can't remember what, I just remember we used to laugh a lot. Lucia told me about her dreams, places she wanted to visit, things she wanted to buy. A car and clothes and a house. She had it all planned. She wanted to work in one of the hotel bars and make a lot of money in no time at all, and then she wanted a husband and two kids and a house on the edge of the village, near the lake. Then I can sit at home, she said, and look out the window and wait for the kids to come home from school.

Once Lucia got sick. She was alone at home, her mother was away in the clinic, and her father was in the shop downstairs. He sold radios and TVs, and he was a nice, rather shy man. She's just got a bit of a cold, he said, and he sent me upstairs to her.

Lucia answered the door in pajamas, and I followed her up to her room. It was my first time in the house, and I had a mildly alarming sense I was doing something forbidden. It was that afternoon Lucia told me about her mother. It's only in summer, she said, she sits upstairs in her room all day long, doesn't speak, doesn't do anything, and my father keeps having to go up and check how she is. He's worried she might try to do it again, said Lucia. Will you make me some tea?

She wasn't really sick, but I made her some tea anyway, it was like a game of house. Lucia told me where to find everything. When I opened the cabinets, I had a feeling I was under observation. Then Lucia walked into the kitchen and watched me and smiled when I looked at her. When she coughed, it sounded like she was pretending.

Lucia showed me photographs. We lay on the bed together, she was under the covers, I was on top. Eventually she asked me to kiss her, and I kissed her. About a week later, we slept together, it was the first time for both of us.

We thought we would go on a circular walk over two mountain passes. We would spend the night in a youth hostel in the next valley. We had been walking all day, had climbed up a long way, crossed stony landscapes, and only late in the afternoon reached our destination, which was a tiny village way up a barren valley. The youth hostel was a small stone house at the edge of the village. On the door was a sign telling you where to pick up the key.

The house was cold and empty. On the ground floor was a kitchen and a little dining room. There was a guest book on the table. The last entry was a couple of days ago. Two Australians had written something about the end of the world. The dormitory was up in the attic. It was dark, because there were only two dormer windows and a single weak lightbulb hanging from the ceiling. I dropped my backpack on one of the narrow mattresses along the wall on the floor, and Lucia took the one beside it. At the foot end of the mattresses were piles of brown woolen blankets. We went down to the kitchen, made coffee, and ate provisions we'd brought with us, bread and cheese and fruit and chocolate.

The sun dipped over the mountain early and it quickly got cold, but the sky was still blue. In a little general store we bought a liter of red wine. Then we strolled up the valley out of the village. We could hear marmots whistle, but we couldn't see them. After a bit, Lucia said she was getting cold. I offered her my jacket, but she declined and we turned back.

The youth hostel was situated next to a stream we could hear even with the windows closed. It was barely warmer inside than out. I opened the wine and we got into our sleeping bags, not undressing, and drank wine out of the bottle and talked. Tell me a story, Lucia said, and I told her about things I wanted to do and films I'd seen and books I'd read.

Lucia slipped out of her sleeping bag to go to the bathroom. When she came back, she sat on my sleeping bag for a minute, then she stripped to her underwear and scooted in beside me.

Autumn came, and Lucia got a job at a hotel bar. I went home and enrolled at university. I had a good record at high school, but I had trouble making the adjustment to college. I found it hard to meet people, and spent most of my evenings alone in the little attic room my parents had found me.

I wrote regularly to Lucia, who rarely wrote back. If she did, it was a postcard that barely said anything, just that she was doing fine, that there was nothing happening in the village, the weather was good or bad or whatever. Sometimes she filled in the space with little drawings, a flower or an Alpine hut, and one time a heart with a drop of blood squeezed from it. The drawings looked like tattoos to me.

The summer after, my grandfather died. I drove out to the funeral in the village with my father. I hoped to see Lucia. She wasn't there. I left messages for her but she didn't get in touch. When we returned to the flatland, we took Grandmother with us.

A couple of times I tried to phone Lucia. Usually her father picked up and said she had just gone out. Once it was her. I said I wanted to visit her, but she didn't seem interested. When I insisted, she said I was free to do what I liked, she couldn't tell me never to come to the village. After that I wrote to her less often, but I didn't forget her either. I had promised her that summer that I would be back, and when I'd finished at college, I applied for the job of teacher at the village school. The headmaster told me it was only on account of my grandparents that I got the job.

YOU WON'T COME BACK, Lucia had said four years ago. Now she said, I never thought you'd be back. I had come up by train at the beginning of the week. My father promised to bring my stuff up to the valley by car that weekend, my books and the stereo and the little TV. But on Friday it snowed and the pass was shut. My father called and said did it matter if he came the following week? I was sitting in my grandparents' little house. I was sleeping in the bed my grandfather had died in, and presumably my great-grandfather before him. I lay under the heavy comforter, my arms pinned to my sides like a dead person's, and I tried to imagine what it would be like if I really couldn't move them, just to lie there and wait for death.

When the rest of my stuff comes, I'll have you around to dinner, I said to Lucia. I'd gone to the bar where she worked. She said she was still living with her parents. She was working a lot, she said, in summer she'd totaled the car, and she wanted to buy another one in the spring. I said my grandparents' garage still had the old Volvo standing in it, she could always borrow that. That piece of junk? she said, and she smirked.

Work at the school was difficult. I had taken courses in education at college, but the kids here were rowdy and badly behaved and didn't make it at all easy for me. My colleagues were no help either. Most of them were local, and the talk at break was about going hunting and village gossip and the weather. Once I rang the father of one especially difficult girl. He was a hotelier, and he treated me like a schoolboy on the phone. A few days later the headmaster came into my classroom after lessons and said if I had trouble, I should talk to him, and not blame the parents for my failures. Astrid stays up half the night watching TV, I said. And then she can't stay awake during class.

The head looked at the cut-paper shapes I'd done with the kids and that we'd hung in the windows. Snowflakes, he said. As if we didn't have enough snow here. He took them down one after the other, slowly and without saying a word. When he was finished, he put them down in front of me and said, You ought to work on the syllabus instead of cutting fancy paper shapes.

He left. I could hear the kids yelling outside. I went to the window. They were fighting, and then, just like that, they all ran out of the yard and disappeared down the street. They all ran off together, and I was put in mind of a swarm of scruffy birds I'd seen scavenging on the rubbish dump outside the village.

The days were short and getting shorter. For a long time that year the snow held off, instead it was cold and rainy, and often I couldn't see the tops of the mountains because the clouds were so low. It's worse than in other years, said Lucia, at least when the snow comes everything gets brighter. She said she sometimes feared she might lose her mind like her mother. We had gone for a walk one afternoon when there was no school, out of the village and up the slope. It was one of the few fine days that autumn. But soon enough the sun disappeared behind the mountains, and only the upper slopes still had light on them.

If only it would snow, Lucia said, then we could at least go skiing. I asked her back for supper, but she said she had no time. On Saturday then, I said, and she said, Oh, all right. She said she could smell snow in the air, and that the old people said it was going to be a cold winter. But that was what they said every year. I tried to kiss her on the mouth, but she turned away and offered her cheek. Tell me a story, she said. You must have stories you can tell. All that time you've been away. I haven't been away, I said, I've been at home.

THE NEXT DAY we went walking again. We went the same way and sat down on the same bench as on the day before. From there we could see the whole village, and the ugly modern hotels on the lake. The sky was cloudy, and soon after we had sat down it started snowing, small flakes the wind blew in our faces and that settled in the folds of our clothes. The snow melted away as soon as it touched the ground. Lucia had got up. I asked her to wait, but she shook her head and ran down the steep slope, leaping from boulder to boulder like a little girl. I watched her until she was back in the village. I stayed a while longer, then I walked

down the road. I got to the school just on time. The headmaster was standing in the doorway, and watched silently
as I walked past him and into my classroom.

On Saturday Lucia came around. I had gone shopping
that morning and cooked all afternoon. Lucia ate in silence. I asked her how she liked the food. She said, Yeah,
and went on chewing. When we were finished, and sitting on the sofa drinking coffee, she got up and switched
on the TV. I said did she have to do that. Not really, she
said. You can tell me a story, if you like. She left the TV
on, but turned the sound down a bit. I've been waiting for
you, I said. I haven't kept you waiting. I mean since that
time . . . since we . . . you know, since we slept together.
Lucia furrowed her brow. You mean you haven't slept with
any other woman? No, I said, and suddenly I felt stupid.
Lucia laughed out loud. She said I was crazy. That's just
weird. I said I'd often thought about her. Lucia got up and
said it was time she went. I switched off the TV and put on
a CD. I asked if she'd slept with a lot of guys. She said that
was none of my business, and after hesitating briefly, Of
course, what else was there to do up here? Then she said
she had brought some condoms, but she didn't feel like
it anymore. She took the little pack out of her pocket and
tossed it to me. Here, they're all for you, she said, and she
put on her shoes and jacket.

A WEEK LATER we went to the movies together. From the beginning of winter, the community center had one screening per week, and we often went to see them together. But Lucia wouldn't come back to my house again. I was allowed to walk her home, and sometimes we would stand around chatting on the doorstep for a while. When she got cold, she gave me her hand and went inside.

Finally, early in December, it started to snow in the village, and this time the snow stayed with us. For one week it snowed almost solidly, then it stopped. It was very cold now, and the sky was clear. At night I saw loads of stars, they seemed to be much nearer than they were down in the flatland. Once, just before Christmas—we'd watched an American comedy together—Lucia said I could come in if I liked. On the landing she kissed me.

Have you had any more practice since? she asked me, laughing. And when I shook my head: Do you even remember how it's done?

She left me standing in the hallway and went into the living room. I could hear her talking to someone, then she came out again. She opened the door to her room, and I just caught her father sticking his head around the corner of the living room door to see who it might be.

When Lucia was sitting on top of me, she got a nosebleed. She leaned forward and cupped her hand under her nose, but even so some of the blood splashed on my face. She laughed. The blood felt surprisingly cool. Later I heard her father in the passage outside. I wanted to stay over, but Lucia sent me away. She said she didn't want anyone to see me. I got home very late.

The following afternoon I went by without phoning beforehand. Her father was friendly as always and told me just to go up. I'd spent the whole afternoon grading papers, and I was feeling drained. Lucia said she had to go right away, she was on shift at six. If I wanted to, I could go along with her. She would buy me a drink.

In the bar there were a couple of guys from the village, and Lucia wanted us to sit with them until it was time for her to start. I didn't feel like it myself, but she had pulled up a couple of chairs. She was on first-name terms with all of them, and sat next to one she called Elio whom I'd never seen before. Elio worked as a mountain guide in summer and a skiing instructor in winter. He talked about his climbing trips and some ski race that was taking place in January, and the foreign girls who all wanted to hop into bed with him. One came back every year, a German woman from Munich. She books private lessons, but let me tell you, we don't do a lot of skiing. Her husband was some bigwig in a bank, and he might show up in the valley for a weekend. She parked the kids on a baby slope. Then he worked out how much he made from private lessons. He said he was in it purely for the money.

I wanted to go, but Lucia told me to stay. She put her arm through Elio's and told him to go on. By now he was on to mountaineering, relating heroic exploits about difficult ascents and dangerous rescue missions. Lucia wasn't looking at me. She beamed at Elio. In the middle of one story I got up and left. At home I didn't know what to do with myself. I turned on the TV. There was a talk show, in which, to the consternation of the audience, a man was talking about living with two women. The women were present in the studio, and they kept saying what a good relationship they had. I felt disgusted and turned the TV off.

I vacuumed the whole house, washed the dishes, and took the empty bottles to the recycling center. I felt a bit better after that. On my way home I looked in on the bar again. Lucia was working now, and the whole place was full of noisy tourists. Elio was sitting at the end of the bar. When Lucia spotted me, she went over to him and took a puff from his cigarette. Then she leaned across the bar and kissed him on the mouth. She looked at me with an evil smile.

THE NEXT DAY I ran into Lucia on the street. I had bought her something for Christmas. She took the parcel from me without looking at it, shrugged her shoulders, and walked off.

There was no school until the new year. My parents, along with my grandmother, came up to the valley and stayed in the house. They went skiing every day, my grandmother sat downstairs knitting or dozing. She had complained because I had taken down some of her pictures, and there was a scratch in the slate surface of the dining table. I was relieved when Christmas was over and they all went away.

During the rest of my time off, I stayed in bed as long as I could, and once I got up I hardly ever left the house. In the late afternoon I turned on the TV. There was the same talk show I'd seen before, only the subject was different. After I'd watched for a while, I turned off the TV and carted it into the garage. I stood there and stared at the thing. Then I took it around to the front of the house, left it on the street, and taped a piece of paper on the screen: TAKE ME. I waited by the window and looked out. From time to time someone would stop and read the sign and look up at the house. But no one took my TV.

On New Year's Eve I called Lucia. We didn't speak for long, she said she was busy. When I tried later, there was just the answering machine. I left a message on the tape. I said, Lucia, and I loved her and I was lonely and I wanted to spend the evening with her. I waited. At nine o'clock I gave up and went out.

The bar was packed, I could hear the music and the din of voices from out on the street. Lucia and a coworker stood behind the bar, Elio was sitting at one end of it again. I sat down next to him and ordered a beer. Lucia didn't look at me. Sometimes she came down in our direction, leaned across the bar and shouted something in Elio's ear, or kissed him, or had a puff from his cigarette. She smoked hurriedly, scanning the room as she did so. The smoke slid around her hand as though caressing it. I felt drunk, even though it was my first beer.

I watched Lucia at work. She laughed with the customers and moved quickly back and forth. She was wearing a skimpy top, and I saw she had a pierced navel, and wasn't as slim as I seemed to remember her. But that only made her more alluring. I so wanted to touch her and kiss her, my whole body ached. And at the same time I saw myself hunkered in my corner, a pathetic lovelorn figure.

Eventually Lucia had some time off. She came out from behind the bar and got between Elio and me. Elio stood up and threw his arm around her shoulder, then he half bent his knees and gyrated with his hips. Then he let go of Lucia to go to the toilet, stumbled, almost fell. Lucia screamed with laughter. She moved slowly to the music, ran her hands down my hips and smiled at me. She said something. I shook my head, and she put her mouth right up against my ear. Great vibe, isn't it? she yelled. Then she disappeared back behind the bar. I got up and left.

I WENT HOME. The TV was still out on the street, covered with snow. It was cold inside, I'd forgotten to fill the stove before going out. As I was on my way to the garage to pick up a few logs, my eye fell on the stack of blue exam books on the kitchen table. What I Really Want for Christmas. I flicked through them. What was it my students wanted, snowboards, game boys, a motor sled? And what had I expected? Justice? Love? Peace on earth?

I heard the bells chiming for midnight, and then cars honking and fireworks going off. I stuffed the essays in the stove and lit them. I watched through the glass panel as they curled in the heat and burned, first slowly, then faster and faster. Before the flames died down, I ripped a few pages out of an education textbook on the floor, and shoved them in too. I ripped more and more pages out of it, and when there was nothing left of it but the cover, I got another one. My eyes were tearing from staring so hard into the flames, and my face felt scorched.

I burned one book after another. I ripped bundles of pages out of the bindings and threw them in the flames. I was surprised how much strength it took to rip up a book. My hands hurt. In the end I went to bed.

The next day I carried on. I was more methodical now, I stacked my books next to the stove and burned them one by one. It took all morning. Then I pulled my notes out of my desk drawers, my diaries, newspaper clippings I'd never gotten around to reading. I burned the lot. The room was full of smoke that billowed out of the open door of the stove.

That evening I went to the bar. There weren't so many people as the day before. Elio was in his corner again. When I sat down next to him, he looked at me doubtfully. Lucia came and took my order. She asked me if I'd made any good resolutions for the new year. I said I'd burned all my books. You're crazy, she said. I'll tell you a story, I said, but it was probably more for my benefit than hers. I told her about how I'd first come to the village, and how I'd met Lucia. I told her about our long hike into the next valley, and our first night.

Slowly Elio drank his beer. He was looking at the bar, it seemed he wasn't listening. Lucia was, though. She was in the grip of a strange unrest, and wouldn't look me in the eye. When I was finished, she leaned across the bar and whispered something into Elio's ear. Then she kissed him on the mouth long and lingeringly. At the same time she looked at me with an expression that was at once frightened and furious. At least she wasn't indifferent to me anymore. I got up and left. At home I wrote her a long letter. When I'd finished, I put it in the stove and burned it.

I didn't leave the house at all the next day. I burned everything I could find: cardboard boxes, my grandparents' photo albums, old wooden skis that were in the broom closet, a broken stool. Whatever was too big I sawed or chopped into pieces with the ax. The tools were old and hadn't been used in a long time, the saw blade was spotted with rust, and the ax was blunt.

The following day I started on the furniture. My grandparents' things were solidly built, and I had no idea how much work it was to destroy something. It was probably easier to kill someone, I thought. The application of pressure to the correct spot, a twist of the neck, a blade slipped between the ribs, the way I had seen it done in films. I thought more in terms of killing Elio than Lucia, but it wouldn't have changed anything. When the shops opened after the holidays, I bought a new ax.

Destruction had a smell. Torn paper, cardboard, ripped cloth soaked in gasoline to make it burn. Wood smelled when it splintered as if it was freshly felled, as though the smell had been secreted inside it the whole time. And then the smells of burning: the sour smoke from paper that I pushed into the stove in great wads, and that slowly turned to ash. The thick smell of burning gas, the acrid smell of varnish that bubbled and blackened before the wood underneath caught fire.

Whatever I couldn't burn I stuffed in garbage sacks that I stowed in the Volvo, first in the trunk, then when that was full on the back seat, and finally on the front passenger seat.

School had begun again. I had gotten much calmer. During class, my thoughts were already on the work of destruction I would continue that evening. Thinking of it seemed to calm me. When I met the headmaster in the hallway, he gave me a friendly nod, and offered me best wishes for the new year.

One weekend I drove out of the village and took a narrow road up the mountain. At the beginning of the road was a sign saying no passenger cars, only farm and forestry traffic. There were very few marks in the snow. I followed the zigzagging road up the mountain. After a couple of miles it came to a sudden stop. I left the car and walked back. When I got home I was frozen to the marrow.

After a week the village policeman phoned and said my car had been found. He was suspicious and asked various questions. He didn't seem to believe whatever cock-and-bull story I told him.

On Sunday I went to church for the first time since I was living in the valley. I sat in the back pew. When the minister asked the congregation to come forward for the blessing, I stayed put. I saw Lucia, kneeling down with maybe a dozen other believers. The minister laid his hand on their heads, one after the other, and spoke the blessing. After the service I tried to speak to Lucia. It was the first time in ages that I'd seen her without Elio. I love you, I said. You're crazy, she said, you're imagining things. She walked off. I followed her and said it again: I love you. But she didn't react, wouldn't even look at me. I followed her back to her house, climbed the stairs after her to the back entrance. She opened the door, went in, and slammed the door in my face.

At the end of January I took the bed apart and sawed and chopped it up in the garage into little pieces that I burned in the stove. That was the last of the furniture. There was only the mattress to come.

On one of the following days I walked up to the place above the village where I'd sat with Lucia. I wiped the snow off the bench and sat down. The sun was already gone over the mountains. After a while I saw Lucia coming up the road. She was walking fast and had her eyes on the ground. Once she looked up at the bench. I waved, but I wasn't sure whether she saw me or not. She walked on a bit, then she turned back and returned to the village.

The next day I was just about to give my students a dictation when I saw Lucia through the window. I told them I'd be back in a minute, and ran out of the classroom. By the time I was on the street, though, she had disappeared. I hesitated for a minute, then I went home, packed a few things, and called a taxi. I knew the driver, one of his kids was in my class. He didn't ask me any questions, and didn't seem to be surprised when I told him to take me to the station.

There was half an hour until the next train, and I was suddenly worried someone might come and prevent me from leaving. The driver had parked his taxi outside the station. He had got out and was smoking and talking on the phone to someone. He laughed, I could hear him from the platform where I was standing. Sometimes he looked across at me, and in spite of the distance, I thought I could make out a triumphant expression on his face.

The train arrived. A couple of skiers boarded with me, but they got off at the next station and I was alone in the car. I opened a window and leaned out. Cold air flowed in. The sky was overcast, and the mountains looked threatening as they passed. Not until the train turned a corner and entered a tunnel did I calm down.

The Result

THE BANDAGE ON Bruno's back felt tight. The wound hardly hurt, but thinking about it got to him and made him sweat more than he usually did. It had been hot for weeks. It was late August, and some people said it would stay hot well into September.

Bruno had worked at reception for thirty years. The past week he had been on the early shift. He was home at three, and Olivia got him to go shopping with her. In the shops she asked him questions he couldn't answer.

Bruno showered before supper. When he came out of the bathroom in clean clothes, Olivia wanted to change his bandage. The thought that she had left the kitchen and waited for him outside the bathroom door bothered him. I'm sure the bandage has gotten wet, she said, and she followed him into the bedroom. It hasn't, he said, it doesn't matter.

Olivia unbuttoned his shirt. He was too feeble to resist, and sank down onto the bed. She sat down beside him, pulled the shirt over his shoulder, and told him to turn around.

Watch out, she said, and already the bandage was off. It doesn't hurt, said Bruno. It looks fine, she said. It was just a couple of punctures, he said. She said he had always had good powers of healing. He said it felt a bit tight. Olivia was immersed in her work. There, she said, and she stroked his hair, now you've earned your supper.

It was seven o'clock. They always ate at seven. It's supposed to get cooler tomorrow, said Olivia, as she heaped Bruno's plate. He wasn't hungry, but he had long since stopped trying to tell her that.

After supper he went out in the garden and stayed out a long time, longer than usual. It was already getting dark when he came in. Clouds had appeared from somewhere. Olivia was in the living room, watching the late news. Bruno went into the bedroom. He got undressed and lay down. Is it raining yet? Olivia asked as she came to bed. Bruno didn't reply.

He was glad he was on the late shift again tomorrow. He didn't have to be at the hotel until three, and could sleep in as long as he liked. Olivia woke him with lunch, and after coffee he was out of the house. They didn't live far from the hotel, and Bruno loved biking home from work. At night the town center was full of young people talking animatedly in the cafes. When he got home, Olivia was usually in bed already, and he went into the bedroom to wish her good night. He kissed her quickly, and she said, Mind you don't stay up too long.

The cold front had reached the town overnight. Suddenly the air was almost twenty degrees colder, and it had gotten darker, almost autumnal outside. When was he expecting the result? Olivia asked him over lunch. She asked him every day, since he'd gone to the doctor a week ago, to get the mole removed. Tomorrow, he said. It's bound not to be anything, said Olivia. Of course it's nothing, said Bruno, just a routine check. Well, better safe than sorry, said Olivia, it's one less thing to worry about. The uncertainty. That's why I had it done, said Bruno. Quite, said Olivia. Will they call you, or do you have to call them?

Bruno had left the number of the hotel with the doctor's assistant. She had promised to call on Wednesday, sometime during the afternoon. The doctor hadn't even thought it necessary to offer any words of optimism. The chances of it being a melanoma were really very

small. Bruno wasn't worried. On the contrary, he was
in a sparkling mood that day, perhaps because it had
cooled down at last. He made a joke when he took over
from his colleague, and personally arranged the flowers in the room where the Christian businesspeople
were meeting in the evening. Then he stepped out onto
the terrace and contentedly surveyed the landscape,
the little section of the lake you could see from there,
and the forested mountains, which seemed to be much
nearer now than when it was hot. It didn't even bother
him when Sergio called in to say he was sick. The student who generally filled in on such occasions wasn't
home, but his mother said he would be back soon. Bruno
called Olivia. He said he would be back late, he couldn't
say how late. Why today of all days? said Olivia. Bruno
didn't reply.

The Christian businesspeople had all gone home.
Marcella emerged from the room with the last of them,
and stopped at the reception desk for a chat with Bruno.

Those Christians are lousy tippers, she said, I hope
they'll at least remember us in their prayers. She asked
what Bruno was doing there still.

Sergio is sick, he said.

What about the student? asked Marcella. What's the
matter with Sergio?

Bruno shook his head. We've known each other for thirty years, he said. He began here shortly after me. You weren't even born then.

Marcella laughed. She said she was thirty-five.

You don't look it, said Bruno. Who looks after your kids when you're at work?

They can look after themselves. My younger girl is ten. My older girl is thirteen. The boy is fifteen.

He had three children too, Bruno said, but they all moved out a long time ago. Marcella said she was just going to straighten out the hall. See you in a minute, she said.

Two middle-aged women left the hotel. Bruno had often been puzzled by the attractive women who stayed as guests of the hotel. They arrived in twos and threes, without their husbands. They shared a room, were out all day, and returned to the hotel in the evening with half a dozen large bags from expensive stores. Sometimes he saw them on his tours of duty by the pool, lying there half naked on their deck chairs. Bruno would stop for an instant and look at them skeptically from a distance. After dinner, the women might leave the hotel once more, and he wouldn't be around to see them return. Sergio had told him that they sometimes had men with them whom they tried to smuggle in past him. As if he cared who they spent their nights with. He was quite capable of imagining the rest, when the men slunk past the porter's desk an hour later, with cigarettes between their lips and frosty expressions.

Bruno thought of Marcella in her black skirt. He imagined her coming home. The children were already in bed, the husband was watching TV in the living room. She went into the bathroom and took off her skirt and underskirt. She washed and went to the bedroom in her underwear and pulled on her nightie.

Bruno thought of the time when his kids had still been at home, all those long, monotonous years, all the mornings and evenings. Sometimes he longed for those meals, where no one had said much, nothing of importance. It was the repetition that made them so lovely, the knowledge that tomorrow and the day after and next week and next year they would be sitting together in exactly the same way. There seemed to be so much time then. Not until the children had moved out did he notice how distant they had remained in all those years. When Bruno saw a disaster movie in which an earthquake or flood or volcanic eruption threatened a town, it wasn't the destruction that moved him or the deaths, only the fate of the man who had become separated from his family and was desperately looking for them in all the confusion. He would have tears in his eyes, and Olivia said what a load of nonsense.

At ten o'clock Bruno called home and said he still didn't know when he'd be back. Olivia sounded worried, but she didn't say anything. He promised her he would call later on.

He thought of the result he would get tomorrow. He thought about the way they would break the news. The doctor would be straight with him. Seventy percent of patients died within five years. Then he would embark on that rigmarole he had seen one of the waiters, a man from Portugal, go through, that endless sequence of tests and therapies. Times when things looked to be improving, and other times when he could barely recognize the man. Sleepless nights, unbearable pain, days of vomiting, and in the end a mean and nasty death.

He stood in front of the hotel. Not many of its rooms were occupied. Only a few of the windows had lights on; in one of them a young man was sitting and smoking a cigarette. He tossed the butt out the window and disappeared. Bruno was terrified, absolutely terrified of the disease that might already have spread throughout his body. He was afraid of losing his life a piece at a time. He had never wished for very much, only hoped things might stay more or less as they were. But maybe that had been enough to provoke fate.

Marcella emerged from the hotel, said good night, and unlocked her bike. Good night, he said, and Marcella waved and rode off.

Bruno looked at the old oil painting that hung next to the front desk. He had almost forgotten it existed, even though he went past it at least twice a day. It was a fare-well scene in the golden light of a breaking storm. The man was wearing chain mail and some sort of surcoat. His hair was braided and he had a drooping mustache that gave his appearance something Oriental, a Fu Man-chu mustache. He would be gone a long time, perhaps he was going on a Crusade, perhaps he would never return to the castle on the lake, and to the woman in the long flow-ing robes. When he started at the hotel, Bruno had often stood in front of the painting. He had kissed the woman and set out into the storm full of joyful expectation. Now all he could see was pain and the inevitability of parting.

The student called a little after eleven. Bruno told him not to bother anymore. He was annoyed, even though there was nothing he could blame the student for. Bruno waited, looked at the wall clock, sat down at his desk, got up again. He fetched the bottle of grappa from the cabinet that he had been given for Christmas by a regu-lar at the hotel, and hadn't opened. It was a good make, the guest had said, but Bruno didn't care for grappa. He poured himself a water glass full and drank it down. He shuddered. He filled the glass a second time. He picked up the phone, put it down again. What was he going to tell Olivia? The truth? And what was the truth? That he didn't want to come home. That he didn't want to spend this last evening with her and her false concern and her useless chatter. He wouldn't be able to stand it if she changed his bandage again, ruffled his hair like a little boy's. He wasn't a little boy, he was an old man, maybe a man with a deadly disease. And he wanted to spend the evening by himself, without lies and without comfort.

He called Olivia and said he wasn't coming home. The student couldn't make it, and there had to be somebody at reception.

Can't be helped, he said. Olivia asked if he'd eaten anything, and said he ought to lie down. Good night, said Bruno, and hung up.

The two women came back just before midnight. They were unaccompanied, but clearly exuberant. They laughed loudly as they walked up the stairs. A little later, Bruno locked the front entrance. If anyone came along, they would have to ring the bell. Bruno could have lain down now, but he walked through the deserted hallways, and went out through a side exit into the grounds. The swimming pool glistened blackly in the darkness.

Bruno switched on the underwater lighting, and the pool shone azure. He loved that color, and the coolness and cleanness and the faint smell of chlorine. The pool was the real glory of the hotel, not the decorated rooms or the gourmet menus or the lounge musicians who sometimes played here on weekends. The pool was different from the lake where he usually swam, it was detached from the natural scene and from daily life. It represented a life he would never live, but that didn't bother him. It was enough that there were some people who did live like that, and that he was near them, and provided service for them. It had never occurred to him to spend his holidays in the hotel, though probably he could have afforded it.

Bruno stood by the side of the pool. Then, not really knowing what he was doing, he began to undress. Slowly and gingerly he went down the shallow tiled steps, leaning forward as though about to plunge into the water. It was cool, but not cold. He stood there and looked at his naked body, which was yellow and pale in the bluish light. Then he lowered himself into the water and swam to the far end of the pool. He swam back and forth, feeling first a little warmer, then cold again. He got out of the pool and brushed the water from his body with his hands, and got dressed. He was aroused, almost euphoric, and felt like laughing or crying.

Bruno slept on the couch in a nook on the second-floor landing. He had wild dreams he was unable to remember later. When it grew light outside, he didn't feel he'd slept at all. His head ached and he was still a little dizzy from the grappa. He put the half-empty bottle back in the cabinet. Then he went to the bathroom, washed his face, and rinsed his mouth out. The cold water refreshed him a little. He went down to the restaurant, which was still closed at this hour. It took a long time for the water in the coffee machine to heat up. Only then did it occur to him that he'd had nothing to eat since yesterday lunchtime. In a drawer he found some cut bread, and there were little individually wrapped pats of butter and cheese in the fridge.

His colleague got in at half past six. He explained to her that Sergio was sick, and she said Bruno should have called her. He merely shook his head. Then he called Olivia. It took a few rings before she picked up. He could hear the radio in the background. He thought of her eating her breakfast by herself, the way she always did when he was on night duty and she let him sleep in. She will eat breakfast by herself all the time now, he thought, she will have to get used to it. And suddenly he felt sorry for her, and he was ashamed of himself.

Did you sleep well? he asked.

Not really, replied Olivia. She said the house felt cold.

Then why didn't you turn the heat on? he said. I'm on my way.

Did you get your result? she asked.

This afternoon, said Bruno. But it's nothing. It won't be anything.

We're Flying

S IX O'CLOCK CAME and went, but Angelika wasn't
really worried. She brought out the garage, but
Dominic didn't want to play anymore. He sat quietly on her lap and leaned his head against her breast.
The last couple of times the bell rang, he had gone
running to the door, only to come back with shoulders
drooping, because it was some other child's mother
or father. All the parents knew Dominic, because he
was usually already there in the morning when they
dropped off their own children and still there when
they picked them up at night. They said hello to him,
and thanked him for opening the door. They asked him
vaguely if he'd played nicely that day. Then as soon as

they saw their own children, they beamed and forgot all about Dominic.

Shall we look at a picture book together? Dominic merely shook his head. When Angelika stood up and set him down on the ground, he held on to her leg. She said she was going to call his home. Let me go, she said. He wouldn't let go. She was annoyed, not with him, but with his parents, and she felt bad about taking out her irritation on him. She was tired and wanted to go home. Benno was coming at half past seven, and she wanted to shower first and relax a bit. She looked at the clock. It was twenty past six.

She broke Dominic's grip and stepped away from him. He was lying in the corner, screaming now, and she tried to call his parents. She dialed all the numbers she found in the book: home numbers, office numbers, and both mobile phones, but no one picked up. She left messages. She made no effort to conceal her irritation. After that was done she felt a little calmer. She went across to Dominic, leaned down over him, and patted him on the shoulder. Someone would be along soon.

Dominic asked if it would be his mama or his papa who was coming. Angelika said she wasn't sure, but one or the other would be there any minute. Dominic asked if any minute was now. No, said Angelika. When was any minute? Now? No, any minute was soon. Now? Not yet. She would tell him. She lifted him off the ground and carried him to the sofa. He took hold of her again. Is now soon? She didn't reply. She was busy doing things, tidying away the last of the toys, opening the windows to let in some fresh air. At seven she called Benno and said she was running late. They agreed to make it half past eight. Dominic sat rigidly on the red sofa and didn't take his eyes off her.

Usually it was his mother who brought him to nursery school and his father who picked him up. He always came at the last moment, sometimes he was late, but this time he was more than an hour late. Angelika's annoyance had lessened. Now she was beginning to worry. She felt uneasy, she felt threatened, she didn't know how or why. I'm going to leave in five minutes, she thought to herself, and in five minutes she thought the same thing. She called her boss but got no reply. She wondered about calling the police to ask if there'd been an accident somewhere, but then she decided not to. She wrote a note to Dominic's parents to say she had taken the boy home with her. She left her cell phone number at the bottom. She shut the windows and bundled Dominic up in his jacket and hat and shoes, and took him by the hand. When she'd locked up, she realized she'd forgotten the note, and she had to go back in again to get it and attach it to the door.

She was often out and about in the city with the children, going to the zoo or the lake or a playground near the day care. But this was different. She felt she was with her own child, and she felt oddly proud—as though taking a child by the hand were somehow difficult. Dominic was quiet, who knew what was going on in his head. He sat down next to her in the streetcar and looked out the window. After a couple of stops, he began asking questions. He pointed to a woman and asked, Why is that woman wearing a hat? Because it's cold. Why is it cold? It's winter. Why? Look at the little dog, said Angelika. Why is the dog little? Just because, she said, there are big dogs and little dogs. Are we going home? asked Dominic. Yes, said Angelika, we're going home. Home to my home.

At the station they had to wait. The bus was late, so they stood in the dark and waited. It had been raining in the afternoon, and the car headlights glistened on the wet asphalt. At least Angelika had tomorrow off. She wanted to go to IKEA with Benno and buy a cabinet for her shoes. She had looked at the catalog and knew exactly which model.

For a while Dominic didn't say anything. When she bent down to look at him, he suddenly stood up on one foot and swiveled on his own axis like a ballet dancer. He spread his arms, and turned around and around until he was wobbling. He kept his eyes fixed on the ground, completely lost in his funny dance. His face was earnest and concentrated. Watch out, said Angelika, here comes the bus. I'm flying, said Dominic.

Angelika lived in a suburb on the edge of town, in a five-story tenement from the 1980s. At the time she moved to the city, she hadn't been able in her hurry to find anything better, and after a while she had gotten used to it, she no longer heard the noise from the airport, and it was close to the forest where she liked to go jogging in summer. Lots of families with children lived here. Eventually Angelika would have children too. She had never discussed it with Benno, and didn't even know how he felt about it. But one thing was for sure: he wouldn't want to live out here. He let her know that each time he came to visit her. Most of the time they met at his place. Only when Angelika was at work late did he sometimes agree to sleep over at hers.

She was amazed by how naturally Dominic followed her up the stairs. On the second floor he even overtook her and charged on ahead. When she stopped in front of her door, he was half a flight up, and she had to call him back. Then suddenly he didn't want to go down the stairs alone, and she had to lead him down.

He stopped in the hall and waited patiently while she took off his wet shoes and his jacket. She asked him if he was hungry. He nodded, and she went in the kitchen to see what she had in the fridge. She cooked some pasta, with sauce out of a jar. While he ate, she flicked through the free newspaper she'd picked up on the streetcar. Dominic was ravenous, cramming the noodles into his mouth with both hands. When she asked him to use a fork, he said he didn't know how. But you manage it at nursery, she said. He pretended to try. Then, when she told him off again, he started to wail. Don't be so silly, said Angelika. Dominic pushed his plate away with a jerk and upset his glass. The water spilled over the table and the newspaper. Can't you watch what you're doing? snapped Angelika, and got up to get a paper towel.

Suddenly her apartment looked ugly and inhospitable to her. No wonder Benno didn't like coming here. She remembered her childhood and the home of her parents, that cozy old house. At the time she had the feeling nothing bad could happen to her in that house, as though it had always been there and would always be there, a refuge and a protection for her. When her parents said a few years ago that they wanted to sell it and move into an apartment, she couldn't believe it. Her father had trouble walking, and her mother said neither of them was getting any younger, and the garden was a lot of work, and what were they both doing, rattling around all alone in that big old house. Angelika said nothing. Her parents hired movers to handle the move. She asked herself if she would ever manage to offer a child such a home. It seemed to her she didn't have the confidence, the security, or the love.

They were still at table when Angelika heard the key in the door. Hello, Benno called from the hall. He appeared in the doorway of the living room, stopped, and said, Well, who do we have here? Angelika explained. Is he going to sleep in our bed? Benno asked with a grin. Because if he is, I can pack up and go home. Angelika said she was sure it was just a misunderstanding. Misunderstanding? said Benno. People leave their kid somewhere, and it's a misunderstanding? He sat down with them at table. Dominic stared at him, and Benno stared back, with the same look of astonishment. Perhaps they flew away, he said. Do you think your parents could have flown away? He flapped his arms like a bird. Dominic said nothing, and Benno asked if there was anything left to eat. I thought you would have eaten already. Not really, said Benno. Angelika said she could make him some spaghetti. Do you want some more? she asked Dominic. He nodded.

When she brought the spaghetti into the living room ten minutes later, Benno and Dominic were sitting on two sofa cushions on the floor. Dominic was sitting behind

Benno and had his arms around his waist. Benno leaned his upper body forward and to the side and back, and was making droning sounds. Dominic was laughing wildly and copying his movements. We're flying, said Benno.

Angelika put the spaghetti on the table and fetched cutlery and a clean plate. Come on, she said, supper'll get cold. Again she thought of her childhood, where such a sentence must have fallen a thousand times, though she seemed only now to understand it. Benno got up. He had his arms out and was still flying. He made for the table. Dominic was holding onto his belt and allowed himself to be towed. He was skipping up and down with delight. Suddenly Benno spun around and grabbed the boy and plopped him on a chair. There, he said, we have to eat something, the plane's run out of fuel.

Angelika watched the two of them eating. Now it was Dominic's turn to copy Benno. He had his head low over his plate and shoveled forkfuls of spaghetti into his mouth, all the while squinting at Benno. Angelika looked at her boyfriend, who seemed unaware of it. He's like a kid himself, she thought. Maybe that was why he was so good with them. She had had a couple of occasions to witness it, when he had picked her up from nursery school. In some ways he struck her as almost being younger than Dominic, who seemed to be aware of everything that was going on, and thought it through and asked questions. Benno didn't ask any questions. He came here, ate, slept with her, and went away the next day. She couldn't imagine him as a father. But then most of the men who came to pick up their kids at day care weren't fathers either. They talked to the kids as if they were kids themselves, and fooled around, and when you asked them something they shrugged their shoulders.

Do I get a beer? Benno asked, and then he asked Dominic, Hey man, do you want a beer? No-o-o, said Dominic emphatically, beer is for grownups.

After supper, Dominic wanted to fly some more, but Benno said the plane had mechanical trouble. He sat on the sofa and switched on the TV. Angelika cleared the table. She brought Dominic a few toys she kept in the apartment for her nephews and nieces. Then she sat down next to Benno, who was watching a cop show. Suddenly she felt very much alone.

Dominic played uncertainly with Legos, and kept looking up at them on the sofa. Benno had put his feet up on the coffee table, and had his arm around Angelika. He undid the top button of her blouse. Stop that, she said, but he carried on, and shoved his hand down her front. When she tried to get up, he held her down. I'm not going to let that runt spoil my fun, he said, and he took off her blouse. If he says anything, I'm out of a job, said Angelika. Benno kissed her on the mouth and talked at the same time, she didn't know what he was saying. He must have seen things at his parents', he said, and anyhow he had to learn sometime. Angelika tried to forget about Dominic, but she couldn't. She remembered how he had cried on the stairs. He had looked at her as though it was her fault his parents weren't coming. I don't like him, she thought, actually I don't like any of them. She lay on the sofa and embraced Benno. He laughed and thrust his hand between her legs. When he tried to undo her belt, she pushed him away. He allowed himself to fall to the floor, and lay there on his back, next to Dominic.

Do you want to fly? he asked the boy, who was staring at him in utter bewilderment. He grabbed him and lifted him onto his belly, where he began tickling him. Dominic squirmed, but he didn't laugh. He assumed the serious expression he had had during his dance at the bus stop. Angelika sat up, straightened her bra, and pulled on her blouse. She felt ashamed of herself.

Do you know where babies come from? Benno asked. Dominic said he had come out of his mama's belly. But do you know how you got in there? asked Benno. I was so small, said Dominic, I was as small as this, and he pinched his finger and thumb together.

Just before nine, Dominic's mother called. Angelika jumped, as she always did when her cell phone rang. The woman's voice sounded half annoyed, half embarrassed. She apologized. Her husband had a late meeting that he hadn't told her about. Angelika could hear his voice in the background, protesting. At any rate, we each thought the other was doing it. They were at the day care, and were on their way here. Angelika gave them directions, with a lot of difficulty. Well, we'll be there soon, said the mother. Dominic's fine, said Angelika. Yes, of course, said the mother with a little laugh, I didn't doubt it. I'll see you in twenty minutes, half an hour, maybe.

She's a lawyer, said Angelika.

Is she good-looking? asked Benno. Rich?

Angelika said she was sure Dominic's parents weren't short of money. His father was a relationship counselor.

What's she look like? asked Benno.

Average, said Angelika.

Half an hour later the bell rang. Dominic had been sitting on the sofa in shoes and coat for the past ten minutes. Good-bye, little fellow, said Benno. Come and see us again, will you?

Dominic didn't answer. Angelika took him by the hand.

When Dominic saw his mother through the glass door, he broke away and ran down the last couple of steps. The two of them faced each other, separated only by the glass. The mother had crouched down and was signaling to the boy. He pressed his hands and face against the cold glass, which misted over with his breath. Angelika unlocked the door. The mother stood up. Angelika saw she had a package in her hand. Is that for me? asked Dominic. That's for dear Angelika, said the mother. As thanks for letting you come and visit her. She handed the present to Angelika, and repeated that she was terribly sorry it had happened, and she was thoroughly embarrassed. A misunderstanding. Angelika had thought of some reply, but then all she said was these things happened, and thank you for the present. I hope you'll enjoy this, she said, and then to Dominic, Right, let's hurry home and get to bed. Say bye-bye. Angelika watched them leave and walk over to a jeep that was parked diagonally to the other cars. She could just make out the silhouette of the father at the wheel. The mother bent down to Dominic and seemed to tell him something. Angelika waved, but they didn't seem to notice. When the door closed behind her, she turned around once more. The car was gone. On the glass she saw the traces left by Dominic's hands. She wiped them away with her sleeve.

Benno was in the shower, Angelika could hear the water. She sat down in the living room and opened the package. It was a bottle of perfume. She sniffed it and dabbed some behind her ears and between her breasts. Benno emerged from the shower. He was naked, with a towel slung around his hips. She saw the bulge of his erection. He sat down beside her and embraced her. She freed herself and said she would have a quick shower too. She locked the bathroom but didn't undress. When Benno knocked on the door, she was still sitting on the toilet, with her face in her hands.

Videocity

"You talkin' to me? You talkin' to me? You talkin' to me?
Then who the hell else are you talkin' to? You talkin' to me?
Well I'm the only one here."

—TRAVIS BICKLE in *Taxi Driver*

T ALL BEGAN with the death of his mother. With their claim that his mother had died. He can hardly remember what came before. Just occasional images: exterior, day. A large garden, colors, fruit trees, a house with a steeply pitched roof. The image is distorted at the edges, as though seen through a wide-angle lens. In close-up the face of his mother. She is laughing and swinging him up in the air. She is holding him by the hands and swinging him around in a circle. His eye is the camera. The garden smudges in the accelerating movement, a green blur. Cut.

A long hallway, gray linoleum, white walls. Rainy light leaks in from outside, dim. He is sitting on a bench next to a woman he doesn't know. They wait for a long time until a doctor emerges from one of the rooms, shakes his head, says something he doesn't understand. The face of the doctor is gray. The woman stands up, takes the boy by the hand, and they leave down the hallway and down a wide flight of stone steps. They walk out of shot, which is held a moment longer. Cut.

A montage: dining rooms, dormitories, gym halls. He is standing there, in too short pants, in a gym outfit, clothes that others have worn before him. Always with other boys. The soundtrack is a babel of noise, an echoey confusion of scraps of words, yells, whistles, the singing of children. The loneliness of never-being-alone. The light goes out and goes on again immediately. The taste of toothpaste, porridge, white bread. Someone is banging around on an upright piano, the clatter of dishes and sounds of liquids being slopped out and scraping noises. He shuts his eyes, opens them again.

Twenty years later. The radio alarm plays "I Got You, Babe." A hand slams on the button and the music stops. A man gets up, sits for a moment on the edge of the bed, his face buried in his hands. He stands up and leaves the room. We track him to the bathroom, then to the landing. The camera pans away from him, moves toward the window, then through it. Outside a street in a poor neighborhood. The asphalt is wet, but judging by the clothes of

the passersby it is not cold. As if on command, the extras
start to move. A man carrying a bouquet of flowers walks
past, the same as every morning, then two women of
thirty or so, presumably foreigners, with long black hair.
Both are wearing jeans and white T-shirts, one of them is
carrying a light blue shoulder bag. They are yards apart,
but even so they seem to belong together, like clones, or
sisters unaware of each other's existence. The front door
of a house opens. The man we saw a moment earlier steps
out onto the pavement. His hair is wild, he looks like an
unmade bed. At a corner bodega he buys a cup of coffee. Then he walks on in the same direction as the two
women.

From street level, a couple of steps lead down to a low
basement premises. VIDEOCITY it says on the glass door.
On the inside of the glass is a red sign: CLOSED. The man
unlocks the door, walks in, and turns the sign around.
A smell of cold cigarette smoke. The room is dark, even
after the man has switched on a light. On the walls are
shelves stacked with hundreds of videocassettes, at the
far end of the room is a counter with a cash register and
a small TV set. Behind it a door leads into a tiny room
with a toilet, an old fridge with a stained coffee machine
on it, and a rickety cabinet that looks as if it's been sal-
vaged from a dumpster. The man plugs in the TV and the

register and starts the coffee machine. Only then does he take off his coat.

All morning no one comes. A little before noon, a short woman of about fifty walks into the shop and looks around. She is wearing blue shoes and a 1950s houndstooth jacket. She has a vaguely stunned facial expression. She seems to have walked in by mistake. She turns and walks out again without saying a thing. It often happens, people walk in here and leave, for no apparent reason. Sometimes they just look in the window, sometimes they walk in under some pretext. They're looking for some film he's never heard of, or they want to buy the life-sized cardboard figure in the window. Sometimes they want change for the meter. He can't do anything, he can't prove anything. They're too cunning for him. Once he saw that someone must have broken in during the night. Since then he's careful to remember all the details of where he leaves everything when he goes. They must have noticed it, because they've stopped coming in at night. They are very cagey.

It's not just the young men in dark suits with name tags. Sometimes there are children or old women, foreigners with some illegible piece of paper they hold in his face, some address they claim they're trying to find. He's remembered the addresses, marked them down on a map, and connected them up. It's not yet clear to him what their significance is. He is unable to trust even his oldest customers. They're sounding him out. They start a casual conversation, ask him if he's seen some film or other, and what he thinks of it. He's very careful with what he says. He doesn't know how many of them are involved. It's not impossible that they're all in league with each other.

The sets are made of wood and stone. They are to very high specifications, you barely notice the difference, but you sense there's something missing. Distant buildings seen against the light look transparent. The horizon retreats as you walk toward it, it seems two-dimensional, a painting. Sometimes he spots mistakes, trivial things, but they can't be accidental. When he taps the wall, it makes a hollow sound. Some things are smaller than they should be in reality. He feels tempted to lift the manhole cover in the street to see what's concealed underneath. But that would be too obvious. When he goes home at night, he thinks he could just keep on going, straight on, but he's convinced they wouldn't allow it. He would lose his way in the streets, he would wind up at a dead end. An accident could be organized.

Every step he takes is watched. At night he can hear people walking about in the apartment above. He's tried to spot the cameras and microphones, but they're so small and so well concealed that he can't find them. He can't exclude the possibility that a computer chip has been implanted in him that records his whereabouts, controls his physical processes, pulse rate, blood pressure, metabolism. He pats himself down sometimes, but he can't feel anything. The chip must be buried deep in his flesh. He doesn't believe they can read his mind. The technology for that hasn't been invented. But they're working on it.

When he showers, he hangs a towel over the mirror. When he goes shopping, he often puts back the package he picks up first and chooses a different one from the back of the shelf. He's noticed the salespeople looking at him. He is almost certain they are mixing things into his food, drugs that alter his consciousness. Hence his forgetfulness, his visual distortions, his racing pulse, his tendency to sweat. Hence the occasional panic attacks. Who knows whether the medications the doctor prescribes aren't the real cause for his condition.

He's stopped going to restaurants long ago. He's not even sure of the coffee at the corner bodega. Sometimes he changes his order to tea at the last moment. Then he monitors his body's reaction very carefully.

For security reasons, he's detached the little TV from the antenna. There's nothing easier than picking up data that travel through a wire. Now he only watches videos.

They are his last connection to the world outside, to the
real world. He sees the same films again and again, runs
them in slow motion and attends to their tiniest details,
to minute slips. A wristwatch in a film set in ancient
Rome. The shadow of a boom falling across a scene.

He's tried to get in touch with film people, written
letters to Jodie Foster and Martin Scorsese. No reply of
course. It was naive of him to suppose his letters would
get through, but back then he saw no other way. Since
then he's learned to use dead letterboxes. He leaves his
plans and protocols and samples behind mirrors in
public toilets or in garbage cans at certain crossings.
He gets the position of the garbage cans from films,
and also whether the messages have been received. His
progress can be charted from film to film. Each film
answers the question put in the one before. The communications are encoded, but he's learned to decipher
them. Sometimes he laughs aloud when he gets their
meaning. He often feels a great hilarity, the cool bliss
of being undeceived. He won't be misled by the voices
in his head anymore: *You can't leave. This is where you belong. You belong to me.*

The sudden clarity, after years of uncertainty. He walks
through the city and laughs. He sees through things. He
could knock over the buildings with one hand, uproot the

trees that have been fixed in the ground like parasols. He has achieved mastery over his body. By pure mind he can control his physical functions.

He knows his contribution is vital. Otherwise they would have pulled him out long ago. A sacrifice will be required of him, but he is willing. The sacrifice will give shape and meaning to his life.

He has forgotten his sandwiches. He wonders whether he dares to buy a hamburger at the bodega. They can't know that today of all days he will go there. If he's quick enough, he can take them by surprise, not give them time to doctor his food. Some risks are unavoidable.

While he's waiting for his hamburger, he sees a woman with a small child walking straight up to him. She is wearing a fawn leather jacket and carrying a black leather bag. They always carry bags, presumably for the technical equipment, the batteries. They may be armed. The child is beyond suspicion. Presumably it knows nothing, it's just there as a decoy. He looks the woman straight in the eye. She should know that it's impossible to trick him. And it works: she turns aside and walks past him. Suddenly she speeds up. When she is a few steps past him, she looks back. Her expression is full of fear. He smiles triumphantly.

He waits until the last possible moment before turning

on the light in his store. The light makes it easier to see him from the street. That's the most dangerous moment of the whole day. Sometimes he walks out of the store and watches it from the other side of the road. If a customer walks in, he hurries across the street to be there.

Between six and eight o'clock is the busiest time. After that the customers dwindle away. It used to be he stayed open until midnight, now he closes at ten or eleven. Ever since the big video chain opened two blocks away he's been getting fewer customers. They are trying to drive him out of business, but he's not about to give up. He mustn't give up. He counts the earnings for the day and puts the money in his pocket. Ever since he's suffered a break-in, he leaves the register open.

He has gotten used to the situation, he is calmer now. On his way to work in the morning, he says hello to the agents. That terrifies them. They never expected him to identify them, and they run away. Good morning, he calls out after them. And in case we don't see each other again, good afternoon, and good evening as well. He wants to burst out laughing, but controls himself. When he goes home at night, there they are again. He hurries down the street and runs up the stairs to his apartment, taking the stairs two and three at a time. He is so boisterous he feels like ringing all the bells and yelling in his neighbors' faces that he knows perfectly well what they're up to. Once he's locked the door after him, he stops for a moment, then opens it again, peeps out into the stairwell, and locks it again. He goes straight to his living room and switches on the radio, so that no one can hear what he's doing. His neighbors have complained about the noise. No surprise there.

Only after he's eaten and showered and has been to the bathroom does he turn off the radio and switch off the light. With heavy strides he goes to the bedroom. That'll fool them into thinking he's gone to bed. Their guard will drop. He waits perfectly still for minutes. He is so tired he thinks sometimes that he'll fall asleep on his feet. His thoughts wander, he loses track of time.

When everything's quiet, when he's calmed down, he creeps back into the living room, switches on the video recorder and the TV. He's rewound the tape to the correct place.

He's playing in the garden. His mother comes, picks him up, spins him around. The garden blurs with the movement, becomes indistinct. The music reaches its climax. He can no longer keep back his tears. He stretches his arms out to his mother, his hands brush the screen. She looks at him and smiles sweetly.

Men and Boys

THE RIVER BATHS were closed, the entrance padlocked. There was a chill rain falling. The lifeguard was nowhere to be seen, perhaps he had gone home or was in the village somewhere. When Lucas clambered over the wire fence, he thought of the drunk who had got in here at night a few years ago and fallen into the pool. They had found him dead the following morning.

He went to the changing rooms, which were in a low whitewashed brick building. Next to the entrance was a sign, MEN AND BOYS. There was no light except what came through the gap between the walls and ceiling, and it was always a bit damp in the cabins, even when it was really hot outside. Lucas browsed along the row of lockers, to see if someone had forgotten a coin, but there wasn't one. About halfway he stopped looking. He went down to the river. The water was high and pale brown. It flowed so fast that there were little eddies marking its surface. Twigs drifted past, they seemed to be going faster than the current. They must have opened the weir downstream, following the storm, Lucas could hear a distant roar of falling water. The rain eased, then stopped altogether. He went back to the cabins and changed.

He remembered summer afternoons when it was hot and all the kids seemed to go swimming. There were various groups dotted about the lawn. Lucas's fellows ran around on the edge of the pool jumping or pushing each other into the water until the lifeguard intervened. Lucas swam back and forth, counting laps. After he'd done a mile, he climbed out, feeling cold and staggering slightly as if he'd forgotten how to walk. His friends lay on big bath towels on the grass. They talked about the summer holidays and where they would go. He lay down next to them on the grass.

Whenever he was with the others, Lucas felt as though his pores were closing, he felt small and painfully self-conscious of his body. He was shut up inside it, he couldn't be human without it. On his own, he could forget about it, then his edges were those of his consciousness, the damp meadow he was walking over, the passing clouds, the blue strip on the horizon, the seam of forest on the river's far bank. Then Lucas could have been just anyone, or even no one.

He lay down on the rough concrete slabs beside the pool. There were leaves floating on the water that the storm had blown off the trees, and a wasp was wriggling about. Lucas put out his hand to rescue the creature, but he was afraid he might get stung. His hand hovered protectively over it. Slowly it drifted farther and farther from the edge of the pool.

Lucas remembered Franziska, who was in the same class as him. They sometimes walked home together from school as far as the railroad crossing, where their paths divided. Often they would stand in front of the crossing sign for a long time, talking. Franziska had so much to say, she never seemed to get to the end of it. But at the class party she didn't want to dance with him, she made some snotty remark and got herself something to drink. And later she was seen dancing with Leo.

Lucas picked three stones from the rosebed that surrounded the pool, washed the clay off them, and dropped them into the water one after the other. Once the ripples had stopped, he could see them lying on the bottom. He lowered himself slowly into the water. It was so cold it took

his breath away. For a long time he stood on the lowest
step of the ladder, up to his belly, and then he slipped in.
As soon as he started to move, the cold abated. He dived
for the stones. The first time he only managed two, he
didn't see the last one until he was on the surface again.
He released them from his hand. When they dropped,
they made a little clucking sound in the water, and then
they sank waveringly to the floor. The second time, Lucas
found all three. He wasn't an especially good swimmer, but he was a good diver. He took a few deep breaths,
pushed off the side, and dived down on a diagonal slant.
He saw the blurry white tramlines and the bottom of the
pool quickly move beneath him. Now he was swimming
just over the floor. After the third line, he felt an ache
in his throat and chest. He had to rise to the surface, he
couldn't make it all the way across. But he carried on, and
the aching diminished. He now had the feeling he could
dive forever. Over the last few yards he expelled the air he
still had in his lungs, and then his head broke the surface
just in front of the edge. He took deep breaths and turned
and swam slowly. He wished Franziska could have been
there and seen him. One time, as she was getting out of
the water, her bikini top slipped and for a second Lucas
caught a glimpse of her small bare breast, and the nipple
dark and erect.

When he left the water he was cold, and he ran to the diving board and back. The surface of the water was smooth once more. Lucas dived the length of the pool, fifty meters, and surged out of the water at the far end with a shout of triumph. Franziska was standing there smiling at him. She bent down, put out her hand, and helped him out. He wanted to hug her, but he wasn't sure how to do it. They just looked at each other and walked to the lawn side by side. In her bathing suit, Franziska walked somehow differently, more confidently, her whole body moving, the hips, the shoulders, the slender arms. She sat down—it looked as though she just let herself drop. Then she sat there on the grass, cross-legged, leaning forward. She talked and talked.

Lucas wandered about, crossed the large lawn, and walked along the fence under the trees, where in some places the bare earth had a shiny gleam, as if someone had polished it. There was a smell of grass and earth, and something sweet like flowers or something rotting. The sun had come out from under the clouds, and its level rays were falling on the ground. Little droplets of water glistened on the leaves and in the grass, and suddenly everything looked very bright.

Lucas wandered across the lawn, hoping to find something, a purse or a watch or a penknife, something.

Down by the river he lay down in the short-cut grass and watched the dirty brown water flowing past. The grass was wet and cold. Everything was clear and shallow. It was a mixture of happiness and unhappiness. It was happiness that felt like unhappiness.

Franziska and her girlfriends were going to the baths. They sat in a circle, they had bought sweets and were talking and laughing. Lucas couldn't imagine what they were talking about, he couldn't remember what Franziska used to talk about with him. Sometimes she wouldn't know what to say anymore. Perhaps that was the moment when people kissed. You had to be quiet before you kissed.

Lucas lay in the grass. He cupped his hands on his chest and made two shallow breasts. A couple of drops of water from somewhere landed on his stomach. A light wind had started up. Lucas shivered with cold.

He stood in front of the changing rooms: WOMEN AND GIRLS. He went inside. Here there were single stalls, there was no general changing room, like for men, who didn't mind changing together. Lucas wondered if women felt more shame, and if they had secrets from one another, and what they were.

Franziska walked in, with a plastic bag with her things under her arm. She locked herself in one of the stalls and

pulled off her jeans and T-shirt. Before undressing fur-
ther, she pulled her bathing suit out of the bag and shook
it out and hung it on a hook. She hurried. She was thinking of the others who were already there, lying in a ring
on the grass and waiting for her to arrive.

Lucas had taken off his trunks and hung them. He
wedged his cock between his legs, and looked down his
body, stroked his hands over his hips. He could be someone or no one. He had a sensation of warmth, his skin
seemed to glow, but inside his body was still cold.

He opened the stall door, and immediately felt much
more exposed. When he stepped out into the open,
someone could see him naked. He didn't dare go on, and
stopped at the entrance. The women walked past him, the
girls in light summer dresses and young mothers and
older women. They vanished into the changing rooms,
and immediately re-emerged in various brightly colored
bathing suits.

Lucas ran over to the men's changing rooms. He hadn't
put his clothes away in a locker, there was a little heap of
them lying on the long wooden bench. He pulled on the
chilly garments. Then he checked the lockers again, to
see if someone had forgotten their deposit, starting with
the first lockers and going on until halfway, when he gave
up and left the building.

The toilets were locked. Lucas tried both doors, the men's and women's. At the back of the little hut was a door that was open a crack. A low monotonous drone was audible. Lucas peered into the unlit room. The noise came from a big pump. On the floor were blue-and-white plastic chemical containers. It smelled of chlorine.

He went inside—it was far warmer there than it was outside—and pulled the door shut behind him. For a while he stood in the darkness. Suddenly he panicked: the lifeguard might return and catch him.

When he climbed back out over the fence, he remembered he had left his trunks in the ladies' cabins. He imagined Franziska picking them up and taking them between the tips of her fingers to the lifeguard, who tossed them in a box where all sorts of lost and forgotten things were kept until someone came for them.

The Letter

I N T H E D A Y S between Manfred's death and his burial, Johanna threw away all his clothes and shoes. Later on, she suspected, she would no longer be capable of it. She threw away his toiletries and medications, unfinished containers of food, little supplies. When it was dark, Johanna carried the big garbage bags out to the car. The next day she drove to the incinerator and dropped the bags herself in the big ditch. It was midsummer, and the smell of garbage was unbearable, even early in the morning. The car was weighed once as she drove in and then again as she left, and the fee was calculated on the basis of the difference in weight. One hundred and ninety-eight pounds, said the man at the register, and he charged the basic fee. You know you could have brought in three times as much stuff for that money. Never mind, said Johanna, and she tipped him. The period of mourning began only after the burial.

It took years before Johanna managed to look through those things she hadn't immediately thrown away. She sorted through Manfred's books, almost all of them manuals on tax and company law from the time he was qualifying. He had been a tax accountant, whose clients were mostly small firms for whom he did the bookkeeping, and individuals whose tax declarations he prepared, often without asking for payment. You're much too good-natured, Johanna would sometimes say, but Manfred merely shrugged his shoulders and said, I see how little people make, we're well off by comparison. Following Manfred's death, Hedwig, his long-serving secretary, had settled affairs at the office, got in touch with clients, returned files and recommended other tax accountants, and finally had the furniture collected by the firm from whom Manfred had bought it not too many years previously. Early on, Hedwig had called now and again, but Johanna had always said, I have no idea about these things, you must do what you think is right. I miss him, Hedwig had said, and Johanna, with a rough laugh: Do you think you're the only one?

Johanna felt guilty when she cleared Manfred's desk, even though he had been dead for seven years now. But she would have to do it sooner or later. She needed the room for Felicitas, who sometimes came to stay for a day or two. Thus far, the little girl had slept in her bed with her, but now she was six, and it seemed to Johanna that she needed her own bed and somewhere to keep her things.

The top drawer was full of the stuff that had been so endlessly fascinating to Adrian when he was a boy. Sometimes Manfred had set him on his lap and pulled one thing after another out of the drawer and told him its story: the Red Sox baseball he had bought during his first trip to America, the Lapland knife, the papier-mâché elephant, a slide rule, a broken pocket watch. Some of these items dated back to Manfred's childhood, others Johanna knew where they came from and what they had signified to Manfred. She held each item in her hand a long time, unable to decide what to keep and what to throw away. Finally she put everything back in the drawer and shut it again. She would ask Adrian if he wanted any of it. She didn't need any of it herself, those things only made her sad.

In the second drawer were files of all sorts of documents, office furniture catalogs and instructions, old papers of no sentimental value that Johanna unhesitatingly threw in the recycling. In one of the folders there were a few issues of a 1970s magazine. On one cover was a black woman with an Afro hairstyle and pointy breasts. Johanna flicked through them. She was surprised by the innocence of the pictures, even though she was bothered by the fact that Manfred had hidden their existence from her. When she hoisted the empty files from the drawer and dumped them in a garbage bag, a bundle of letters slipped out and fell to the floor. Johanna picked it up and pulled off the rubber band that held it together. There were perhaps twenty small envelopes, addressed to Manfred's office in an attractive hand. The letters had been sent within the space of a single year, the date on the cancellation stamp was perhaps thirty years old. Johanna hesitated, then she took one of the letters out of its envelope and began to read.

ADRIAN DIDN'T HAVE much time. When Johanna opened the door, he was in the process of saying good-bye to Felicitas. He greeted his mother perfunctorily and said Iris was waiting in the car. We won't be that late, he said. She can stay the night if you like, said Johanna, I've cleared out the office. You've got your own room now, she said to Felicitas, who had taken her hand and was beaming

at her. Is that really OK? asked Adrian. Come to breakfast tomorrow, said Johanna, there's something I want
to talk to you about. Thanks, said Adrian, and kissed
his mother on the cheek. He stroked Felicitas's head and
said, See you tomorrow, sweetie. You can stay here yourselves if you like, Johanna added, but Adrian said over
his shoulder, going down the stairs, he would rather go
home, thanks all the same.

When Felicitas was in bed, she started to ask her
grandmother about her grandfather. She always tried
anything not to have to go to sleep. Johanna had often
told her what a good man Grandfather was, and how he
had helped lots of people, but on this occasion she was
curt, she didn't feel like thinking about Manfred now.
Why did he die? Felicitas asked. We all have to die, said
Johanna, he smoked too much. My papa smokes too much
as well, Felicitas said. Does everyone die if they smoke
too much? If you're unlucky, said Johanna. Your grandfather's in heaven. I don't think he can see us. A little while
ago, Felicitas's guinea pig had died, and now she was pic-
turing it up in heaven along with her grandfather, a vi-
sion that was clearly too much for her. Go to sleep now,
said Johanna, and sweet dreams.

In the morning they were speaking about something
else, but when Felicitas caught sight of a photo of her

grandfather on the sideboard, she asked if that was taken in heaven. No, said Johanna, that was in Italy, in Tuscany, where we were on vacation. You've been there too, remember, with your mama and papa last year. I don't remember, said Felicitas. It seemed to make her sad. And there followed another round of questions about heaven that Johanna couldn't answer. No one knows what it looks like. No one has ever come back from there. It's farther away than the stars. Yes, she said, I'm going to go to heaven as well, and so will your papa and mama, and you too.

At breakfast Felicitas started again. Grandfather's in heaven, she said, and I'm going to go to heaven too. Iris looked at her mother-in-law critically. Adrian didn't say anything, it still wasn't possible to talk to him about his father's death, even though the two of them hadn't been close. I'm going to go to heaven too, Felicitas said again. Sure you will, said Iris, but there's plenty of time until then. Then she wanted to leave, and Johanna only had a moment in which to show Adrian Manfred's things. She watched his face, and for a moment saw a boyish joy that suddenly was extinguished. He took out the slide rule and slid the scales along each other. I've never understood the principle of these, he said. Look, Felicitas, this is how people used to do calculations before there were computers. Do you want any of it? asked Johanna. Adrian hesitated. We've got so much stuff already, Iris said. What about the watch? asked Johanna. It doesn't work, said Adrian. Johanna felt disappointed, even though she herself didn't want to keep any of it either. She accompanied them out to the car. Iris put Felicitas in her car seat. Adrian hadn't got in yet. Are you all right? he asked. I've been a bit tired recently, said Johanna, I'm not sleeping well. Wasn't there something you wanted to talk to me about? he asked. She said it wasn't urgent, later when he had time. Call me, he said.

Johanna called Hedwig, the secretary, and they met at a cafe. Johanna got a shock when she saw Hedwig. She had stopped dyeing her hair, and she was in flat shoes and glasses. She couldn't deal with the contact lenses anymore, she said. The two women had nothing to say to each other—they never had. Manfred's office had been a world of its own, Johanna had never had anything to do with it. Manfred hardly ever brought his work home with him. When Johanna asked him about it, he would gesture dismissively and say, Oh, the usual. Sometimes she would pick him up from the office and caught him seeing out a client or bantering with Hedwig, and each time she thought he was an utter stranger. He seemed different there from the way he was at home, more decisive, more humorous, more alive. It was this man who had got those letters, and written others whose content Johanna could only guess at, from the replies of his mistress. *Your last letter made me blush. Your erotic fantasies turned me on. I think about you all the time.* Johanna had meant to ask Hedwig about the woman, but she couldn't now, she would have felt too ashamed. And would his secretary know anyway? Johanna couldn't imagine that Manfred would have let her into the secret of his double life. In fact she couldn't imagine the double life itself.

She only went to the cemetery out of a sense of duty. When she tended his grave before, she had felt very close to Manfred. Now it was as though he really was dead, as though the bond between them had torn, the connection that had lasted beyond his death. It occurred to her to track down Manfred's mistress and demand the return of his letters, so as to undo the deception. But it was all such a long time ago, and the woman had signed using her first name only. And what difference would it have made to destroy those relics? In the end it hardly mattered who Monica was. Perhaps she was one of many. Johanna thought of one of Manfred's clients, the manager of a restaurant where they sometimes ate. She had cried at the funeral, at the time Johanna hadn't thought anything of it, but now she was suspicious. Many of Manfred's woman clients had gone to the funeral.

She had meant to talk about all this with Adrian, but when he next called, she didn't say anything about it. She tried to persuade herself it was that she didn't want to damage his image of his father. Privately, though, she knew that it wasn't his father he might lose respect for, but herself, the injured party. She tried to think of someone else she could take into her confidence, but there was no one. The neighbors were out of the question, and most of the other people she knew in the village she had met through Manfred. He had grown up here, and knew everyone, man and woman. Because she had been his wife, she was still greeted by many people today in the street, but she wasn't on friendly terms with any of them. Once, a couple of years ago now, she had taken an Italian course, but the others there were all much younger than she was, and when it was over, the group split up. She thought of the man who had taught the course, who wasn't a local. They had got along well together, but what was she going to say to him? He probably wouldn't even remember who she was.

ON HIS FORTIETH BIRTHDAY Adrian threw a big party. For all my friends, he said, and he asked his mother if she would look after Felicitas. Johanna was there from the afternoon on, and played with her granddaughter while Iris and Adrian made salads. The party was to be held in the garden. The weather was being a bit unpredictable, and at the last moment Adrian had a big tent set up in the garden, in case it rained. The guests started arriving at six, work colleagues of Adrian's and old school friends whom Johanna hadn't seen in twenty years, but whom she immediately identified. Back then, she had been on easy terms with all of them, and it felt a little weird to her to be formal. Felicitas had gone off somewhere with some other kids. Johanna had followed them, but had quickly seen she wasn't welcome. She went back out to the garden. Adrian was busy over the grill, Iris was welcoming the new arrivals and introducing them, if they didn't know each other. Johanna stood on the fringes with a fixed smile on her face. She didn't want to bother anyone, didn't want anyone to see how unhappy she felt.

Clouds had filled the sky, it looked as though it could start raining any minute. The meat's ready, called Adrian, and a line of people formed in front of the grill. Johanna went inside to get the children, then sat down with them at their junior table and tried to keep them vaguely under control. From time to time one or another of the parents would go up to the table and ask if everything was all right. One young woman remained standing behind a rather quiet toddler, laid her hand on his head, and asked him if he wasn't tired yet. Only then did she seem to notice Johanna. She extended her hand and said, Why, how are you, we haven't seen each other in ages. Johanna hesitated. Eva, said the young woman, I used to wear my hair longer. Now Johanna remembered. Eva had done an internship at the same time as Adrian, and for a while the two of them had been an item. She and Manfred had been fond of the girl, and both were disappointed when one day Adrian announced that they had broken up. He hadn't given a reason, and Johanna hadn't asked him for one either. Of course, now I remember, she said. And this is your little boy? Yes, this is Jan. Johanna took the little boy's hand in hers. He looked at her rather rigidly. And who's your daddy? she asked. Eva said she and Jan's father weren't together anymore. I'm sorry, said Johanna. Eva laughed and said, I'm not!

The older children had jumped up and run over to the sideboard, where Iris was serving dessert. The little ones followed them. Eva picked up Jan, but he wriggled so hard that she had to put him down and let him run after the others. I think they can look after themselves, said Eva. Wouldn't you like to come and sit with us?

After dessert, Johanna put Felicitas to bed. As she came back down the stairs, she saw Eva standing in the hallway, jiggling a stroller. It's started raining, said Eva in a hushed voice. I think he's gone to sleep.

Shall I turn the light off? Johanna whispered.

There's no need, said Eva, once he's asleep, it's not easy to wake him. She turned on the baby monitor and put the microphone next to the stroller.

But then, instead of going back out to the garden, she went into the kitchen, and, not bothering to switch on a light, took one of the empty champagne glasses that were standing around and filled it at the faucet. Johanna had followed her and said, Hang on, I'll get you a clean glass, but Eva had already drunk from hers. Even so, Johanna took a glass from the cabinet and filled it, and stood there rather cluelessly until Eva took it from her and set it down on the side.

God, I'm so tired, Eva said, running her fingers through her hair. Man problems.

Johanna was silent. She wasn't sure what the young woman expected from her. Well, time will tell, she said, and she sat down at the kitchen table.

Eva laughed. You never know, she said. He's married, I'll spare you the rest . . . I've heard it so many times, and now it's happened to me. At least he was open with me from the start.

Her lover was a German teacher, like herself. They had met at a teachers' refresher course and fallen in love immediately. But he had two children, and wasn't prepared to leave his wife. He's afraid he'll lose the children, said Eva, and anyway his marriage seems to be OK. It's such a wonderfully banal story. Johanna didn't say anything, and Eva carried on. Her lover lived in Lucerne, maybe that was an advantage, the fact that they didn't see each other that often. They met every couple of weeks. He visited her, she didn't know what he told his wife, and she didn't want to know, either. For a weekend at a time they lived together like man and wife, and then he went back to his family. Eva laughed. It's peculiar, I'm not even jealous of his wife.

If his marriage is OK, said Johanna, then what makes him into an adulterer?

Eva shrugged her shoulders. Do you think it's immoral? I tell myself it's his responsibility, she said, after all he's the one who's cheating on his wife. Do you think I should get rid of him?

But that wasn't the question that interested Johanna. What sort of person is he? she asked. Does he talk about his family with you? What do you talk about?

He's a perfectly normal guy, said Eva, he doesn't talk about his family much. That's fine by me, it's none of my business.

But is that normal? asked Johanna, more vehemently than she meant to. Is it normal for a man to have a mistress? Surely it can't be?

In the bit of light that came in from the hall, she could see that Eva was smiling. Adrian never told you why we broke up, isn't that right? she asked.

What would you say to his wife? asked Johanna. What do you tell her if she calls you up and asks you what you're doing?

I don't know, said Eva. They were silent. Then Eva said, I would tell her that it's of no importance, and she doesn't have anything to worry about.

There were sounds in the hallway, someone had come in from outside and was going to the toilet. Johanna heard a man's voice. Are you ready? And then the flush, and the door, and a woman saying, I think he's nice. Just coming, said the man. Again, the door, and then the woman's voice. I'll wait outside. Eva shrugged her shoulders, and said she'd better get going too.

JOHANNA MUST HAVE BEGUN her letter five times. Dear Eva, I've been thinking about what we were talking about. I'm familiar with the other side of the problem, I was the victim of a man's cheating. No, she thought, I wasn't a victim, I didn't know anything. My husband committed adultery, she wrote, but she didn't like the phrase either. My husband cheated on me. And why should Eva care? She had wanted to tell her to leave her lover, she was damaging herself and him and his family. But was that really what she believed? What if she hadn't found the letters, but had thrown them away unread? It wasn't Manfred, it was she who had hurt herself because she hadn't been content to leave things alone. And wasn't it actually her fault if Manfred had cheated? He must have missed something in their relationship. Maybe—and this was the most comfortable version—it was something physical. *Reading your letter made me blush. Your erotic fantasies turned me on.* Johanna had never written sentences like that to her husband. Sex in their marriage had been a wordless affair for something that was transacted in darkness, and wasn't discussed. Perhaps you had to be apart from a man to desire him in that way, to be able to write him sentences like that. She had never been away for more than a day or two at a time. Then she had written Manfred postcards that didn't have anything on them that the postman couldn't read.

She got out the mistress's letters and read them again, trying to read the words without thinking of Manfred, as the product of a passion that could surmount any obstacle and any distance. She read them all from beginning to end, then she crumpled them up and threw them away. For the first time in a long time, she thought about Manfred without thinking of his infidelity. She thought of his joie de vivre, his patient, helpful manner, and his self-irony. She thought of the intimacy between them, his tenderness to her, and how much she missed him. And suddenly she felt perfectly sure that he hadn't lacked anything in their relationship, and that he hadn't committed adultery for want of anything, but from that excess of love and curiosity and wonder with which he encountered everything in life, children, animals, nature, his work, the whole world. She ripped the letter she had begun off the legal pad, and started writing to Manfred, quickly and without thinking, sentences the likes of which she had never written before.

Years Later

WECHSLER HAD DRIVEN for two hours when he saw the looming shape of the mountain on whose slopes the village nestled and from which it took its name. From the distance its mass had always suggested to him the body of an enormous animal that had come down ages before to lie down in the plain, and had gradually been overgrown with grass and forest.

It was more than twenty years since he had left the place where he had grown up, the village where he had married and worked on his first jobs as an architect. After his marriage with Margrit broke up, Wechsler had moved into the city and begun a new life. He had met with success and his memories of living in the village faded.

February had been unseasonably mild, but a few days ago there was another snowfall. There was still a little snow in the vineyards that covered a large part of the slope. The regular rows of vines might have been cross-hatching from one of Wechsler's sketches. The landscape instantly looked familiar to him. Only as he drew closer to the village did he see how much had changed in the time he was away. There where corn and sugar beets had been planted now stood monstrous industrial build-ings, painted in all kinds of colors and sprawled self-importantly over the plain. Wechsler remembered his first little restoration jobs in the village. At that time he had argued for months with the authorities about the color of some shutters. Now it seemed people were free to build just exactly as they pleased out here.

Wechsler parked his car in the marketplace he had once crossed to go to school. Sometimes he had sneaked off to the butcher's after class and watched him at his work. He could still remember the apprehensive eyes of the calves, tethered in the open, waiting for it to be their turn. The butcher's shop no longer existed, now it was lingerie. Round the square, ugly new buildings had been put up, office blocks, a shopping center, even a hotel.

It was almost noon. Wechsler went into a restau-rant he remembered from long ago. The inside hadn't

changed. It was paneled in dark wood, and the tables
were set, but Wechsler was the only person there. The
waitress asked him if he wanted lunch and sullenly took
his order for coffee. She was just bringing it to him when
the cook came out. He was wearing a stained apron, and
for a moment Wechsler thought it was the landlord of the
old Linde, who had let them drink beer in his pub even
though they weren't yet sixteen. It must be his son, who
wasn't much older than Wechsler. Twenty years ago he
had been a good-looking ladies' man. Now he was pale
and fat, and had the puffy face of a drinker.

The cook stepped up to Wechsler's table and shook
hands with him, as seemed still to be the custom in these
parts. Wechsler asked after his father. The cook looked
at him suspiciously and said his father had been dead
for many years. Wechsler explained he used to live here
once, and he asked after some of his old friends. The cook
gave him what information he could. Some of Wechsler's
friends had moved away, others were dead. A few of the
names the cook had never heard before.

But you do remember Wechsler, the architect? And his
wife, Margrit?

The cook nodded and made a vague gesture, as if to
say it was all a long time ago. His face looked suddenly
tired.

The divorce was a bit of a scandal, said Wechsler. To begin with, the wife contested it. Hodel was the lawyer in the case. I'm sure you remember.

Hodel had since become a notary, said the cook, he ate lunch here every day. Then he excused himself. He was needed in the kitchen. Wechsler called the waitress and said he had had a change of heart, he would have lunch here after all.

At twelve o'clock the bells in the nearby church began to toll, and the restaurant started filling up. Most of the customers came in small groups, and greeted the waitress by name. Wechsler had the feeling that these people, whom he didn't know, had taken possession of his past. He had moved away and others had replaced him. The old village existed only in his memory.

Hodel entered the restaurant. He stopped in the doorway and looked around, as though the place belonged to him. Wechsler recognized the lawyer right away, even though he had grown old and bald and seemed shrunken. Their eyes met, and when Wechsler half got to his feet and smiled and nodded to Hodel, the latter came over to his table.

I'm so sorry, he said, with a questioning look in his eyes. I meet so many people . . .

Wechsler identified himself. Hodel's face brightened, and he said, Well, well. A revenant. How are you?

The men shook hands and sat down. After a glance at the menu, Hodel ordered casually, as befits a regular. The waitress smiled when he asked her to bring a bottle of wine, the barrique, not the house wine.

Even the wine's improved, Hodel observed.

He had kept seeing Wechsler's name in the paper, he said, people in the village were proud of him. The indoor pool he had built . . . The outdoor pool, you mean, Wechsler corrected him. What was it that brought him back to the village, Hodel asked, and nodded when Wechsler said the cemetery chapel was being renovated. He had come to have a look at it. He wasn't yet sure whether to bid for the contract or not. Hodel grinned and said the business with his wife had long since been forgotten and forgiven. Today, divorces were almost part of the *bon ton*. Suddenly Wechsler wished he had gone to a different restaurant. He didn't want to be reminded of his early years. Time had passed, he had remarried, had become a father, and was expecting the birth of his first grandchild. He was happy with his life.

I'll walk you to the cemetery, if you've no objection, Hodel said over coffee. The exercise will do me good.

All through lunch, Hodel had talked only about himself, his work, and his wife and two sons, who were living in the city. Wechsler would have liked to be rid of his old friend, but he didn't want to be impolite. He was tired after the food and the wine, and everything disgusted him. Hodel insisted on paying for lunch. That was the least he could do, he said, after all, he had made quite a bit of money off him. Besides, without knowing it, Wechsler had helped him get some nooky on the side.

Did he have much recollection of his first wife? Hodel asked, as they strolled along the busy street going to the cemetery. Of course, said Wechsler. He was going to say something else, but refrained. A young woman with a stroller was coming the other way, and Hodel stepped aside, walking so close behind Wechsler that he seemed about to jump on him.

She had her reasons for not wanting to grant a divorce, he said. Tongues were wagging. She was told she was no longer wanted in the church choir. Who could have guessed . . .

Margrit came from a religious family. Her father had been opposed to her marrying a man of a different faith, and the divorce was a calamity as far as he was concerned. He threatened his daughter, even though she was innocent, and at that point Wechsler was already living in the city with another woman. Margrit had been a highly emotional woman, sometimes almost wildly so, but she couldn't shift her father over. Wechsler left the conduct of the case to Hodel, giving him free rein. He had never heard what it was that had changed Margrit's mind. He wasn't sure he wanted to know now.

Rumors travel quickly here, said Hodel with a brash laugh. If she'd been found the guilty party in the divorce, that would have brought disagreeable financial consequences.

At that time, he hadn't been too particular about the way things got done, Hodel said, but that was long ago, and he had no cause to feel shame anymore. By now he had become a respected citizen, and was on good terms with all the people that mattered.

It might be that one or another person doesn't greet me on the street, but anyone who doesn't make enemies in this business must be a complete incompetent.

Reaching the cemetery now, they came to a stop in front of the chapel. When it was first built in the 1960s, its progressive style had divided opinion, now it just looked seedy, and the facade was grimy with dirt.

It was colder inside than out. There was a smell of chemical cleaner and candle wax. Wechsler looked around and took pictures of the interior with his digital camera, even though he was already sure that he wasn't going to bid for the contract. Hodel didn't budge from his side. He was silent now, except once to clear his throat.

Just one after another, he said when they were outside again. Do you want to look at the grave?

Without waiting for a reply, he led the way down the row of graves. He stopped in front of an unobtrusive white marble. Wechsler joined him, and for a while the two men stood silently side by side, hands in their coat pockets, staring at the stone, on which only Margrit's name and dates had been carved. Hodel sighed deeply.

This is the worst, he said. His voice sounded altered, quieter, cracking. I'm not saying I was a better person when I was younger. But getting old is no fun at all.

He turned around and gestured at a workman who was just in the process of digging a new grave with a little bulldozer.

You never know whether it's your turn next, he said. If only they could at least dig the graves by hand . . .

Wechsler suddenly felt an urge to cry. But in Hodel's presence he restrained himself. He shook his head and walked on. He sat down on a bench under a group of fir trees at the edge of the cemetery. Hodel had followed him. He stood in front of the bench, and looked over at the cemetery wall, behind which the railway line ran.

If you fall, she said to me one time, then at least make sure you fall hard, he said quietly. There was something going on between her and the landlord of the Linde. When he got rid of her, she started drinking. Maybe she was drinking already. After that, she had, let's say, various relationships. I think she loved you more than you thought.

He had helped Margrit out a couple of times, said Hodel, not out of pity, he freely admitted. Desperate women were the best lovers. You could do anything you liked with them, they had nothing left to lose. Even when she was already on the bottle, Margrit was still a good-looking woman. It was only at the very end that you could see the disintegration.

Why didn't you call me? Wechsler called out in a sudden fury. I could have helped her.

She said she'd written you a letter, said Hodel, smiling cautiously.

Wechsler raised his hands and let them fall against his thighs. He had always just worked, he said, he hardly had any time for his children and his second wife.

The old stories, said Hodel. A train passed on the other side of the wall, and he stopped until the noise went away. Then he said he had paid for the stone. In the village people were still scratching their heads about where the money had come from, but the mason was discreet. He was another of Margrit's admirers, incidentally.

We've gotten so ugly, said Hodel, shaking his head. He said he had to go now. Wechsler should let him know ahead of time when he would be back. He held out his hand to Wechsler without looking at him, and left.

The snow wouldn't lie for long, thought Wechsler. The air was cold, but the sun had some force. He sat on the bench a while longer, then he got up. He stopped in front of Margrit's grave. He thought of the girl she had been when he first met her, her happiness, her lightness, and how he and Hodel and others had wrecked her life. He wanted to cry, but couldn't. He squatted down and plucked a few dry leaves off the plants that were grow- ing on the grave. Then he stood up and walked out of the cemetery without looking back.

Children of God

I T WAS THE first Michael had heard of the girl. His housekeeper was telling him about her: she claimed—Mandy did—that there was no father. She lived in the neighboring village of W. The housekeeper laughed, Michael sighed. As if it wasn't enough that church attendance was way down, that the old people sent him away when he tried to visit them in their home, and the children cheeked him in Sunday school. It was all Communism, he said, or the aftereffects of it. Ach, nonsense, said the housekeeper, it was never any different. Did he know the large sugar-beet field on the road to W.? There was a sort of island in the middle of it. A clump of trees had been left standing by the farmer. Since forever, she said. And that's where he has assignations with a woman.

What woman? asked Michael. What farmer? The one who's there, and his father before him, and his grandfather before that. All of them. Since forever. We're only human, after all, them and me. Each of us has his needs.

Michael sighed. He had been the minister here since spring, but he hadn't got any closer to his flock. He came from the mountains, where everything was different: the people, the landscape, and the sky, which here was so infinitely wide and remote.

She claims she's never been with a man, said the housekeeper, the baby must be a gift from God. That Mandy girl, she said, was the daughter of Gregor who works for the bus company. The little fat driver. He gave her a good spanking, she was black and blue all over. And now the whole village is scratching its head over who the father might be. There aren't a lot of men living there who are candidates. Maybe it was Marco the landlord. Or a passing tramp. She's no oil painting, you know. But you take what you can get. That Mandy, she's not the brightest either, said the housekeeper: maybe she didn't realize. Up on the ladder picking cherries. All right, all right, said Michael.

MANDY CAME TO THE VICARAGE while Michael was eating lunch. The housekeeper brought her in, and he asked her to sit down and talk to him. She just sat there with downcast eyes and didn't speak. She smelled of soap. Michael ate, and kept sneaking looks at the young woman. She wasn't pretty, but she wasn't ugly either. Perhaps she would turn to fat later. Now she was plump. She's blooming, thought Michael. And he sneaked a look at her belly and her big breasts, very prominent under the rather garish sweater. He didn't know if it was pregnancy or food. Then the young woman looked at him and immediately lowered her eyes, and he pushed away his half-eaten lunch and stood up. Let's go out in the garden.

The year was far along. The leaves were turning on the trees. The morning had been misty, now the sun was trying to break through. Michael and Mandy walked together in the garden. Your Reverence, she said, and he, No, please just call me Michael, and I'll call you Mandy. So she didn't know who the father was? There was no father, said Mandy, I never . . . She stopped. Michael sighed. Sixteen, eighteen, he thought, no older than that. My dear child, he said, it's a sin, but God will forgive you. Thus saith the Lord God of Israel: Every bottle shall be filled with wine!

Mandy tore a leaf off the old linden tree where they had come to a stop, and Michael said, Do you know how it is when a man lies with a woman? You mean, with the peter, said Mandy, and she blushed and looked down.

Perhaps it was in her sleep, thought Michael, apparently such things happen. They had studied it in school, Mandy added, and quickly: Erection, coitus, and rhythm method. All right, all right, said Michael, school. That was the upshot of having so many Communists still sitting on school boards.

Holy mother of God, said Mandy, I've never . . . All right, all right, said Michael, and then, with sudden vehemence, Well, where do you think the baby's come from then? Do you think it's a gift from God? Yes, said Mandy. He sent her home.

ON SUNDAY, Michael saw Mandy among the few who were at the service. If he remembered correctly, she had never been before. She was wearing a simple dress in dark green, and now he could see her condition plainly. She should be ashamed of herself, said the housekeeper.

Mandy was all at sea. Michael could see her craning around. When the others sang, she didn't. And when she came forward at the end to receive Communion, he had to tell her, Open your mouth.

Michael spoke about steadiness in adversity. Frau Schmidt, who was always there, read the lesson with a quiet but firm voice. See that ye refuse not him that speaketh. For if they escaped not who refused him that spake on earth: be not forgetful to entertain strangers: for thereby some have entertained angels unawares.

Michael had kept his eyes closed during the reading, and he felt he could almost see the angel who came to visit men, an angel that had Mandy's face, and whose belly in its white robes bulged like Mandy's in her dress. Suddenly it got very quiet in the church. Michael opened his eyes and saw that everyone was looking at him expectantly. Then he said: We can speak with confidence. The Lord is my helper, and I will not fear what man shall do unto me.

After the service was over, Michael hurried over to the door to see out his old biddies. He had shut the door behind the last of them when he saw that Mandy was kneeling at the altar. He went up to her and laid his hand on her head. She looked at him, and he saw she had tears running down her cheeks. Come, he said, and he led her out of the church and across the road to the cemetery. Look at all these people, he said, they were all sinners: but God took them to Himself, and He will forgive you your sins as well. I am full of sin, said Mandy, but I have never been with a man. All right, all right, said Michael, and he touched Mandy's shoulder with his hand.

But when he touched Mandy, it was as though his heart and his whole body were filling with a joy he had never felt in his life, and he shrank back, as though he had burned himself. And if it's true? he thought.

AND IF IT'S TRUE? he thought that afternoon, as he walked down the road to the next village. The sun was shining and the sky was wide and cloudless. Michael felt tired after lunch, but his heart was still filled with the joy that had flowed from Mandy's body into his own: and if it's true?

He often walked to one of the other villages on a Sunday afternoon, striding quickly down the tree-lined roads in rain or shine. But on that day he had an objective. He had called the doctor who lived there, a man by the name of Klaus, and asked if he might talk to him: no, he couldn't tell him what about.

Dr. Klaus was a local man, the son and grandson of farmers. He knew everyone and everything, and the word was that in an emergency, he would treat sick animals as well. He lived alone in a big house in W., following the death of his wife. He said if Michael promised to keep God out of it, he was welcome and might come. He was an atheist, said the doctor, no, not even an atheist, he believed in nothing, not even that there was no God. He was a man of science, not faith. A Communist, thought Michael, and he said, All right, all right, and suppressed a yawn.

The doctor served schnapps, and because Michael had a question, he drank the schnapps, drank it in one swallow, and then another glass that Dr. Klaus poured him. Mandy, said Michael, whether . . . and . . . He was sweating. She claimed her baby wasn't the outcome of union with a man, that she had never, no, that no man had known . . . My God: you know what I'm trying to say. The doctor emptied his glass and asked whether Michael meant the Lord had a hand in the business, or maybe a peter. Michael stared at him with an empty, despairing expression. He drank the schnapps the doctor had poured him, and stood up. The hymen, he said quietly, almost inaudibly, the hymen. That would be a miracle, said the doctor, and here in our midst. He laughed. Michael excused himself. I am a man of science, said the doctor, you are a man of faith. Let's not mix things up. I know what I know; you believe whatever you like.

On his way back, Michael was sweating still more profusely. He grew dizzy. Blood pressure, he thought. He sat down on the grassy edge of a large beet field. The beets had already been harvested and were lying in long heaps along the road. In the distance he could see a strip of woodland, and in the middle of the enormous field was the little island that his housekeeper had spoken of, a few trees sprouting from the dark earth.

Michael stood up and took a step into the field, and then another one. He walked toward the island. The damp soil clung to his boots in great clumps, and he stumbled, reeled, walking was difficult. Be of good heart, he thought, howbeit we must be cast upon a certain island. He walked on.

Once he heard a car drive past on the road. He didn't look around. He crossed the field, step by step, and finally the trees came nearer and he was there, and it really was like an island: the furrows of plowed land had divided and opened, as if an island had erupted from the land, and torn the soil aside like a curtain. This island was maybe half a yard in elevation. At its edge grew some grass, beyond was shrubbery. Michael broke a twig off one of the bushes and scraped some of the earth off his soles. Then he walked around the island on the narrow strip of grass. In one place there was a gap in the vegetation, and he climbed through it and got to a small clearing under the trees. The tall grass was trampled down, and there were a couple of empty bottles.

Michael looked up: between the tops of the trees he could see the sky, it seemed not so high as over the field.

It was very quiet. The air was warm, even though the sun was far gone to the west. Michael took off his jacket and dropped it on the grass. Then, without really knowing what he was doing, he unbuttoned his shirt and took it off, and then his undershirt, his shoes, his pants, his shorts, and last of all his socks. He took off his wrist-watch and dropped it on the pile of clothes, and then his glasses and the ring his mother had given him for pro-tection. And stood there the way God had made him: as naked as a sign.

Michael looked up at the sky. He had never felt more connected to it. He lifted his arms aloft, then he felt the dizziness of a moment before, and he toppled forward onto his knees, and knelt there, naked with upraised arms. He began singing, softly and with a cracked voice, but it wasn't enough. And so he screamed, screamed as loudly as he could, because he knew that out here only God could hear him, and that God heard him and was looking down at him.

AS HE WALKED back home across the field, he thought about Mandy, and she was very near to him, as though she was in him. So he thought, without knowing it, I have given shelter to an angel.

Back in the vicarage, Michael went straight to the old sideboard, and got out a bottle of schnapps that a farmer had given him after the burial of his wife, and poured himself a little glassful and then a second. Then he lay down, and only woke when the housekeeper called him down to supper. He had a headache.

And what if it's true? he said as the housekeeper brought in supper. What if what's true? Mandy. If she's conceived. By whom? Is not this land also a desert? said Michael. How do we know that He doesn't direct His gaze here, and that this child has found favor in His eyes, this Mandy? The housekeeper shook her head angrily: Her father's a bus driver. Well wasn't Joseph a carpenter? But that was a long time ago. Didn't she believe that God was still alive and in our midst? And that Jesus will return? Sure. But not here. What's special about Mandy? She's nothing. She works in the restaurant in W., she helps out.

With God nothing shall be impossible, said Michael, and verily, I say unto you, that the publicans and the harlots go into the kingdom of God before you. The housekeeper made a face and disappeared into the kitchen. Michael had never managed to persuade her to eat with him: she had always said she didn't want there to be talk in the village. Talk about what? We're only human, she said then, we all have our needs.

AFTER SUPPER Michael went out again. He walked down
the street, and the dogs in the yards barked like crazy,
and Michael thought, You would do better to trust in God
than in your dogs. That was the Communists' doing: he
should have talked them around, but he hadn't done it.
There were no more people in the church now than in the
spring, and you could hear of immorality and drunken-
ness every day.

Michael went into the retirement home and asked for
Frau Schmidt, who read the lesson every week. If she's
still awake, said Ulla, the nurse, unwillingly, and disappeared. A Communist, thought Michael, bound to be. He
could tell, he knew what they thought when they saw him.
And then, when someone passed away, they called him
anyway. So that he gets a decent funeral, Ulla had said
once, when he was required to bury a man who hadn't
been inside a church in his life.

Frau Schmidt was still awake. She was sitting in her
comfy chair watching *Who Wants to Be a Millionaire*. Michael shook her hand, Good evening, Frau Schmidt. He
pulled up a chair and sat down beside her. She had read
nicely, he said, and he wanted to thank her for it again.
Frau Schmidt nodded from the waist. Michael took a
small leather-bound Bible from his pocket. Today I'd like
to read you something, he said. And while the TV quiz

host asked which city was destroyed by a volcanic eruption in 79 A.D., Troy, Sodom, Pompeii, or Babylon, Michael read aloud, and steadily more loudly. There shall come in the last days scoffers, walking after their own lusts, and saying, Where is the promise of his coming? for since the fathers fell asleep, all things continue as from the beginning of the creation. But, beloved, be not ignorant of this one thing, that one day with the Lord is as a thousand years, and a thousand years as one day.

And he read, the day of the Lord will come as a thief in the night; in which the heavens shall pass away with a great noise, and the elements shall melt with fervent heat, and the earth also and the works that are therein shall be burned up.

All the while Michael read, the old woman nodded: she rocked back and forth, as if her whole body were one great yes. Then finally she spoke, and said, It's not Sodom, and it's not Babylon. Is it Troy?

The day is perhaps closer than we imagine, said Michael. But no one will know. I don't know, said Frau Schmidt. He will come like a thief in the night, said Michael, standing up. Troy, said Frau Schmidt. He shook her hand. She didn't say anything, and didn't look when he left the room. Pompeii, said the quiz host. Pompeii, said Frau Schmidt.

No one will know it, thought Michael as he went home. The dogs of the Communists were barking, and once he bent down to pick up a stone and hurled it against a wooden gate. That made the dog behind bark still more loudly, and Michael hurried on, so that no one would spot him. He didn't go back to the rectory, though, he walked out of the village.

It was half an hour to W. A single car passed him. He saw the beam of the headlights a long way ahead, and hid behind one of the trees lining the road until it was safely past. The island was nothing but a dark stain in the gray field, and it seemed to be closer than during the day. The stars were glittering: it had turned cold.

There was no one on the streets in W. The lights were on in the houses, and there was a single streetlamp at a crossroads. Michael knew where Mandy lived. He stopped at the garden gate and looked at the small single-story house. He saw shadows moving in the kitchen. It looked like someone was doing the dishes. Michael felt his heart grow warmer. He leaned against the gate. Then he heard breathing very close by, and suddenly a loud, yelping bark. He jumped back and ran off. He wasn't a hundred yards away when the door of the house opened, and the beam of a flashlight showed in the darkness, and a man's voice shouted, Shut yer noise!

ON ONE OF THE following days, Michael went to the restaurant in W., where his housekeeper had said Mandy was helping out. And so it proved.

The dining room was high-ceilinged. The walls were yellowed with cigarette smoke, the windows were blind, the furniture aged, and nothing went with anything else. There was no one there but Mandy, standing behind the bar as if she belonged there, with her hands on the counter. She smiled and lowered her gaze, and Michael had the sense of her face glowing in the gloomy room. He sat down at a table near the entrance. Mandy went over to him, he ordered tea, she disappeared. Please no one come, he thought to himself. Then Mandy came back with his tea. Michael added sugar and stirred. Mandy was still standing beside the table. An angel at my side, thought Michael. He took a hurried sip and burned his mouth. And then, not looking at Mandy, nor she looking at him, he spoke.

But of that day and hour knoweth no man, no, not the angels of heaven, but my Father only. But as the days of Noah were, so shall also the coming of the Son of man be. For as in the days that were before the flood they were eating and drinking, marrying and giving in marriage, until the flood came, and took them all away; so shall also the coming of the Son of man be.

Only now did Michael look at Mandy, and he saw that she was crying. Fear not, he said. Then he stood up and laid his hand on Mandy's head, and then he hesitated, and placed his other hand on her belly. Will it be called Jesus? Mandy asked softly. Michael was taken aback. He hadn't considered that. The wind bloweth where it listeth, he said, and thou hearest the sound thereof, but canst not tell whence it cometh, and whither it goeth.

Then he gave Mandy the little manual for young women and expectant mothers that the church provides, and from which he drew all his understanding, and he said Mandy should come to instruction, and to service, that was the most important thing, she had plenty to catch up on.

MONTHS PASSED. Autumn gave way to winter, the first snows fell and covered everything, the villages, the forest, and the fields. Winter stretched out over the land, and the acrid smell of woodsmoke hung heavy over the streets.

Michael went on long walks over the countryside, he went from village to village, and he went again across the large sugar-beet field, that was now frozen, to the island. Once again he stood there and raised his arms aloft. But the trees had lost their leaves, and the sky was distant.

Michael waited for a sign. None came: there was no new star in the sky, no angel on the field to talk to him, no king and no shepherd and no sheep. Then he felt ashamed and thought, I am not chosen. She, Mandy, will receive the signal, it is to her the angel will appear.

Mandy was now coming in from W. on her moped every Wednesday to class, and every Sunday to church. Her belly was growing, but her face was growing thinner and pale. After service she stayed behind in church until everyone was gone, and then she sat with Michael in one of the pews, speaking quietly. Her baby was due in February, she said. If only it had been Christmas, thought Michael, if only it had been Easter. But Christmas was soon, while Easter was the end of March: they would see.

Then the housekeeper put her head through the door, and asked if the minister proposed to eat his lunch today. All the trouble she went to, she said, and not a word of praise, nothing, and then he left half of it. Michael said Mandy should stay for lunch, there was enough for two. For three, he added, and both smiled shyly. Why don't we just open a restaurant, said the housekeeper, laying a second setting. She banged the plates down on the table and stalked off without a word, and certainly without wishing them *Bon appétit*.

Mandy said her father was tormenting her, he insisted on knowing who the father was, and he went into a rage when she said it was Almighty God. No, he didn't beat her. Only slaps, she said, her mother as well. She wanted to leave home. They both ate in silence. Michael very little, Mandy twice helping herself to more. Do you like it? he asked. She nodded and blushed. Then he said, why didn't she live here in the rectory, there was room enough. Mandy looked at him timidly.

You can't do that, said the housekeeper. Michael said nothing. If you do that, I'm out of here, said the housekeeper. Still Michael said nothing. He crossed his arms. He thought of Bethlehem. Not this time, he thought. And the thought gave him strength. I'm moving out, said the housekeeper, and Michael nodded slowly. So much the better, he thought: he had already concluded that this housekeeper had been a Communist, and who knows what besides. Because she always said she was only human, and because her name was Carola, which was a heathen name. He had heard the stories about her and his predecessor, a married man. In the sacristy, they said, among other things. That woman had nothing to say to him. She least of all. And she wasn't even a good cook.

The housekeeper disappeared into the kitchen, and then she left the house, because it wasn't right and it wasn't proper. And Mandy moved in: she was the new housekeeper, that was the agreement worked out with her parents. She was even paid. But Mandy was already in her fifth month, and her belly was so big that she snorted like a cow when she went up the stairs, and Michael was afraid something might happen to the baby one day when she lugged the heavy carpets out to beat them.

Michael was just returning from one of his walks when he saw Mandy beating the carpets in front of the vicarage. He said she ought to take it easy, and carried the carpets back into the house himself, even if it was almost more than he could do: his body wasn't very strong. Everything has to be clean by Christmas, said Mandy. That pleased Michael, and seemed to him to be a good sign. Other than that he hadn't found much evidence of faith, even if she liked to swear Holy Mother of God, and was firmly convinced that her baby was a baby Jesus, as she put it. She did say she was Protestant. But not so very much. Michael was in doubt. He felt ashamed of his doubts, but there they were, poisoning his love and his belief.

From now on, Michael did all the housework himself. Mandy cooked for him, and they ate together in the dark dining room, without speaking much. Michael worked far into the evenings. He read his Bible, and when he heard Mandy come out of the bathroom, he waited for five minutes, he was no longer able to work, that's how excited he was. Then he knocked on the door of Mandy's room, and she called, Come in, come in. There she was, already in bed, with her hand on her brow, or else on the blanket, over her belly.

On one occasion he asked her about her dreams: after all, he was waiting for a sign. But Mandy didn't dream. She slept deeply and solidly, she said. So he asked her if she really hadn't ever had a boyfriend or anything, and if she'd ever found blood on her sheets. Not during your period, he said, and he felt very peculiar, talking to her like that. If she is the new mother of God, then what sort of figure will I cut, he thought. Mandy didn't reply. She cried, and said, didn't he believe her? He laid his hand on the blanket and his eyes got moist. We should be called the children of God, he said, therefore the world knoweth us not, because it knew Him not. What Him? asked Mandy.

Once she pushed the blankets back and lay before him in her thin nightie. Michael had had his hand on the blanket, and then he raised it up, and now it was hovering in the air over Mandy's belly. It's moving, said Mandy, and she took his hand with both of hers and pulled it down so that it pressed against her belly, and Michael couldn't raise his hand, it lay there for a long time, heavy and sinful.

. . .

CHRISTMAS CAME AND WENT. On Christmas Eve, Mandy went to her parents, but the next day she was back again. There were not many people in church. In the village there was talk about Michael and Mandy, letters had been written to the bishop, and letters were written back from the bishop. A call had gone out, and a representative of the bishop had traveled to the village on a Sunday, and had sat with Michael and spoken with him. On that day, Mandy had eaten in the kitchen. She was very excited, but when the visitor left, Michael said everything was fine: the bishop knew there was a lot of bad blood in the district, and that some old Communists were still fighting against the church, and sowing division.

With the passing of time, the baby grew, and Mandy's belly got ever bigger, long after Michael thought it couldn't possibly. As if it wasn't part of her body. And so Michael laid his hand on the growing baby, and felt happiness.

The terrible thing happened when Michael went off on one of his afternoon walks. He realized he had left his book at home. He turned back, and half an hour later had returned. He quietly let himself into the house and tiptoed up the stairs. Mandy often slept in the daytime now, and if that was the case now, he didn't want to wake her. But when he stepped into his room, Mandy was standing there naked: she was standing in front of the large mirror in the door of the wardrobe. And she was looking at herself from the side, and so confronted Michael, who could see everything. Mandy had heard him coming and had turned to face him, and they looked at each other, just exactly as they were.

What are you doing in my room? asked Michael. And he hoped Mandy would cover her nakedness with her hands, but she did not. Her hands hung at her sides like the leaves of a tree, barely stirring. She said she had no mirror in her room, and she had wanted to see this belly she had grown. Michael approached Mandy, so as not to have to look at her anymore. Then his hands touched her hands, and then he thought about nothing at all, because he was with Mandy, and she was with him. And so it was that Michael's hand lay there, as if it had been newly brought forth: an animal from out of that wound.

Then Michael did sleep, and when he awakened, he thought, my God, what have I done. He lay there curled in bed, and with his hand covered his sin, which was great. Mandy's blood was her witness and his proof, and he was surprised that the elements did not melt with fervent heat, or the heavens pass away with a great noise: to slay him and punish him with lightning or some other event. But this did not transpire.

. . .

NOR DID THE HEAVENS open when Michael hurried along the street on the way to W. He was on his way to the island in the field, and he walked rapidly and with stumbling steps across the frozen furrows. Mandy had been asleep when he left the house, Mandy, whom he had taken in and to whom he had offered the hospitality of his house.

He reached the island and sat down in the snow. He could not stand any longer, so tired was he and so sad and lost. He would stay there and never leave. Let them find him, the farmer and the woman when they came here in spring to commit adultery.

It was cold and getting dark. Then it was night. Michael was still sitting on his island in the snow. The damp soaked through his coat, and he shivered and felt chilled to the bone. Let us not love one another with words, he thought, nor with speech. But with deeds. So God had led him to Mandy, and Mandy to him: that they might love one another. For she was not a child, she was eighteen or nineteen. And was it not written that no one should know? Was it not written that the day would come like a thief? So Michael thought: I cannot know. And if it was God's will that she conceive His child, then it was also His will that she had received him: for was he not God's work and creature?

Through the trees Michael could see only a few scattered stars. But when he left their cover and stepped out onto the field, he saw all the stars that can be seen on a cold night, and for the first time since he had come here, he was not afraid of this sky. And he was glad that the sky was so distant, and that he himself was so small on this endless field. So distant that even God had to take a second look to see him.

Soon he was back in the village. The dogs barked, and Michael threw stones at the gates and barked himself, and aped the dogs, their stupid yapping and howling, and he laughed when the dogs were beside themselves with rage and fury: and he was beside himself just as much.

In the vicarage the lights were on, and as soon as Michael stepped inside, he could smell the dinner that Mandy had cooked. And as he took off his sodden boots and his heavy coat, she stepped out into the kitchen doorway and looked anxiously at him. It had gotten cold, he said, and she said dinner was ready. Then Michael stepped up to Mandy, and he kissed her on the mouth, as she smiled up at him. Over supper they discussed one possible name for the baby, and then another one. And when it was bedtime they squeezed each other's hands, and each went to their own room.

As it got colder and colder in January, and it was al-most impossible to heat the old vicarage, Mandy moved one evening from the guest bedroom into the warmer room of the master of the house. She carried her blanket in front of her, and lay down beside Michael as he moved aside, without a word. And that night, and in all the nights to come, they lay in one bed, and so learned to know and to love one another better. And Michael saw everything, and Mandy was not ashamed.

But was it a sin? Who could know. And hadn't Mandy's own blood affirmed that it was a child of God that was growing, a child of purity? Could there be anything impure about purity?

Even if Michael hadn't thought it possible, his word reached the people and the Communists of the village. They were touched by the wonder that had occurred, and one couldn't say how: for such people came to the door and knocked. They came without many words, and brought what they had. A neighbor brought a cake. She had been baking, she said, and it was no more trouble to bake two than one. And was Mandy doing all right?

On another day, Marco the publican came around and asked how far along they were. Michael invited him in, and called Mandy, and made tea in the kitchen. Then the three of them sat at the table and were silent, because they didn't

know what to say. Marco had brought along a bottle of cognac, and set it down in front of them. He knew full well,
he said, that it wasn't the right thing for a small baby, but
maybe if it had a colic. Then he asked to have it explained
to him, and when Michael did so, Marco looked at Mandy
and her belly with disbelief. Was that certain? he asked,
and Michael said no one knew, and no one could know. Because it was pretty unlikely, Marco said. He had picked up
the cognac again, and was looking at the bottle. He seemed
to hesitate, but then he put it back on the table, and said,
three stars, that's the best you can get hereabouts. Not the
one I serve my customers. And he was a little confused,
and he stood up and scratched his head. Back in the summer you rode pillion on my bike, he said, and he laughed,
think of it. They'd gone bathing, the whole lot of them, in
the lake outside F. Who'd have thought it.

When Marco left, Frau Schmidt was standing in the
garden, with something she had knitted for the baby.
With her was Nurse Ulla from the retirement home,
whom Michael had suspected of being a Communist. But
she was bringing something herself, a soft toy, and she
wanted Mandy to touch her as well.

It was one after another. The table in the front room
was covered with presents, and the cupboard housed a
dozen or more bottles of schnapps. The children brought

drawings of Mandy and the baby, and sometimes Michael was in the pictures too, and perhaps an ass or an ox as well.

Before long the people were coming from W. and the other villages, wanting to see the expectant mother, to ask her advice on this or that matter. And Mandy gave them advice and comfort, and sometimes she would lay her hand on the arm or the head of the people, without saying anything. She had become so earnest and still that even Michael seemed to see her anew. And did all that needed to be done. In the village, various quarrels were settled during these days, and even the dogs seemed to be less ferocious when Michael walked down the street, and on some houses the straw stars and Christmas wreaths were back up on the doors again, and in the windows, because the whole village was rejoicing, as though Christmas was yet to come. Everyone knew it, but no one said it.

One time, Dr. Klaus came to see that all was well. But when he knocked on the door, Michael did not welcome him in. He sat upstairs with Mandy, and they were quiet as two children, and peeked out of the window until they saw the doctor leaving.

The next day, Michael went to W. to see the doctor. He poured schnapps, and asked how things stood with Mandy. Michael didn't touch the schnapps. He merely said everything was fine, and they didn't need a doctor. And these stories that were making the rounds? He that is of the earth is earthly, and speaketh of the earth, said Michael. Be that as it may, said the doctor, the baby will be born on earth, and not in heaven. And if you need help, then call me, and I'll come. Then they shook hands, and nothing more was said. Michael, though, went back to the retirement home in the village and spoke to Nurse Ulla. She had four children herself, and knew the ropes. And she promised him she would assist when the time came.

Then in February, the time came: the baby was born. Mandy was assisted by Michael, and by Nurse Ulla, whom he had called in. As word spread of the impending event, people gathered on the village streets to wait in silence. It was already dark when the baby was born, and Ulla stepped up to the window and held it aloft, that all might see it. And it was a girl.

Michael sat at Mandy's bedside, holding her hand and looking at the baby. She's no beauty, said Mandy, but that was more of a question. And Nurse Ulla asked the new mother where she meant to go with her baby, as she would no longer be able to run the minister's household anymore. Then Michael said: He that hath the bride is the bridegroom. And he kissed Mandy in full view of the nurse. And she later told everyone of it: that he had given his word.

Because the child could not be called Jesus, they called it Sandra. And as the people in the village believed it had been born for them, they didn't mind that it was a girl. And all were contented and rejoiced.

The following Sunday attendance at church was greater than it had been for a long time. Mandy and the babe sat in the front pew. The organ was playing, and after it had played, Michael climbed up to the pulpit and spoke as follows: Whether this is a child that has long been awaited in the world, we do not know, and may not know. For you yourselves know perfectly that the day of the Lord so cometh as a thief in the night. But ye, brethren, are not in darkness. For they that sleep sleep in the night; and they that be drunken are drunken in the night. But let us, who are of the day, be sober.

That which is born of the flesh is flesh, said Michael, and that which is born of the Spirit is spirit. But we, beloved, should be called the children of God.

Go Out into the Fields . . .

BACK THEN, THE time you left Trouville and climbed the narrow path up the hill, and then crossed the harvested field to get a good view. The earth clung to your soles in thick clumps, the leather was sodden. There was this kid, a boy, ten years old or even younger. He watched as you crossed the field, set up your folding chair, and started sketching the landscape. First he watched you from a distance, then he slowly came closer, step by step, wary as a cat. His clothes were old and dirty, their color like the earth from which he emerged. His hair was slightly reddish, almost transparent when the sun struck it in the odd moments when it broke through the clouds. His nose was blocked and he sniffled persistently. He kept his mouth slightly open to breathe, which distorted his otherwise pretty face, and gave it an expression of stupidity.

YOU GIVE HIM a cloth from your paint box, a little scrap of linen you normally use to clean brushes.

Here, wipe your nose.

The way he stares at you. He wipes his nose and then wipes his neck too, as though he was sweating. But the weather is cool and he's jacketless. It's a gesture he must have copied from his father.

Do you live near here?

He nods and takes his cap off.

Is that your field?

He nods again, takes a step closer, and tries to take a peek into your sketchbook. His shoulders are hunched, as if in the expectation of blows. You can see in his face how the question has come about, via many detours. And then his fear of asking it. But his curiosity is too strong.

Why are you doing that, monsieur?

Why are you doing that? The most terrible of questions. The question you don't even dare ask yourself. He doesn't ask what you're doing. He doesn't seem to be stupid. He must have watched other painters.

Has he ever seen a painting? Maybe a saint in church. But a landscape? How futile it must seem to him, you standing there in his father's field in your muddy boots, trying to capture the mouth of the river and the sea and the few houses in his village, the only one he knows.

You buy yourself off with a coin. He thanks you with a bow, and he's gone, and you work on, quickly, so as not to miss the moment. You've almost missed the fishing boats in the river mouth. They're on their way back to port.

It will rain later, and you will ask yourself where the boy is now, and whether he has a roof over his head. His question worries you. You ask yourself what quarter the clouds are coming from. Who cares? Weather is for farmers.

You are just hand and eye now. You hum a tune from Mozart, your Mozart. To paint the way he composed, with such facility and lightness. To paint in such a way that no one will ask any questions.

Why are you doing that? Because you're a painter. Nothing else, just a painter.

WHEN YOU TRANSFERRED the sketch in your studio, when you tried to remember the light and shade, and the reflexes on the sea—were there reflexes on the sea?—and the colors and the hues, all you could think about was the boy and his question. The question you never asked yourself. Why are you doing that?

You could just carry on like that. You will carry on like that. Already you have material for a whole lifetime. Sketches. Folders full of sketches, a head full of landscapes ready to be painted. And every day there are more. Every landscape you see is a job for you. The sun rises and sets for you, the wind blows the clouds across the sky for you, the grass and the trees grow for you.

Why are you doing that? Why not? The pictures are good. You know how good they are. You love your pictures more than anything. Your little sketches. The walls of your studio are covered with them. And you love working in the open, being outdoors, contemplating landscapes, painting. Nothing but the changes in the light, the slow, almost imperceptible movement of the shadows. How irritating it always was, when you drew the street urchins in Rome and they ran off before you were finished. They left you with a load of unfinished sketches. Landscapes don't run away.

You don't paint them to show them off. You don't exhibit your sketches. When your friends call on you in your studio, they want to see the big pieces you will exhibit, the landscapes with mythological or biblical scenes. They pass judgments that are baffling to you. You ignore them.

You'd rather do it wrong in your way than do it right according to the prescription of those twenty people. They all know better, give you advice, as if you didn't know that you can't pull off the big things, and why you can't. The biblical figures, the mythological figures, basically they don't interest you. Your true love is for the sketches, the little mood pieces.

If you could manage to depict the moment in just the way you sensed it, so that the boy in Trouville would recognize his village. That he might see the beauty of the village, the beauty of the moment. But who cares about such things?

Old Sennegon loved sunsets. In Rouen he went walking with you every evening. He told you Bible stories, always the same ones. It was as if he needed some pretext to be with you. The stories didn't interest you. Stories and the past—they never interested you. What interests you is the present, the moment. Father Sennegon walked two paces ahead of you, his hands crossed behind his back. He spoke slowly and thoughtfully, and suddenly he stopped and said, Look, look at the colors of the clouds. As if you had been looking at anything else anyway.

You sat down on a bench and silently watched as the sun went down. Very slowly it grew dark. The changes were barely perceptible. Then, the second sun dipped below the horizon, everything was different. That terrible moment in which the light seems to die. You kept painting dusks, as if you wanted to stop time, to escape the certainty of death.

YOU ARE TWENTY-NINE YEARS OLD. Soon you will leave your parents and travel to Italy. You must travel to Italy, if you are serious about becoming a painter. You are looking forward to the journey, but you're a little afraid of it too. Everything will be different. You will meet new people, sleep in strange beds, learn another language. You are thinking about the women in Rome. You have visited the rue du Pelican once or twice, but the women in Rome are different. Michallon told you stories about them. And on that occasion you were interested in stories.

You've bought a suitcase and clothes for the journey, a broad-brimmed hat, paints and brushes. You are prepared. In a couple of days you will leave. When you walk through Paris now, everything looks completely different. It's as though you were seeing it for the first time, it looks fresh and exciting. The beauty of the city is frightening to you. The last look is like the first.

You paint a self-portrait. Your father requested it. He wanted you to leave a picture of yourself. He will get on better with your picture than with you. He won't lose his temper with you for not getting up in the morning, for being absentminded, for wandering around aimlessly.

For the first time you look at yourself in the mirror with a painter's eye. You're not good-looking, but you like yourself. You smile. You will paint yourself smiling, with that smile with which you seduce women and drive your father white with rage. When he shouts at you and tells you to get on with it. You smile, and no one can do anything to you. You don't shout, you just smile.

You sketch your face. You capture your likeness. You have always clung to pictures. When you were sent out on errands during your apprenticeship, you stopped in front of galleries and looked at the pictures, always the same pictures. Once, when one of them was suddenly not there—it was a study of Valenciennes—in your excitement you walked into the gallery to ask after the painting, to see it one last time. It was as though you'd lost a loved one. But then you didn't dare. You said you'd gone in the wrong door, and you blushed and ran off.

You cling to pictures, your pictures. You don't really want to sell them. You've been known to buy pictures back. They are part of you, part of your life. You look at them. They don't change. When you put out the lights at night, you know they're there in the dark.

If only you'd drawn Victoire, while she was alive. You'd never have been a painter without her. It broke your father when she died. After that he didn't care what happened. He gave you the money he'd set aside for her. If you'd drawn her, she would still have been there. But drawing people, that was something you only learned to do afterward. Once you'd learned to see.

You learned: the world is flat, space is composed of blurs, shadows. Gradations. There is no time.

Long after you've died, long after the boy you saw on the field above Trouville will have died, your pictures will still be around. They will have barely changed. If only you'd said that to him: Once we're both dead, this picture will still be there and show your village the way it has long since ceased to be. But who will look at it, once we're both dead? Children always put you in mind of death, of your death, of the passage of time. Perhaps that's why you never wanted a family.

All I really want to do in my life is draw landscapes. That's what you wrote to Abel Osmond from Italy, shortly after you'd turned thirty. Draw landscapes. I won't change from that. That resolution will keep me from entering into any firm bonds, such as marriage.

As if the one excluded the other. Were you kidding him, or only yourself? You're a sketch artist, that's the reason. Whether it's a landscape or a woman, you're incapable of deciding. A fleeting touch, a brief glance, that's enough for you. So brief that nothing changes. The eyes, the shoulders, the hands, the bottom. Pictures of women. But such brief moments come with a price. Even in Rome.

Your passion is seeing. The act of love for you is painting. The other, the physical thing, is tedious for you, it just distracts you from work. You make love the way you eat, when you're hungry, quickly, without concentrating. You were never especially picky. For your bed the lovely Italians, for emotion the lovable French. And as a painter, as you wrote Abel, I prefer the former. Roman prostitutes. They do their work for a fixed price, and when it's done they leave with a smile.

You never really loved people, you were afraid of loving them, of losing them, of dependence on them. Love makes you vulnerable. Perhaps that's what makes you so popular: because you don't expect anything from people, you're indifferent to them. You were always generous. You helped lots of them without making a fuss. You buy your freedom. You want to be left in peace.

You don't like people for the same reason you don't like the sea. Back then, on the field in Trouville, you looked out at the sea, and it became clear to you that you don't like it. Because it keeps changing. It's dangerous. You can drown in it. You need terra firma underfoot. You wish the world would freeze over. Strange that you never painted snow.

YOU WOULD HAVE TO BE ABLE to take the moment of love into yourself, and live from the memory. But memory is deceptive. You remember the feelings, not the appearance of things. Once you tried to draw Anna from memory, your dear, sweet Anna. But as soon as you had the pencil in your hand, her face blurred. Your recollection was just a feeling. A feeling has no nose, no cheeks, no mouth. You can't trust your feelings, they're too inexact. Whereas exactitude was always your commandment. When you paint, you can't leave anything unresolved.

Memory cheats you, and you cheat memory. You paint it over, you destroy it. The world has no colors. Colors are interrelated, one entails the other. You obey colors. This green, this brown, this blue, you saw them for the first time when you mixed them on your palette. Your world is made up of lines and surfaces and colors. Your light is white lead.

How frightened you were the first time you painted your own likeness. How your face changed under the brush. It became a landscape, an approximate landscape, a surface. For a moment you were afraid you would lose your face.

I paint a woman's breasts no differently than I paint cans of milk. The forms and the contrasting tonalities: that's what matters. When you said that, did you think of Anna's breasts?

Her love only makes you impatient. You would have to sleep with her to free yourself of her, you would have to paint her. Why won't you paint me, she once asked in jest. Why does she want you to paint her? She thinks it would be proof of love. She doesn't know that it would destroy your love, that it could do nothing else. What you contemplate changes, becomes a picture. When you contemplate her, her face freezes. However much you fight it, you see lines, planes, colors. If you were to paint her, you would discover her beauty anew, the beauty of her picture. You would love the picture. Anna would be nothing in comparison.

YOU COULD HANG IT UP in your studio. Then you'll always have me with you.

You know that modeling is hard work. You have to keep still for a very long time.

I don't mind that. It's what I've done all my life.

I can't paint you, because I can't see you. My feelings for you cloud my eye. I can't paint what I love.

She laughs. She's flattered, but then she looks at you with an expression of reproach.

If you loved me . . .

She doesn't get to the end of the sentence. It's up to you. But you just kiss her hand. No one can keep silent like you. She reflects.

Don't you love the landscapes you paint?

I love my pictures. The landscapes don't mean anything to me.

VIEW OF VILLENEUVE-LES-AVIGNON, View of the Church of Saint-Paterne in Orleans, The Woods at Fontainebleau, Trouville, The Mouth of the Touques. You give your pictures titles, as if that's what they were for: one particular church, a bridge, one village rather than another. You love these villages, these landscapes, but when you paint them, you have to be indifferent to them. You said it in jest, but it's true: you work out of a passionate indifference.

It's hard to explain and hard to understand. You paint what you see with the maximum of precision, but you don't care about the precision of the depiction. You try to capture the feeling, the inexact feeling, as exactly as you can. What counts is decisiveness.

Your regard is cold, but not unfeeling. The coldness

of the regard is an absolute precondition. You mustn't be moved when you want to see clearly. To see something with cold regard means being nothing but eye. Otherwise it's not possible to feel your way into a landscape or a person. To feel your way means above all to forget yourself, to be beside yourself. It's not proximity that's your objective. The foreground is always messed up, if you don't wholly disregard it. You have decided against nearness. Nearness is warmth, nearness is when you're in love.

WHEN YOU WERE IN TROUVILLE the next time, you climbed up on the hill again, to check over a few details. You have to go out into the fields, not to the paintings, how often you used to say that to your colleagues, the ruminants, who copied the great pictures in the Louvre and reckoned that doing it made them great too. Bertin had sent you there, with a commission to copy some of the canvases, but you only ever drew the painters, those pathetic creatures, contorting their features, doing their best. Go out into the fields . . .

You climbed up the steep hill. It was chilly, but you were sweating. You were still tired after your lunch. In the distance you heard the breaking waves and a dog barking. This time you walked along the edge of the field, so as not to muddy your shoes. Then you had that view again of the village and the river mouth and the sea.

And suddenly you had the extraordinary feeling that the landscape was wrong, that it didn't accord with the reality you had created. Later on, you will paint this feeling over and over again. The young reader. She interrupts her reading, looks up from her book, and no longer knows the world. You will paint the wonderment in her eyes. Her smile is your smile. She knows that she is invulnerable. She lives in her own world, a world in which no time passes, in which there is no death.

YOU ARE STANDING at the edge of a field above Trouville. It is your field, and you look down at your village and your sea and your sky, at the lead white light.

When you go back to the village in the evening, you see the boy you saw before. He is squatting on the ground beside the path, playing with a piece of wood. He pushes it around on the ground, a cow, a pig, who knows what he sees in it. You ask him. He looks up at you in apprehension, as though you'd caught him doing something forbidden. Perhaps he doesn't recognize you.

A coach, monsieur.

As if you were able to see it.

Where is it going?

To Paris.

That's where I'm going soon. Do you have room in your coach?

He laughs. He's laughing at you. You've fallen for it.

It's just a bit of wood.

A bit of wood, a piece of paper, a canvas. Call it a coach, a bridge, a landscape. Call it a person. It's a game. Any child knows that.

What are you doing it for?

He looks at you with that expression of utter blankness of which only children are capable. Then he stands up and runs away. He has left his toy behind at your feet. You stoop to pick it up. It is just a bit of wood, a wretched piece of wood.

THE RIDGE

Summer Folk

WILL YOU BE coming alone? the woman on the telephone asked me again. I hadn't managed to catch her name, and couldn't place the accent. Yes, I said. I'm looking for somewhere quiet where I can work. She laughed a little too heartily, then asked me what my work was. I'm a writer, I said. What are you writing? An article about Maxim Gorki. I'm a Slavist. Her curiosity bugged me. Is that right? she said. She seemed to hesitate for a second, as though not sure whether to pursue the subject or not. All right, she said, come. Do you know how to get here?

In January I had taken part in a symposium on female characters in Gorki. My presentation on *Summer Folk* was to appear in a Festschrift, but I hadn't managed to find time in my crowded university schedule to take it out and polish it. I had kept my calendar free for the week before Ascension and was looking for a place where I could hope to remain completely undisturbed. A colleague recommended the Kurhaus. As a child he had spent many summer vacations there. The then-owner had gone out of business, but he heard the hotel reopened a few years ago. If you're looking for somewhere really quiet, that will be perfect. I used to hate it when I was a kid.

Buses only went up to the Kurhaus in summertime. She wouldn't be able to meet me, the woman said on the phone, without giving me a reason, but I could walk up from the nearest village, it wasn't far, no more than an hour or so.

THE BUS WOUND UP through steeply terraced farmland. There weren't many passengers, and when we reached the end of the line, I was the only one remaining, apart from a couple of schoolboys who quickly disappeared into various houses. I had packed just a couple of changes of clothes, but with a stack of books and the laptop, my backpack still probably weighed forty pounds. What have you got in there? asked the bus driver, dragging it out of the luggage bay. Paper's heavy, I said, and he looked at me doubtfully.

In front of the post office were a couple of signposts pointing in various directions. I followed one little lane, which turned into a path crossing a steeply inclined meadow, and then down into a narrow wooded gully. At the edge of the wood were larches and oaks, the interior was all spruce. All over lay felled trees, dried-up skeleton pines, with a few last traces of snow under them. The ground was boggy, and my feet sank deeply into the black mulch. I repeatedly felt spiders' webs catching on my face and hands. I saw no signs of other hikers, presumably I was the first this year.

After a while, I realized it was quite some time since I'd last seen a signpost, and sure enough, the path soon lost itself among the trees. I didn't feel like turning around, so I headed down the slope, which grew steeper and steeper. In places I had to grab hold of roots or branches, once I slipped a few yards and tore my pants. The rushing of the stream below grew louder, and when I reached it, I found the path again. The stream was a rapid mountain brook, with gray water. Its broad bed of gravel and light-colored stones looked like an open wound cut into the dark of the rest of the landscape. I was making better headway now, and after about half an hour I came to a little boardwalk. The ground below the supports had been washed away, and a fallen tree had come to rest squarely across the boardwalk. The impact had sheared off the rails and smashed some of the planking. I cautiously made my way over it. On the far side of the ravine, the path climbed sharply up, and I started to sweat, even though the air in the forest was cool.

It wasn't for another two hours till I saw the Kurhaus looming through the trees. Five minutes more and I was standing in front of an impressive art nouveau structure. The valley ground was already in shadow, but the hotel, standing a little higher, caught the full evening sun and was dazzling white. All the shutters except one on the ground floor were closed, there was no one to be seen, and only the rushing of the brook to be heard. The double doors at the front were open, and I walked in. The lobby was almost dark. Through the colored glass of the inner door panels a few rays of sun fell on the worn Persian rug covering the flagstones. The furniture was sheeted over.

Hallo-o, I called softly. There was no reply, and I walked through a pair of swing doors that had the words *Dining Room* over them in old-fashioned script. I found myself in a large room with two or three dozen wooden tables, all with upturned chairs on them. In the far corner of the room was an illuminated table with a woman sitting at it. Hallo-o, I called out, a little louder than before, and walked across the room toward her. Even before I got to her, she was standing up and coming to meet me with hand outstretched in greeting, saying, Welcome, my name is Ana, we spoke on the telephone.

She had to be about my age, dressed like a waitress in black skirt and white blouse, with sleek, shoulder-length black hair. I asked if the hotel was closed. Not anymore, she said, and smiled. On her table was a plate of ravioli, half-eaten. Just one moment, said the woman. She sat down and, gulping it down, finished her dinner. It didn't seem to bother her that I was standing there watching her eat. I hadn't had anything to eat since lunch, and was starting to feel hungry, but I wanted to go to my room first, shower, and get out of my clothes. When she belatedly gestured toward a chair, I sat down facing the woman. Tell me about your work, she said. I told her once again what I was doing here. She wiped her mouth on the napkin and asked, What do you find so interesting about that? I shrugged my shoulders and said, I had been invited to the conference. Gender studies was hot at the moment. And why always women? she asked. I said I didn't know, I supposed men were less interesting. She took a sip of wine and washed down the last of her food. I'll show you to your room now.

In the lobby she disappeared behind the front desk and rooted around inside it. After a while she pushed a pad across to me and asked me to fill in the form. I wrote in my details. When I turned the page to look up the last few entries, she took the pad from my hand and put it away. Would you mind paying in advance? I said that was fine. Seven days full board, she did the math, that makes four hundred and twenty francs, including tax. She took the bills from me and said she would give me the change later. And a receipt please, I said. She nodded, emerged from behind the desk, and walked toward the wide stone staircase. Only now did I notice that she was barefoot. I picked up my backpack and set off after her.

She was waiting for me on the second floor at the start of a long, gloomy passageway. Do you have any special requests? she asked. When I said I didn't, she opened the very first door and said, Then why don't you just take this one here? I stepped into the room, which was small-ish and without much in the way of furniture, except a poorly made bed, a table and chair, and a dresser with an old china basin on it containing a jug full of water. The walls were whitewashed and bare, except for a crucifix hanging over the bed. I headed straight for the French window that opened onto a tiny balcony. You shouldn't go out there, said Ana from the corridor. I asked her where she slept. What's it to you? I just wondered. She looked at me crossly and said just because she was on her own here didn't mean that I could walk all over her. I hadn't had any ill intentions, and stared at her in surprise. I asked what time dinner was. She frowned, as though concentrating hard, then said I should just come when I was ready. Then she vanished, only to reappear briefly in the doorway and drop a set of sheets and a towel on the table beside me.

THE BATHROOM AND TOILETS were at the far end of the corridor. I got undressed and stood under the shower, but when I turned on the tap, there was nothing but a faint gurgle. The toilet didn't flush either. I went back to my room in my underwear, and washed with water from the jug and put on some clean clothes. Then I went downstairs, but there was no sign of Ana. Opposite the dining room was a somewhat smaller room, with *Ladies' Saloon* over the door. There were a few armchairs in it—sheeted as well—and a big pool table. There was a white ball and a couple of reds on the green baize, and a cue leaning on the table, as though someone had just been playing. The next room, called *Smoking Room,* seemed to function as a library. Most of the books were old and dusty, by authors

I'd never heard of. Then there were a handful of classics, Dostoyevsky, Stendhal, Remarque, and in amongst them some tattered paperback American thrillers.

I went back out to the lobby and from there to the ballroom, which was bigger than all the others and completely empty, except for a rolled-up carpet. An old brass chandelier hung from the ceiling, which rested on fake marble pillars. It felt cool everywhere, and not much light came in through the closed shutters. In the kitchen downstairs it was even darker. There was a massive cast-iron stove that evidently ran on wood, and a sideboard loaded with dozens of used wineglasses and stacks of dirty plates, as though there had just been a banquet at the hotel. I went back up to the ground floor and then headed outside.

The shadows of the tall old pines that stood some distance away from the Kurhaus had grown a little longer by now, and were just grazing the white walls. I walked once around the building. On one side was a small graveled area with a few metal tables and folding chairs lying about, and some deck chairs. There I finally saw Ana. I sat down next to her and asked her how she was enjoying the last few rays of sunshine. It's been a long winter, she said, without opening her eyes. I looked at her. She had unusually heavy eyebrows and a strong nose. Thin lips gave her face a hint of severity. Her legs were folded under her, and her skirt had ridden up a little. The top two buttons on her blouse were undone. I couldn't get rid of the feeling that she was displaying herself to me on purpose. At that point she opened her eyes and ran her palm over her brow, as though to wipe away my gaze. I cleared my throat and said, The showers don't work. Didn't I tell you? And the toilet doesn't flush either. You'll just have to improvise, she said with a friendly smile, at least the snow has mostly gone by now. When does the season begin here? I asked. She said that depended on various factors. For a time we sat silently side by side, then she pulled herself up, straightened her clothes, and said, I thought you were looking for somewhere quiet to do some work. I'm not so sure about that anymore, I said, and when she stared at me questioningly, I wouldn't mind getting something to eat. She said dinner was at seven, and she got up and left.

I WENT TO MY ROOM to try to do some work. Distracted by my hunger, I went out on the little balcony to smoke a cigarette. I remembered that Ana had warned me not to use it, but it looked sturdy enough, only the iron railings were corroded and in some places rusted through. The gorge was directly under my feet, and I could hear the loud rushing of the brook. When I turned, I saw Ana lying on the deck chair again, in the graveled area.

I was down in the lobby on the dot of seven. Shortly afterward, Ana came in from outside. Oh, it's you, she said, you'd better come along. She led the way into the kitchen, lit an oil lamp, and led me into a small pantry stacked with cans of ravioli. Ravioli all right? she asked. Is that all you've got? Quickly she spun around, as though to see what the choices were, and then she listed them by heart anyway: Apple sauce, green beans, peas and carrots, tuna fish, artichoke hearts, and sweet corn. I said I'd take the ravioli. She reached down one of the cans and pressed it into my hand. Back in the kitchen, she showed me where to find silverware and plates, and handed me a can opener. Don't lose it, we'll be needing it. Is there anywhere I can heat it up? She furrowed her brow and said, Do you expect me to light the stove for the sake of that one single can? Anyway, I wouldn't know how. What about some wine, then? I asked. She disappeared and came back with a bottle of Austrian white, which she set down in front of me. That's extra, she said. Now enjoy your dinner, I'll be upstairs.

She left me the lamp and walked confidently off into the darkness. I shook the cold ravioli out onto a plate and went upstairs to the dining room. It tasted truly awful, but at least it filled me up. I returned the empty plate to the kitchen and left it on the side, with the other dirty dishes. I thought about leaving, but by now it was too late. So I sat in the library to work, with my laptop and bottle of wine. I found an outlet, but there was no power. The light didn't work either. Luckily my laptop battery was full. I read back over my talk and saw that it needed less work than I thought. I tried to concentrate on the text, but I was tired from the long walk, the wine, and the unfamiliar altitude, and I kept dropping off. At ten o'clock I stumbled upstairs to bed through the pitch dark building, without having seen Ana again.

I RAN INTO HER the following morning in the dining room with a plate of apple sauce in front of her. Help yourself, she said, and pointed to a big jar of the stuff on the table. I said I hadn't managed to find a working outlet for my laptop and the lights weren't working either, perhaps there was a fuse somewhere that had blown. We don't have any power, said Ana, as though it was the most natural thing in the world. While I was still eating, she got up and left the room. A little later, I saw her disappearing between the trees with a towel and a roll of toilet paper.

My battery was dead, and seeing as I didn't have a printout of my talk with me, there wasn't much more I

could do. I read around in *Summer Folk* and in Gorki's
correspondence, and jotted down a few notes, but it didn't
make much sense. The sensible thing would be to leave as
soon as possible. But instead of packing and looking for
Ana, I went into the Ladies' Saloon and played billiards.
At noon, there was a table laid for two in the dining room.
No sooner had I sat down than Ana came in with a can of
ravioli. I put it in the sun to warm it up a bit, she said. It
didn't seem to be any warmer than the day before. Don't
you like it? she asked.

I said I couldn't do my work without electricity. She
looked at me as if I was some kind of weakling and said,
Surely you'll find something to occupy yourself with.
I have to hand in the manuscript in two weeks, I said.
Why do people write such things, she said, who's really
interested? That's not the point. I have a deadline, and
I have to stick to it. She smiled mockingly and said, But
you don't even want to leave. Ana was right. I wanted to
stay here, I didn't know why, maybe it was for her sake.
Don't get your hopes up, she said, as though she'd read
my mind.

FOR THE NEXT FEW DAYS the weather remained fine, and
I often lay out and dozed on one of the deck chairs. I read

a lot, and played billiards or solitaire. Ana was around, but each time I asked if she wanted to play cards with me or practice cannons, she would shake her head and disappear. When I went into the library, I would find her sitting there, staring out the window. I pulled a book off a shelf at random and started reading. If I happened to get to a bit I liked, I would read it out loud, but Ana never seemed to be listening.

After the jug in my room was empty, I washed in the stream every morning, the way Ana did. I hung back in the dining room until she was finished, and then I headed out. I had found a good spot, where the banks were flat and the stream had a quiet flow. In the soft earth I saw traces of bare feet, and assumed it was the same spot that Ana used as well. When I dipped my head in the ice cold water, it felt as though it was exploding, but after that I would feel refreshed for the entire morning. Only the noise of the rushing brook was starting to bother me a little. There was nowhere you could avoid it, even inside the hotel you could hear it everywhere. I kept thinking of Ana, the whole day we circled one another restlessly, to the point that I was often unsure who was tracking whom.

She didn't cook and she didn't clean, I even had to make my own bed. The only services she performed were opening cans and setting the table. One time I remarked that I wasn't exactly getting my money's worth. Ana's face darkened in a scowl. She said it would be better if I stopped wasting time on Maxim Gorki and started thinking about my own attitude toward women. That has nothing to do with it, I said, surely you can at least expect running water and electricity in a hotel. You're getting much more than that, Ana snapped back. I didn't know what she meant, but I was careful to stay off the subject in future.

I tried to imagine what the place would be like with visitors in summer, with the dining room packed, someone playing the piano, and children running up and down the corridors, but I couldn't manage it.

The stack of dirty plates in the kitchen grew. One time I counted them. If Ana used three plates a day, then she must have been here all winter. I asked her if she was some kind of housekeeper. If you like, she said. I didn't believe her, but by then it was a matter of some indifference to me why she was here.

FOR LUNCH WE usually ate tuna with artichoke hearts, in the evening we lit a fire outside and heated a can of ravioli on a stone. The sun left the valley early and it got cold quickly, but even so we sat by the fire a long time in the

evening, drinking wine. We had barely exchanged a word
all day, and while Ana wasn't any more talkative than before, she did at least listen to me. I didn't feel like talking
about myself, I didn't want to think about my home life,
which seemed remote and irrelevant. So I started telling her about *Summer Folk*. She responded to the various
characters as if they were real people: she got annoyed
with Olga for complaining all the time and called the engineer Suslov a bastard. Varvara and her ravings about
the writer Shalimov left her cold. How could she fall for
such a man, she said indignantly, he's just a bad seducer.
What would a good seducer be like, then? I asked. He
would have to be honest to the woman and himself, said
Ana, and shook her head disapprovingly. Her favorite was
Maria Lvovna. I knew the famous monologue from Act IV
pretty much by heart, and was asked to recite it several
times by Ana. We are summer folk in our country, we've
traveled here from somewhere. We bustle about, look for
some comfortable niche in life, we do nothing and we
talk all the time. Yes, said Ana, we all need to change.
We need to do it for our own sakes, too, I said, so that we
don't feel our awful solitude so much. Ana looked at me
suspiciously, and said I wasn't to start getting any ideas.
You would fit well into the play, I said. In a letter, Gorki
said all his female characters hate men and all his men

are rotters. Then you would fit into the play yourself, said Ana. By the flickering firelight I couldn't be sure of her expression.

I never found out where Ana slept. When we went back inside at night, each of us with an oil lamp, she said I should go on ahead, she would be along in a while. Once I waited for her in the corridor outside my room. I had turned my lamp off, and listened in the darkness for a long time, but I couldn't hear anything, and in the end I just went to bed.

Half dreaming, I imagined Ana coming into my room. In the middle of the night I awoke and saw her silhouette in the pale moonlight. She got undressed, pulled aside the covers, and climbed on top of me. It all happened in complete silence, the only thing that could be heard was the distant rushing of the brook through the thin windows. Ana was rough with me, or perhaps I should say she treated me like an object she needed for a particular end, but for which she had no particular regard. When she had satisfied her hunger, she left, without a word passing between us.

IN THE MORNING, as usual, Ana was already sitting at the breakfast table when I walked into the dining room. Not really thinking what I was doing, I stroked her hair on my way to my seat. She gave a jump and cringed. I tried to start a conversation, but Ana didn't answer, and only looked at me with a grim expression, as though she knew about my dream. As she always did, she gulped down her food and got up as soon as her plate was empty.

After breakfast I browsed through some illustrated volumes in the library, and later I went along to the Ladies Saloon and knocked billiard balls around. There was no sign of Ana, and she didn't come in for lunch either. I ate downstairs in the kitchen, and then I went back up to the library and started reading one of the American thrillers. In the early afternoon I heard a car outside. When I looked out the window, I saw a couple of men getting out of an old Volvo in the driveway. For a moment I thought of hiding somewhere, but then I just stayed put and went on with my book. It was maybe an hour later, and I had just thrown aside my thriller in irritation, when the double doors swung open and the two men walked in. They looked at me in amazement, and one of them—not replying to my greeting—asked me what I thought I was doing. I'm reading, I said. And how did you get in? asked the man. Through the door, I said, and got up. I'm a guest at the hotel. The Kurhaus has been closed since last autumn, said the man. The owner has gone bankrupt. The hotel is going under the hammer next month.

And then he introduced himself, his name was Lorenz and he was the official receiver in the next-door community. The other man was a prospective buyer, an investor by the name of Schwab, who already owned a few other hotels in the area. I told them about Ana, and went to the lobby with them, and in a drawer behind the front desk retrieved the guests' register with my own entry. Even so, the receiver remained suspicious. Had I not suspected anything was amiss? he asked. A hotel with no running water and no electricity. True, he hadn't canceled the telephone, how was he to know that someone was going to squat in the building? I didn't say anything, what could I have said? And where is this enigmatic woman? he asked. I said she would be here at seven, seven was when we always had dinner. The receiver looked at me doubtfully, and said he would be grateful if I would pack my things. I would be able to get a ride with them later. They would take another hour or hour and a half to finish what they were doing. I said I had paid until tomorrow, but he didn't respond, and said to the investor that he would now show him the basement floor. I went up to my room to pack.

When I was done, I climbed up to the higher floors for the first time since I was here. They looked exactly like the one I was staying on. I opened the doors to all the rooms, but none showed any sign of occupation. From the top floor, a narrow staircase led up to the attic, which was crammed full of old furniture, Christmas decorations, cardboard boxes full of envelopes and toilet paper. A stack of straw wreaths lay next to an old sign with *Yuletide Ball* written among painted icicles. I found a dozen horn sleighs and big dusty Chianti bottles, but no sign of Ana. Even so, from the time I started searching the building for her, I had the feeling she was around, and would pop up somewhere at any moment.

After I had searched the whole building without finding anything, I sat down in one of the chairs in the lobby, not bothering to pull off the sheet. Eventually the two men emerged from the dining room. Herr Lorenz had a paper roll under one arm. He looked at his watch and made a gesture of impatience. Six o'clock, he said to his companion, I don't want to keep you any longer. If you want to wait, replied Herr Schwab, I'm not in any particular hurry. I'm curious about this woman myself. He turned to me and said, surely I knew where they kept the wine, and couldn't I bring up a bottle for us? I'll do that, said Lorenz quickly, and vanished downstairs. What do you think of the place? asked the investor, is it bearable? He wasn't quite sure himself. Two bankruptcies in short order didn't exactly bode well, but perhaps it had just been badly run.

We sat in the dining room, and drank the bottle of

Austrian white that Lorenz had brought up. At a quarter past seven, Schwab said he didn't think the woman
would appear, presumably she had seen the car parked
outside and had panicked. If she even exists, said Lorenz. She exists, I said. Lorenz nodded and said, It's all
right, I believe you. We sat fifteen minutes more. The
receiver locked the door, and said he would send the police up here tomorrow, to keep an eye on the place. While
we drove down the valley on the winding road, I thought
about Ana, and wondered what she would do now, what
she would eat, where she would spend the night. I was
certain that it wasn't the car that had frightened her away,
but me, with my thoughtless contact that morning.

I spent the night in a little bed-and-breakfast that the
receiver recommended. In the morning I went home. I
had a week left to finish my paper, and I worked hard on
it for the next few days, often thinking of Ana. Only now
did I understand what she meant in saying that what I
got from her was much more than electricity and water.
After I had sent in my contribution, I called the receiver.
It took him a moment to place me, then he said the police had been up to the hotel and looked everywhere, but
apart from the empty cans and the dirty plates, they had
found no sign of a woman anywhere.

The Natural Way of Things

'M NOT SAYING they tricked us, said Alice, but they
didn't tell us the truth. That's what always happens, said
Niklaus with a sigh, and he put a finger in the pages of
the guidebook he had been browsing. It's always different from what you imagine. You mean, it's always different from the way the travel agents describe it, said
Alice, and it's always worse. Whatever, said Niklaus.
They had had this conversation at least five times since
they got here. Alice had expected the rental to be bigger, better equipped, and with a better-kept garden. She
expected life to be different, thought Niklaus, that's the
problem, no sagging sofas or grimy ovens. And the oven
is filthy, said Alice. Five minutes to the beach! she said

with a sarcastic laugh. You hardly ever use the oven, said Niklaus. And as for whether it's five or eight minutes to the beach, what difference does it make, we're on vacation. Of course it wasn't just about the five minutes. It was about Alice feeling cheated, duped, and about Niklaus being passive and not sticking up for her. You let them get away with anything, she said. He changed the subject. What do you think about driving to Siena?

ORIGINALLY, SIENA WAS an Etruscan settlement, said Niklaus. Under the Romans its name was changed to Sena. The high point of its development was in the thirteenth century. That was when the university was founded and the town hall built.

Trying to avoid the hordes of tourists, they had gone down little alleyways and had gotten lost. Niklaus was reluctant to take out the little map in the guidebook, even though it was obvious to anyone that they were tourists. When he finally did, they had long since left the historic district and were standing on a busy traffic street that wasn't featured on the map. Normal life, he said. Makes an interesting change, don't you think? But Alice had seen everything she wanted to see, the Palazzo Publico, the Art Museum, the Campo, and the Cathedral. Normal life was something she could see at home. Now her feet were hurting, and the rain could begin again at any moment. You don't have a clue where we are, do you? I think, said Niklaus, turning the map in his hands, we must be somewhere around here. Alice hailed a taxi. It didn't even slow down.

On the way back, Alice moaned about the tourists choking the old town, just to buy a few ugly souvenirs. They had no idea of the treasures in the museums or the beauty of the architecture. If you don't know something, how can you have any feeling for it? she said. You don't know what they're looking for, said Niklaus, I expect they'll derive some good from it, otherwise why would they all have come here? They come because they come, said Alice. And when they return home, they'll go on about the toilets being dirty or clean. And the food expensive or cheap. That's what life is reduced to for them, eating and excreting. She laughed bitterly. I know, you're right, said Niklaus. He was sorry he'd suggested the outing.

THE NEXT DAY it rained buckets. Alice and Niklaus read all morning. When the rain eased up around noon, they went to the beach, but it was full of noisy families and games of beach volleyball. They hadn't been there long when it started raining again. Alice handed Niklaus his umbrella and put up her own. They watched the bathers hurriedly packing their things and racing past them laughing to take shelter under the awning of the beach restaurant. Serves them right, said Alice. Her mood seemed to have brightened slightly.

On the way back they shopped for groceries at a little store on the main strip. Afterward, on the street, Alice made fun of the other customers who had addressed the storekeeper in loud German and seemed perplexed that he didn't understand. They could at least learn *pane* and *prosciutto* and hello and thank you.

Outside the cottage next to theirs was a shiny black SUV with tinted windows and Stuttgart plates. The trunk stood open. On the road were suitcases and bags, a kid's bike and a tricycle. A man emerged from the house and walked toward them. Alice greeted him in Italian. The man didn't reply. Perhaps he didn't hear you, said Niklaus as they crossed the garden into their own house. Alice shrugged her shoulders. I only hope the kids make as little noise.

Inside it felt humid, and there was a smell of old furniture and cold cigarette smoke. There should be a law against smoking in vacation villas, said Alice. If the chimney worked, we could at least have a fire. They got the quilts out of the bedroom and spent the afternoon on the sofa reading.

OVER THE NEXT FEW DAYS they didn't really get to see much of their new neighbors. The weather had cleared, and when Alice and Niklaus had their breakfast on the terrace in front of the house, the SUV was already gone, and they didn't see it until they returned from dinner at the end of the day, and there were lights on next door. Alice and Niklaus hadn't so much as laid eyes on the woman and children. Maybe they don't exist, suggested Niklaus. Once they spent all day in the hills, touring wine estates, and bought a lot of wine and olive oil. When they returned at around five o'clock, the black Hummer again wasn't there, but an attractive young woman was lying in a deck chair in the garden. She had on a skimpy flowered bikini and was doing sudokus. *Buona sera*, said Alice, but the woman didn't respond any more than her husband had a few days earlier. After Niklaus and Alice had freshened up, they went out into the garden too, to read before dinner. No sooner had they sat down than their neighbors' car pulled up, and the man and two small children got out and went into the garden. Niklaus saw the man bend over the woman in the deck chair and give her a kiss, before vanishing inside. The children didn't greet their mother, they had been quarreling as they stepped out of the car and were still bickering over something or other. The mother seemed to have no intention of intervening. She lay on her deck chair, puzzling over her numbers. Once, with an angry hissing tone and in broadest Swabian, she called out, Cut it out, the pair of you, but she didn't even look up, and the quarrel went on as heatedly as before.

Alice lowered her newspaper and looked up at the sky. Niklaus pretended to be engrossed in his book. After a while, she threw it down and went inside. Niklaus waited a moment, then followed her. He found her sitting at the living room table, staring into space. He sat down opposite her, but she avoided his gaze. She was breathing fast, and suddenly she fell into a furious sobbing. Niklaus went around the table and stood behind her. He thought of laying his hand on her shoulder or stroking her hair, but in the end he only said, Just imagine if they were our children.

Alice had never wanted children. When Niklaus found that out, his first reaction had been relief, and he saw that it was only convention in him that had assumed he would one day start a family. On the occasions they had talked about it, it had been to assure each other that they had come to the right decision. Perhaps there's something wrong with me, said Alice with a complacent expression, but I find children boring and annoying. Perhaps I have a wrong gene somewhere. They both worked hard and enjoyed their work, Alice in customer service at a bank, Niklaus as an engineer. If they had had children, one of them would have had to sacrifice his career, and that was something neither of them was prepared to do. They traveled to exotic countries, had been on a trekking holiday in Nepal and a cruise to the Antarctic. They often went to concerts and plays, and they went out a lot. All that would have been impossible with children. But sometimes Niklaus wondered if having a family might entail not just a loss of freedom, but perhaps a certain gain as well, perhaps he and Alice might have been more independent of each other, without the exclusivity of love and irritation.

Alice had grown up as an only child, while Niklaus's siblings had no children themselves, so he and Alice knew only other adults. When friends of theirs came to have children, they usually lost contact soon after. If families came to visit, Niklaus and Alice were usually tense and impatient, and reacted clumsily to the clumsy efforts of the children to make friends. Then Niklaus would feel ashamed of himself. He had never regretted not having children, but sometimes he regretted that he had never even felt the desire to have any.

FROM NOW ON, the Stuttgarters were often in their garden. Half the time the children would be squabbling, and the rest of the time they contrived to be just as noisy. The older of the two was a girl of about six. Every so often, for no evident reason, she liked to issue a piercing scream. Her brother was maybe half her age. He was capable of keeping himself amused for fully a quarter of an hour at a time by bashing two objects together. He would only stop when his father yelled at him. Then the mother would yell at her husband, and he would shout loudly back. The coarse dialect didn't exactly improve matters. At other times Niklaus would see through the shrubbery between the two properties how the man knelt in the grass beside the woman in her deck chair, and rubbed her with tanning lotion. She would have her bikini top off, and he was kneading away at her breasts, seemingly unconcerned whether anyone could see him. Eventually the two of them would disappear, and a quarter of an hour later, Niklaus would hear one or another of the children banging on the front door, calling for the parents.

Alice could stand the noise for ten minutes at most. A few days later, the mere sight of the neighbors in their garden made her turn on her heel. They took their meals indoors now, when they didn't go to the local trattoria. Niklaus would propose trips, but Alice turned them all down. She was at war, and had to guard the terrain. Why don't you say something? she demanded. Niklaus looked blank and shrugged his shoulders. What can I say? If they were playing music outside, or making noise at night, then I could complain. I can't tell them not to talk. Children can't help being noisy. A rotten upbringing isn't punishable. Common is what they are, said Alice, and Niklaus nodded thoughtfully.

WHEN NIKLAUS WAS SITTING alone on the terrace, he would catch himself repeatedly looking across to the neighbors' garden. The woman lay out on her deck chair all day long, doing her puzzles. She had taken to sunning herself topless. She had small firm breasts that reminded Niklaus of those of the Polynesian women in Gauguin's paintings. He felt a desperate desire to go over and touch them.

Sometimes the man would take the children to the beach, and Niklaus would prowl restlessly around the property, imagining how he might get into conversation with the woman. He would make some casual remark, and she would ask him where he was from. Oh, Switzerland, we only ever drive through it. Then she would realize the laundry was still in the machine. She would put on her top and he would follow her inside, where it was cool and quiet. She would look him long in the eye. Well, what about it? she would say, and take him by the hand.

When Niklaus turned around he saw Alice standing at the window. She seemed to be observing him. He went inside. Alice hadn't stirred, she was still standing by the window, as though he were still outside. He laid one hand on her shoulder; she tried to shrug it off, but he wouldn't let her, and spun her around to face him, and kissed her. It took a while before Alice responded, and after a bit she freed herself, and said with a sarcastic laugh that the laundry must be finished. Niklaus followed her into the little room off the kitchen where the washing machine stood and watched as she took out their clothes, giving each individual item a shake. He followed her into the garden and helped her hang up the wet clothes. She kept the underthings separate, and draped them indoors on a little rack, as she did at home. I have the feeling nothing gets properly dry here, she said. Her voice sounded softer than usual. That'll be on account of the high humidity, said Niklaus. And they don't get properly clean either, said Alice. This time she didn't resist when Niklaus kissed her.

THEY LAY SIDE BY SIDE in silence. Alice had covered herself with a sheet, even though it was hot. Her expression kept changing, switching among the most diverse feelings: surprise, mockery, tenderness, grief. She seemed unable to decide on any one of them. Niklaus tucked his hand under the sheet and stroked her breasts, which were satin soft and had grown fuller over time. They hadn't slept together in ages, in fact he couldn't remember the last time. If you think . . . , he began, and stopped. Alice turned to him quickly, smiled affectionately, and looked away again. He wanted to talk about what had just happened, wanted to use the intimacy of the half hour to influence the day ahead of them, but in the end he just asked Alice what she felt like doing. Should we drive somewhere? She said she was hungry, but to Niklaus it was as though she had said, That felt so good. We still are a couple. I'm glad. We could have something to eat in town, he suggested. No, said Alice, I feel faint, I need something right away. She took a deep breath and stood up. For a moment she remained standing by the bed, looking down at Niklaus. He liked lying in front of her like that, naked and relaxed and vulnerable. Alice often made comments about his weight, and he knew she went for slimly built men, but she was looking at him with devotion. I'll just have a quick shower, she said. Niklaus got up too. He heard cries from outside. He went over to the window and saw the Stuttgarters evidently on their way to the beach, weighed down with bags and inflatable toys and a cooler. All four of them had on colored clogs and ridiculous sunglasses, the mother had put on a skimpy beach dress and the father was in shorts and a T-shirt with BABEWATCH on it in big letters.

IN THE AFTERNOON Alice and Niklaus set out on a trip for the first time in almost a week. They were going to the nature reserve, not far from their village. They were most of the way there when Alice realized she had left the binoculars behind, so they turned back.

Only a few of the parking spots at the visitors' center were taken. With this heat, everyone was at the beach—who but they would think of going birding? They followed a dusty gravel path, with bushes on one side and a narrow creek on the other, toward a wood. Niklaus felt tired from lunch and he was sweating, but he was in good spirits, whistling away to himself. Alice didn't speak much, not even to complain about the heat. When they reached the wood, it was barely any cooler than it had been out in the open. Niklaus kept stopping to consult a brochure about the reserve he had found in their house. If we keep heading in this direction we should reach the sea in half an hour or so.

In fact it was an hour later when they finally reached the sea. Alice kept herself to a few ironic remarks about Niklaus's sense of direction. There were supposed to be nightingales in the park, but they didn't see anything except a common buzzard and a few gray herons and moorhens on a pond.

There were lots of pieces of driftwood on the sand, limbs, sometimes whole trees, worn smooth by the wind and the waves and bleached silver by the sun. Alice took her shoes off and paddled in her bare feet. Do you fancy a dip? asked Niklaus. Alice looked at him questioningly. I'm sure there's no one around.

They quickly undressed and ran into the water. They were both excited, and kept glancing around at the shore. Imagine if someone steals our clothes, said Niklaus. Then we'll have to stay in the woods, said Alice, and eat berries and hunt wild boar. And I'll break into remote farmhouses at night, and steal eggs and the odd bottle of Chianti, said Niklaus.

After their swim they lay in the sun to dry, then they brushed the sand off each other. Alice giggled when she saw Niklaus had an erection. Not that as well, she said. She left her hand on his thigh a moment, as though thinking about something, but then she got dressed.

It was getting dark when they returned to the visitors' center, their car was the last one in the parking lot. Since they didn't feel like cooking, they thought they would have a bite in town. It was midnight before they got back. Next door, the lights were still on.

THE FOLLOWING DAY Alice and Niklaus had breakfast outside. There was no sound from next door. They spent the entire morning reading. It was quiet. The SUV was out on the street, their neighbors had to be home, but they didn't put in an appearance in the garden, not even in the afternoon. Maybe someone complained, said Alice, or maybe they've got food poisoning, and they're all lying in bed with stomachaches. The silence didn't seem quite real to her, she kept looking up from her book. Just be glad, said Niklaus. I never said they had to shut themselves away in the house, said Alice, of course kids need to run around and let off steam. It's just a matter of how they do it. At one point a man in a suit showed up on the property and went inside; a little later he went away again. Later on another man came, but he didn't stay long either.

I wish it was always this way, said Alice when things continued quiet the next day. They sat in the garden and played Scrabble. Alice had brought the dictionary from home so that they could look up any contentious words, but there were none. They both seemed a little distracted. Once, Niklaus saw someone walking past the windows next door, but he couldn't quite make out who it was. I keep thinking about them, said Alice, it's almost as though they were less intrusive when they were noisy. At least I could tune it out.

In the late afternoon they went down to the beach. They rubbed each other's backs with sunscreen, and Niklaus felt as though Alice's touch had changed since they had slept together, not more tender perhaps, but more aware. He too took his time about it, and noticed how Alice liked it when he pressed his fingertips against her spine and over her shoulder blades. It looks as though the vacation has turned out all right after all, she said. One week of rain, one week of fine weather, said Niklaus, I don't think we can complain. Do we need anything? Bread and prosciutto, said Alice, we've still got some cheese. And something for tomorrow. I feel like cooking. Do you have money on you?

THE SHOPKEEPER, who usually greeted them boisterously, today merely nodded and mumbled something. Wonder what got into him, said Alice, filling up their basket. Olives? she asked, holding up a jar of black olives. Niklaus nodded, and went over to the wine section, to look at the prices and compare them with what they had been quoted at the estates. When he turned, he saw Alice standing at the meat and cheese counter. The shopkeeper was jabbering away to her. Niklaus went outside and read the headlines of the German newspapers on the rack. A moment later, Alice came out of the store, looking upset. She walked off, not turning to look for him. He caught up to her in a few quick strides and asked what the matter was. That little boy is dead, she said, the father ran him over. He was backing up into the road, and didn't see him behind him. They walked silently back to their vacation home. Niklaus put the shopping away. Alice stood leaning against the kitchen table, watching him. What shall we do? she asked, when he had finished. There's nothing we can do, said Niklaus, we don't even know their names. We could ask them if they need anything, said Alice. It must have happened the day we spent at the nature reserve. The shopkeeper said the father's cries could be heard all over town. I'm glad we weren't here then, said Niklaus, and he felt rather cowardly. That evening, they ate standing up in the kitchen.

. . .

WHEN NIKLAUS AWOKE, it was just getting light. He checked his watch, it was a few minutes past five. Alice was gone. He found her in the living room. There was no light on, and she was by the window in her nightgown. When he came in, she quickly turned to him and then looked away again. He came up behind her and laid his hands on her shoulders. For a while they stood there in silence, and then Alice said, They're leaving. Only now did Niklaus see that the back of the black SUV was open. Look, said Alice, and Niklaus saw the man from Stuttgart coming through the garden carrying a suitcase that seemed to be very heavy. Together they watched him come and go a few more times. Last of all, he carried the damaged tricycle to the car. He could find no room for it, and pulled out some of the already packed things, looked at everything in bewilderment, and packed everything back in. Then he went into the house.

Maybe that's why I never wanted to have children, said Alice very quietly. Because I was afraid of losing them. We're bound to lose each other sometime anyway, said Niklaus. That's not the same thing, said Alice, that's in the natural way of things.

Niklaus went into the kitchen to put on the coffee. Then he heard Alice calling him. He went to her, and put

his arm round her bony shoulders. Now! she breathed,
as though something long-awaited was at last happening, and she pointed. The man had left the house again,
he was supporting the woman who walked beside him
with slumped shoulders and lowered head, leading their
daughter by the hand. The woman was wearing a heavy
wool sweater over her summer dress. The man walked
her to the car and helped her get in, as though she were
handicapped or very old. The little girl stood quietly next
to the rear door, until the father came around for her, and
carefully strapped her into the child seat. Last of all, he
got in himself. Through the window, they heard the engine start, then the headlights were switched on, and the
car rolled very slowly away.

Niklaus heard the coffee machine spluttering in the
kitchen, but he didn't pay it any attention. He pulled off
his pajama bottoms and drew Alice to him by the hips.
Urgently he raised her nightie and reached a hand up between her legs. They made love standing up, more force-
fully than a few days before. Alice didn't say a word, he
was hardly aware of her breathing.

Holy Sacrament

REINHOLD STOOD BY the window, looking out. A couple of men were walking by, and instinctively he took a step back. If he was honest, he was afraid of the people here, they were so moody and sullen. Their coarse language repelled him, and their humor shocked him. His predecessor had been like them, a rough, noisy man who went out drinking with his flock on Saturday night and preached to them on Sunday.

When Reinhold took the job a year ago, he had been full of good intentions. He had looked forward to the move to Lake Constance, and thought people in the south would be more open. He had been mistaken. Whatever he turned his hand to had failed. All sorts of things were held against him, the use of bread instead of wafers for Communion, and grape juice in place of wine, altogether the way that he didn't officiate in the style they were familiar with here. Word was that he neglected the elderly of the parish, while the fact that he was on first-name terms with the confirmands put a few more noses out of joint. He had wrecked things with the lady organist because he let his wife play guitar in the service a couple of times, and with the sexton because he kept too close an eye on the books.

Reinhold drew the curtains and went next door. Brigitte was watching TV. He had stopped telling her about his troubles, she was finding it hard enough to make the adjustment, and becoming a minister's wife was never her idea. He sat down next to her on the sofa. On the TV there was a little boy who claimed to be able to "read" the letters in alphabet soup with his mouth. Brigitte laughed. Isn't he something? Reinhold said nothing, he knew what was on her mind.

He lay there in the dark, unable to sleep. He could hear the TV in the living room. He asked himself what he might have done wrong. He had reached out to people, explained himself, and, at moments, been conciliatory. But all that seemed only to whip up the people against him even more. He no longer had the strength to fight, and barely enough to do his job. There was a time when the Sunday service had been the high point of his week, now he dreaded the stony faces and the cold silence with which his parish met him. When he read the Bible, its verses no longer spoke to him, and when he stood in the pulpit, he felt nothing but embarrassment. Twice already he had canceled worship because he was lying in bed with cramps.

THE ALARM WENT OFF at seven, Brigitte must have forgotten to adjust it for Sunday. When Reinhold leaned over her to turn it off, she awoke. She asked him if he minded if she didn't come to church today. She wasn't feeling well.

Reinhold shivered when he pulled off his pajamas in the bathroom. Out of the corner of his eye he could see the reflection of his pale, stringy body. Hurriedly he turned away and got under the shower. Over coffee, he went over his sermon once more. He would speak on Romans 9. Nay but, O man, who art thou that repliest against God? Shall the thing formed say to him that formed it, Why hast thou made me thus?

Then, still far too early, he set off. It was cold and damp. The area had been fogbound for weeks, and the forecast was for more of the same. No one was out and about at this time, only a few tousled seagulls pecked around in the overflowing trash cans in the little pedestrian precinct. The church was still locked. Reinhold was relieved not to have run into anyone. He walked down the dark nave to the vestry. There was an electric heater there, but still it was so cold he could see his breath. Reinhold pulled on his surplice, and read the Luther prayer that one of his predecessors must have pinned on the wardrobe door. O Lord God, dear Father in heaven, I am indeed unworthy of the office and ministry in which I am to make known Thy glory and to nurture and serve this congregation. But Reinhold didn't even feel unworthy. He sat there, brooding, until he happened to hear the church door fall shut, and a few minutes later a few random notes from the organ. For a long time his only communications with the lady organist had been via email, and the sexton did his job in silence and without looking at him. Reinhold's hands were stiff with cold. He started marching up and down, to get his blood moving. His predecessor had been in the habit of greeting his congregation at the door, but Reinhold needed these moments of silence, and he only entered the nave during the organ prelude. That, too, was taken amiss.

When he heard the organ, he cleared his throat, gave a little tug at his surplice, and emerged from the vestry. With rapid strides and eyes lowered, he went to his place behind the pulpit and sat down in such a way that the congregation could see him in profile. When the organ finished, he waited a moment for the last echo to die away, then he stood up and walked behind the altar, where the bread and grape juice were standing along with two lighted candles. The church was empty.

It took a moment for Reinhold to grasp the fact. No one had come to Communion. Only the sexton was standing by the mixing console, and up in the loft was the organist, with her back to him. He was sure she was watching him in the little rearview mirror that was fitted up there. He breathed deeply, then he said, Peace be with you. Let us pray. He hesitated, as though waiting while the congregation got to their knees, then he spoke the prayer as he did any other Sunday. Amen, he heard himself say. Let us sing Hymn 127, verses one through three. No sooner had he spoken than the organist began to play, her slight body and head in vigorous motion, though her playing lacked feeling and lacked love. The sexton stood there, holding his unopened hymnal in both hands. Dearest Jesus, speak to us. Reinhold sang loudly, though his voice cracked. If at least Brigitte were here, he thought, but maybe it was better that she wasn't, to experience this final humiliation.

At the end of the second verse, the organ suddenly stopped, and Reinhold saw the organist get up and leave. Now there was only his own voice to be heard, and the footfall of the organist, hurriedly and not at all discreetly clambering down the narrow flight of steps from the loft. She stopped in front of the sexton, whispered something to him, then slipped on the coat she had been carrying over her arm and left the church. The sexton followed her out, and the door crashed shut.

Dear Jesus, when to you we come in need, allow our prayers to succeed. The last words echoed away in the empty space. Reinhold waited for complete silence, then he leafed through the big Bible to the text for this Sunday, and began to read from the Epistle to the Romans. I say the truth in Christ, I lie not. He stumbled and had to cough. He took a sip of grape juice from the eucharist and continued. I have great heaviness and continual sorrow in my heart. For I could wish that myself were accursed from Christ.

He had meant to speak on the relations between Christians and Jews, on developments in the Middle East, and on quarrels and reconciliations in general, but now he felt like the boy on TV yesterday, as though he had to laboriously spell out every word, every letter. After the reading he prayed and sang once more. Then he called out, as loud as he could, We are all invited to share in the holy sacrament. And suddenly he felt as though he could see the church full of people, full of the shadows of those who for hundreds of years had celebrated Mass, had been baptized and married here and been given comfort as they lay dying. They arose, they came to him, and he gave them the bread and the wine, an endless stream of humanity. At that moment a bright ray of sunshine fell through the stained-glass windows of the church, and the space was transformed, becoming an explosion of light. The beams cracked and the organ boomed, it sounded like mighty breathing, an awakening from a long sleep.

Reinhold felt the blood shooting to his head. He took the basket with the bread, and he proceeded down the aisle and out of the church. The fog had begun to lift, in one or two places there was a glimpse of blue sky and in the east the sun lit up the earth, as it had on the very first day. In the square in front of the church, various community members stood in little groups. They seemed to have been waiting for him, perhaps the lady organist or the sexton, who were also standing there, had alerted them. Even Brigitte was there.

Reinhold walked up to them and held the basket aloft. The staff of life, he cried out. The people looked at him with hostility and shrank away. Then Reinhold heard a mewing cry, and raising his head, saw a gull hovering in the air above him. He took a piece of bread from the basket and threw it up, and with a tiny flick of its wing, the gull leaned forward and caught it in its beak. It flew so close to his head that he could feel the draft of its wings. And suddenly he was mobbed by a whole flock of seagulls. He threw bread around in gay abandon, and finally flung the whole empty basket into the air. All are invited, he shouted merrily. The seagulls' mewing sounded like crazed laughter, and Reinhold too was moved to laugh; in fact, he couldn't stop laughing, for at the end of many weeks of darkness, he finally saw the light.

In the Forest

T HE HUNTER MUST get into position very early in the morning. By the time Anja is awake, he's already there. He keeps very still, and he is so far away that she can only just make him out, but even so, she has a sense of knowing him and being close to him. All day she thinks about him. When she zips herself into her sleeping bag at night, she imagines him approaching her sleeping place, to watch over her while she sleeps. His gaze is calm and friendly. He picks up her clothes, sniffs them, as though looking to find a scent. Then quietly he takes off, climbs up the ladder into his high stand, and waits.

Even before the sun reaches Anja, she is woken by the confused singing of many birds. She lies there a moment longer, looks secretly across to the high stand, and sees the hunter sitting there, and her heart starts to beat faster. She takes a little more time in the mornings now, and risks getting to school late. She notices herself moving more consciously, and she feels her body's beauty and freshness, as though it were she observing it and not he. She is in her underwear, but she is in no hurry to get dressed. She stretches, combs her hair, squats down to wet her hands in the dew, and looks around, as though she were seeing the forest for the first time. She hums a tune and wonders if the hunter can hear her. It's a shy form of courtship. Because all the time Anja knows she would run off if he left his stand and took so much as a single step in her direction.

I LIVED IN THE FOREST for three years, that's the most Anja will say on the subject, even years later. It was no secret, even the children knew, but at that time it was grownups who were asking questions that Anja didn't want to answer, couldn't answer. The school psychologist was asking them, after she'd been found. Why? Others gave answers for her: a broken home, father and mother both violent and both alcoholics, often disappearing for days on end. No, Anja said, this has got nothing to do with my parents. No one could understand that she wasn't running away from something, but toward something.

When she looked out of the kitchen window at the wooded hill on the other side of the expressway, she didn't feel anything. You could only feel the forest when you were in it. That was the thing that made it so special, the way you could step into it as if into a room. You needed to be in it to be able to absorb it and be absorbed by it. She didn't go into the forest much anymore, and people didn't understand that either if they happened to know her story, and took her for some kind of forest creature. She didn't pick mushrooms, she didn't watch birds or animals, she didn't know more names of trees than other people. Nor was she one of those bleeding hearts who got agitated about every tree that was cut down. On the contrary, it was a relief to see how people dominated the forest, which sometimes seemed to her like a disease, something that proliferated and spread. Only the noise of chain saws still bothered her, because back then it signified the threat of being found. The routes taken by the foresters were less predictable than those of the hikers, the joggers, and even the hunters, who had their fixed places that they liked to drive up to, if they could, in their pickup trucks. But over time, Anja noticed that the lumberjacks didn't proceed without a plan either, and that they tackled a forest a piece at a time. Once or twice, because of that, she had to move camp, which was bothersome but not threatening.

All this was twenty years ago. In the meantime she had trained as a bookseller, had worked, married, had two children. What was left of her old self were memories and a sensitivity, an alertness, that Marco mistook for nervousness.

THERE WAS ALWAYS SOMEONE Anja was trying to catch up to, her parents, her school friends, dream characters she didn't know and who still seemed to be somehow familiar to her. She was always running after people, in the certainty she wouldn't be able to catch them. Anja wanted to be quicker, but it was as though her limbs were lead, and the air was a viscous soup that required a violent exertion for each movement. She sought to free herself, but that only made the invisible bonds tighten around her. Then she woke up, her forehead burning, her pajamas soaked in sweat. The screaming had awoken her, it was two in the morning. Anja pulled the covers over her head, but she could still hear the screams, hear things being knocked over, the crash of the front door. Often she was all alone in the apartment in the morning. The door was ajar. On the floor lay the wreck-age of whatever had fallen over in the night, a sort of still life with destroyed objects.

School was the only secure place. Where Anja liked best to be was in the physics lab on the lower ground floor, with its dim light and metallic smell, or in the li-brary, among the tightly packed shelves full of the past. When the library was closed, she hung around the school grounds until it grew dark. The worst weren't the shouts or the blows. The worst was coming home, and no one there. The expectation, the certainty, practically, that they would arrive sometime in the night.

YOU HAVE TO LEARN to live without expectations, that's the only way of getting by. Patience by itself isn't enough, because in fact nothing happens. In the forest there is no future and no past, everything there is either instanta-neous or takes place over periods that cannot be mea-sured in mere years. Sometimes Anja imagines what it was like when the whole country was covered with forest. Then she climbs up the lookout tower, peers down at the city, and sees nothing but trees. She sees the trees in the parks and gardens and along the streets, envoys from a past or future time, and everything in between loses its

brashness and its significance. Even the old town, the
houses that are many hundreds of years old, seem no
less provisional to her than her shelter of branches and
canvas.

Eventually the ice will return and efface everything
that people have built and made. Glaciers will lie over
the land for thousands of years, rivers of ice miles deep,
and what they will finally leave behind will be a new
landscape; there will be new rivers and valleys, the
moraines will form chains of hills, enormous piles of
rubble that will soon be colonized by the first pioneer
plants. Trees will grow on the humus, a thin forest to
begin with, then ever thicker. Wild animals will come
over the mountains in the south: insects, birds, deer
and antelope, and with them their predators, foxes and
wolves and lynxes and the first man. And then it will all
be as though nothing had happened.

THEY WERE JOGGING through a residential district, past
small detached houses. There were people working in the
gardens, people walking their dogs, children playing on
the streets. The gym teacher was out in front, along with
the fast runners. A little way behind was the main group,
followed by three or four slower girls, the overweight

ones or the artsy ones, who didn't care. Anja brought up the rear. She made an effort, she wanted to be quicker, but her legs felt leaden.

By the time they reached the edge of the forest, the others were out of sight. After a few hundred yards along a narrow footpath, she reached a dirt road, which led straight up. Way ahead she saw the others, heard the distant padding of their feet on the gravel, their shouts and laughter. Anja stopped. She had a stitch, and she was panting hard. Her T-shirt was sweated through, and now that she had stopped running, she felt a chill. She leaned down to touch her toes, took a couple of deep breaths, and slowly set off again. The others disappeared round a bend, and it was quiet.

Something has changed. To Anja it feels as though she's considering the forest for the first time, as though the forest were turning to her. Her thoughts have stopped, and so too has time, everything is connected to her, becoming a single, exquisite feeling, the light, the smells, isolated sounds that make the sudden silence still deeper. She stands there, studying the play of the light in the treetops. She touches the trunk of a beech tree, its cool silvery bark. Later, whenever she is tempted to give up and return to her parents' apartment, she will evoke this moment. And then time once more stands still, and nothing matters, and she can get through the night, the week, the year.

She had thought the class would take the same route back, but no one came down the hill toward her, and by the time she finally reached the lookout tower, there was no one there either. She climbed up the tower and stared out over the forest and down over the city, where the first lights had already come on.

The next day, Michaela asked what had kept Anja. I told the teacher you weren't feeling well, and had stayed home. Thank you, said Anja. She had been home. Her parents weren't in, and she packed a few things in a backpack, clothes and books and something to eat and a sleeping bag, and she left.

That was her first night in the forest. She wasn't afraid, on the contrary, she felt freer than she had in a long time. In front of a fire she had built, she sat and thought until it started to get light. Over the weeks and months she thought less, and learned just to be there, in a state of alert indifference.

SNOW FALLS FROM A BRANCH, it's like the opposite of a noise, this fall without acceleration that changes the depth of the silence and the configuration of space. Relieved of the weight, the branch rebounds upward in slow motion, and loose snow crystals drift through the air.

The deer sink deep into the snow on their thin legs. Anja watches them from the lookout, their strutting movements, their breath steaming with exertion. When it starts to get dark, she sees the lights coming on in the city. Now she yearns for a home, a room, a warm bed, and a fridge full of things to eat. It's a yearning she is unable to satisfy. She knows too much about what life in the houses is actually like.

In the forest her dreams are different, more alive, even though nothing seems to happen in them. In these dreams, she crosses the terrain, quickly but without haste. Perhaps they are like animal dreams.

It is very quiet at night. If Anja happens to wake, it's on account of the cold. There are some nights when she puts on all her clothes in layers and layers, and it's still not enough. Then she lies awake for a long time, but it feels as though morning won't come unless she falls asleep. Hours later, the quiet bleeping of her alarm wakes her. She quickly turns it off. Though she's a long way from any street or footpath, she's afraid someone could hear the sound and find her.

Anja has her clothes in the sleeping bag with her, so that they're not quite so cold in the morning. She gets dressed in the dark and crawls out of her shelter. Outside, she stretches, cleans her teeth, drinks some water, eats a hard-boiled egg and a couple of slices of bread. She stole the food yesterday. She's due to get her allowance in a week, her father has at least got it together to set up a standing order, but it's never enough to last her through the end of the month. Carefully she wraps the eggshells in a napkin and packs it in her schoolbag. She doesn't want to leave any traces.

AN HOUR BEFORE the beginning of classes, Anja was at school. Luckily, the sports hall was already open. It was cold in the girls' shower room. Anja piled her clothes in a corner and walked right across the changing room, naked as a wild animal. She turned on the water and took a jump back, waited for steam to rise. She showered for a long time, but the hot water seemed only to warm her skin, the chill inside her would take all morning to thaw.

Once she was almost caught. She was just putting her clothes on when she heard the changing room door, footsteps, and the door of the shower room. She stood motionless in the corner, holding her breath. She heard a man clearing his throat and, shortly after, the door falling shut. She waited another fifteen minutes before daring to go out.

She had the afternoon off. Michaela asked Anja if she felt like coming back to her house to eat. She knew her friend had trouble with her parents, and often invited her back. Michaela's parents treated Anja like a sick child, which she sometimes enjoyed and sometimes found unbearable. After lunch the girls sat on Michaela's bed together, listening to music and talking, but at three, Anja said she had better go, she had some things to do.

On such clear days she couldn't stand to be indoors. And the light would start to fade at five. She went to the grocery store. There weren't many customers, and she had to take care she wasn't caught. She stole three small cans of tuna, a jar of mayonnaise, and some chocolate biscuits. She bought a pack of gum, to deflect attention. She thought the checkout girl eyed her suspiciously, but perhaps that was just her own bad conscience. It wasn't until she was back in the forest that she heaved a deep sigh and felt free once more.

SHE HAS CHOSEN her sleeping place carefully, a little dip on an incline. That way she's hidden from sight, but if she walks or crawls a few steps, she can overlook a big piece of forest. She builds a fireplace from a few rocks. At night the firelight can be seen reflected in the treetops, a little dome of light, but at night she's all alone in the forest. The last people here are the joggers who come in groups, and in winter have little miners' lights on their headbands. They make an amazing amount of noise. But noise doesn't protect you, as Anja learned quickly. You have to be very quiet, learn to disappear in the forest, become invisible and inaudible. She was always puzzled that the walkers hardly ever leave the footpaths, that all of them stick to the paths that others have used before them. Three years in the forest have taught Anja that you can blaze your own trail.

MARCO RECKONED she was unhappy because she didn't want to go to the cinema with him, and because she didn't like it when he asked people back to the apartment. Ever since living out here, Anja had stopped seeing her friends—she had long ago broken with her parents—and she didn't like to visit his family either. Marco concluded she was depressed. He didn't understand that it all seemed like a waste of time to her, every moment she wasn't on her own.

For ten years they had lived in the city and done a lot together, gone to clubs and concerts, hung out with friends. Anja had her job, and everything was good. Her time in the forest was long ago, and she felt she could lead a perfectly normal life. It was when she got pregnant that she noticed herself beginning to change. The doctor said that was to be expected, it was hormonal, but Anja could feel something returning to the surface that had long been buried. Without really thinking about it, she had done what was expected of her, and deceived Marco and herself. Now she felt she was waking up, her senses were sharpened, and nothing was obvious anymore. She thought about the forest more often, and about the way she had felt when she was there, that strange mixture of unconsciousness and a higher pitch of being. She began to withdraw.

After the birth, they looked for a bigger apartment. Anja gave up her job, she simply didn't go back once her maternity leave was over. Marco's earnings alone weren't enough for most apartments in the city. After looking for some time, they found a four-room apartment in a new development on the edge of one of the exurbs. The apartment buildings stood between the expressway and the business park. They were occupied almost entirely by young families, there was a school and a kindergarten smack dab in the middle of the complex, and a good direct bus line into the city. Marco's work was nearby, his commute was half an hour less per day. He asked Anja if she would be happy there, if she felt sure. To begin with, she hardly left the apartment. Then, by and by she started to explore the area and take possession of it.

IT'S AN EVER-CHANGING no-man's-land, construction going on all the time, and even the finished buildings look like prototypes. Next to the shopping center and the media mart an OBI home improvement store is going up, and there are a couple of big pet stores, a carwash, and an erotic megastore. On one of the last empty lots there are used cars for sale, but even this lot is spoken for. The area is riddled with access roads. There are young saplings on the slope, made fast to stakes in the ground, as though to stop them from running away. There is heavy traffic all day long, with one rush hour at lunchtime and another at the end of business hours; the middle of the afternoon brings a slight letup. When Anja goes out exploring with the stroller, she hardly sees anyone, only the occasional cyclist zipping past her on a racing bike.

She is pregnant again, and walking is getting harder and harder, but only a few days before her due date she sets off once more. When, exhausted, she looks for some-where to rest, she can't find a bench anywhere, and ends up having to sit on the grass by the side of a road, with the stroller next to her. The traffic pulls up at a red light, the cars are just a few feet away. The drivers stare, but Anja couldn't care less. Only when one winds down his window to ask if she needs help does she stand without a word and walk off.

OUTSIDE, IT WAS COLD and rainy. The children were out of the house, but Anja had no energy to do any chores, the mess didn't bother her or the dirt. The idea of fixing up the apartment, tidying it, making it nice, was alien to her. She paced through the rooms, sat on a chair, picked up a magazine. By lunch she had no idea what she'd done all morning. She ate whatever happened to be in the house, with the children. She didn't often cook, sometimes she stuck a pizza in the microwave or she took the kids to McDonald's.

Marco had made her see the doctor about what he felt was her listlessness. But the doctor had just gestured dismissively and prescribed Vitamin B. Maybe it's the others that aren't normal, she said to Marco that night, the ones who are always out and about doing something. But Marco shook his head and stared at her as though she was mad.

What she liked best were those days when the kids were away in the afternoon as well, at school or on play dates with friends. Then she would wander around the neighborhood, or if the weather was bad go to the mall or one of the supermarkets. She had started shoplifting again. Once, she was caught, it would never have happened before. A security guard had gone up to her after she passed the checkout, and asked her to follow him. He was very polite, a young man with good manners and a neatly trimmed beard. He took her to a back room and asked her to empty her bag. It gave Anja a strange feeling of satisfaction, to spread out her things in front of him, the key ring with the little toy sea lion, paper tissues, her purse, coins and paperclips, and various leaflets she had picked up. When she pulled out a lacy bra with the price tag still on it and laid it on the table, she fixed the young man with her eyes, and he looked away. Then with a casual gesture he pushed away the things that weren't hers, and said, You can put away the rest.

The amount at issue was not large, but the store manager made a huge fuss, and threatened that if it happened again, she would be banned from all branches of the store. The way he carried on, it was as though she had robbed him personally, and he seemed to expect her to be remorseful. Asked what made her do it, Anja shrugged her shoulders. I just did it, was all she said, all she could say. She paid the fine unprotestingly. The affair seemed to embarrass the security guard, but Anja got a kick out of the whole business. Still, she would have to be more careful in future.

She kept running into the young man after that. Now that she knew him, she was surprised she hadn't noticed him before. When they saw each other in the aisles, they looked each other in the eye briefly but didn't speak. Anja was certain that he remembered her, and that made her happy. It was as though they shared some dark secret. Sometimes Anja saw him walking along behind her. Then she would purposely take things off the shelves and turn them around in her hands, as though wondering whether to take them or not. When she saw the security guard eating in the store cafeteria, she would sit down close to him. More important than seeing him was knowing that he could see her. It was as though his glance in some way ennobled her.

WHEN ANJA ENTERS THE FOREST, it feels to her as though she has stepped outside herself. She sees herself as a stranger, a girl walking among trees. She dreams of the forest in a similar way, always seeing herself from

above, from a height of fifteen or twenty feet. She once
read somewhere that people dying could see themselves
like that, as their souls left their bodies.

The lookout tower is at the center of a complex web of
places. There are places for fair weather and places for
foul, places to sleep in and others that she only spends
time at in the daytime. When it rains, she often sits in
a shelter for forest workers, or she climbs up into one of
the high stands on the edge of a clearing. The main thing
is to stay on the move.

She sometimes runs into Erwin in the shelter. He went
to elementary school with her, but it was only in the forest
that they got to know each other better. Erwin is training to be a forest warden. He never asks Anja what she's
doing there, and why she wants to know where they're
going to be working next. Sometimes he loans her some
money, though he doesn't have much himself. For a time
they meet almost every day. After work, Erwin goes to
the shelter. To begin with, she was afraid he might have
fallen in love with her. But all he does is bring her books
he wants to talk about with her or that he thinks would
interest her. *Tuiavii's Way,* Erich Fromm on love, books by
Nietzsche that he doesn't understand, and *Walden*. Erwin
is someone who thinks he understands himself, but almost nothing he says is original. Even so, Anja likes

being with him. They are close. She hasn't told him her secret, but he knows the forest.

A strong west wind has been blowing all day, and by evening it's become a gale. The treetops are individually seized by the wind and hurriedly let go, hundreds of small motions that in their totality become enormous, a rushing and soughing. Look, says Anja. But Erwin doesn't seem to notice. He is thinking about his books. When he leaves, she says she is going the other way. You always seem to be going the other way, he says. Yes, she says, and laughs, it's true.

For some reason it's a time of frequent nosebleeds, almost one a day. She leans over so that her clothes aren't soiled, and lets the blood drop on the ground. Fascinated, she watches the dark splotches on the forest floor. She feels light-headed, as though something has cleared in her. Sometimes she catches the drops in her hand and licks them up.

THE DIFFERENT PLACES are connected by paths that are not logging roads and not trails, which she will only use at night or in bad weather. They are paths known only to her, that she has discovered over the months and years, and that she has walked again and again, safe paths that

are hard to spot. She has hiding places where she keeps
her clothes, her school things, one or two personal items,
little dumps with cans of food she has stolen or bought,
those few times she had money to spend, food she can
eat cold when it's raining and she can't start a fire. Early
on, she sometimes lost things, she isn't sure why, maybe
wild animals took them. Since then, she has become
more cautious, more adept. In winter she heaps leaves on
the hiding places to keep the food from freezing. Winter is the most difficult time, but also the most beautiful.
When there is snow on the ground, and she has the forest
all to herself for days on end. The only thing she's afraid
of is that her footprints might give her away.

Once all humans used to live that way, she told the
school psychologist. It's the others who're not normal,
sitting in their houses behind their lowered blinds. He
looked at her pityingly, and she thought, you wouldn't last
a week in the forest. There it was never a question of why.
Everything was just the way it was, food was food, sleep
was sleep, warmth was warmth.

The psychologist looked at her the whole time. When
she walked out, he followed just behind. He had a little
shiny car, he offered to give Anja a lift somewhere, but
she refused. When he drove off, she saw the child seat
in the back, and a little sticker in the rear window in the

shape of Lake Constance. Anja felt nothing but contempt
for him.

SHE NEVER MANAGED to find out whether the hunter had
betrayed her or whether it was her own fault. Perhaps she
had dropped her guard. The forest wasn't about power or
fleetness of foot, the only thing that mattered was alertness, attention, living wholly in the present. That was an
advantage animals had over humans, for them memory
was only experience, and not another world in which you
could lose yourself.

It was just before her final exams, Anja was eighteen and
could do as she pleased. Even so, one morning a policeman
visited the classroom to ask her some questions. He was
friendly enough, but the fact that afterward they all spoke
to her as to an invalid, that offended her. Michaela's parents
offered to put her up temporarily. She declined and moved
back in with her parents, who were intimidated by the police and treated her like a stranger. After a few weeks, she
managed to persuade her father to pay the rent for a staff
room in a nurses' hostel. No sooner had she moved in than
she stopped going to school. It was spring, and the exams
were in fall. Anja was a good student, and everyone urged
her to stick it out, but she stood her ground.

It wasn't difficult to find a job. Anja had always spent a good deal of time in the bookstore when she was feeling low, or it was raining. The bookseller knew she had no money, and had given her reading copies of recent publications and asked her afterward how she'd liked them. Anja had done errands for her, or minded the shop when she had to be away for a while, to go shopping or to a doctor's appointment. She had been pleased when Anja turned to her to ask if she would take her on as an assistant.

During her training, Anja lived in an attic room above the bookstore. Apart from the customers and her boss, she had very little contact with people. Erwin visited the shop from time to time, and now it was she who was recommending things to him, books, novels, stories, to divert him from his introverted musings. Eventually he stopped coming. To begin with, she didn't even notice, later she heard from another customer, who had also been to school with her, that a forestry worker had died and Erwin had been responsible. He had been cutting down a tree, the other fellow wasn't paying attention and had been crushed. The customer explained how there had been an inquiry but no charges had been filed. Anja wondered about writing Erwin, but she didn't know what to say, and eventually it was too late for that. Soon after, she heard that he had given up his job, and begun to train as a psychiatric nurse. When she bumped into him on the street a few months later, he had joined a free church, and wanted to talk to her about God. She gave him the brush-off. Back home she cried over him.

HAVE YOU HAD YOUR BREAK TODAY? Anja sees the poster everywhere. She has taken the kids to McDonald's. The little one is telling her how his neighbor gave him an apple to eat. That was months ago, and he's told her a dozen times, but it doesn't bother him. The only significance the story can have for him is that it's something he remembers. To Anja, it's as though he's using his memory to escape from her. She watches a world come into being in him to which she has no access. After lunch, the two boys argue over the presents that came with their Happy Meals. One of them wants the other's, but he's not prepared to swap. Anja sends them out, and tells the older one to take his brother to kindergarten. He sulks and fusses, and only agrees after she promises him an ice cream.

When the children are gone, she gets herself some coffee, then she goes to the shopping center. This is her territory, she knows every nook and cranny of it by now. She walks through the shops as though she worked there. On the ground floor there's a discount bookstore, it's a chain, and the stock is all best sellers and cheaply produced coffee table books on popular topics. Marco thought she might apply for a job helping out there, just a few hours a week. He probably thought it would do her good. But Anja has had enough of books. Ever since they've been living out here, most of life strikes her as a waste of time, especially television. Only music is an occasional exception.

She likes the provisional quality of the buildings in the shopping center, which will be knocked down after a couple of decades and replaced by others. She likes the piles of merchandise, the soulless items sealed in plastic. She is capable of walking around for hours on end and picking up the things on display. She tests the fabric of clothes, sniffs them, tries them on. In the food sections, she opens packaging and quickly crams some of the contents into her mouth.

The customers in the stores seem somehow incomplete, they are missing something in their present, provisional setting. Anja doesn't perceive them as people, not even the salespersons. On the rare occasions she is addressed, she gives a start and mutters something, No thanks, just having a look, and goes on her way.

She concentrates so hard on her walking that it ceases to be automatic. Her sensitivity becomes extreme, the cracks between the tiles irritate the soles of her feet. When she comes home after such expeditions, she is exhausted and can barely tolerate the children, and yells at them over everything and nothing.

FOR A TIME, Anja lives in a clump of pines so dense that almost no light gets in. Only the moss on the forest floor glows with a fluorescent green. She has been on edge for months, and this is the safest place. Like a diseased animal, she has retreated here. It's difficult to force herself to go to school every day, the only thing that gets her up in the morning is her fear of being found. When Michaela asks her to come around after school, Anja shakes her head. She spends whole afternoons in her sleeping bag under an old army groundsheet that she bought at a flea market. The ground under her is covered with a dense layer of pine needles that set up a little cracking and rustling. It's been a long winter, in some spots the snow is still there in late March. Once it's thawed away, Anja dares to leave her pine refuge. She sets up on the edge of a clearing, on a little piece of boggy meadow ringed by trees that's hard to get to. Only animals come here, and sometimes a hunter. A week before Easter it finally gets warm, and the forest seems to change from one day to the next.

Anja hears the twittering of the birds and the quiet rush of distant traffic on the highway, and shouting children crashing through the undergrowth. A low-flying plane approaches slowly, seems to hang overhead forever, and moves away. The wind picks up and shakes the last of the dry leaves on the trees, which make a sound like rain. When she shuts her eyes, the space seems to expand; when she opens them again, the colors are unexpectedly pallid. Only the green of the pines is strong, and that of the fresh grass, just starting to peep up among the old dead grass, crushed by the snow. Everything here is alive, even dead wood is swarming with creatures, with funguses and beetles and ants. At the far end of the meadow is a high stand, creaking in the wind.

In autumn, there's a hunter sitting up there. Anja has got up, put her clothes on, and brushed her teeth, when she suddenly becomes aware of him. Perhaps he made a noise, or she had a sense of being watched. He hasn't leveled his rifle at her, even though for a moment she's afraid she might get shot. Then fear gives way to a feeling of security. She carries on calmly, stowing her things under the groundsheet, and dives into the bushes.

The man comes again. For a whole week he's sitting up there every day, watching her. He must realize she's seen him, but he gives no indication of it, not so much as a nod or a little wave of the hand. She relishes the attention, but at the same time she can feel something being broken. The spell is shattered. One morning the hunter is no longer there. For a while, Anja carries on as before, waits for him to come back. She is impatient, comes up with various theories. For the first time she feels bored in the forest, and the cold weather gets on her nerves. She can feel that she won't last out much longer. When she is found shortly afterward, she is almost relieved.

WITHOUT BEING WHOLLY AWARE of it, Anja expects to find the hunter in the bookshop. Even though they've only seen each other at a distance, she is sure she would recognize him. He has dark green trousers, a fleece top, and a funny little hat. His rifle is slung over his shoulder. He doesn't say a word, only looks at her and smiles. His smile is kind, but it spells danger. Anja shrinks back, hides behind a bookcase, waits for him to come after her. She flees from him, luring him farther into the darkness of the shelves, the vaults full of books, full of boxes. She hurries through a labyrinth of passageways she has never seen before. The hunter is close behind. He won't let her escape.

ANJA MET MARCO. He liked to visit the shop from time to time, to order books on automatics and robotics. They got

talking, and finally he asked her out for coffee, so awk-
wardly that she couldn't refuse. He courted her, she knew
for ages that he would eventually try to kiss her, she was
almost counting on it. It took a couple of dates before he
finally got up the courage, and then everything happened
very quickly. They married when Anja was pregnant.

Shortly after their tenth anniversary, Marco con-
fessed one evening that he had a girlfriend. For weeks he
had been troubled and nervous, and Anja couldn't really
say she was surprised. The indifference with which
she greeted the news infuriated him. She didn't hold it
against him, he had to get rid of his agitation somehow,
and the way he did it was blaming her, and shouting at
her, and then immediately apologizing and weeping and
then shouting again. Be quiet, she said, the children.

The separation passed off without strife or scenes.
Only when Marco asked her to forgive him, she impatiently shook her head. She kept the apartment and the
kids. Marco and his new girlfriend moved back into the
city. The kids spent more and more time with their father,
and before long got on with the girlfriend better than
they did with Anja. Each time she handed the children
over to Marco, he would ask her casually whether she was
seeing anyone. He was hoping she would remarry, so that
he could stop paying her support. Anja would have been

happy for that to happen, but she didn't need a man, or companionship wasn't what she needed.

One time, the security guard sat down at her table. It felt as though he was in breach of a tacit agreement between them. Anja shook her head in annoyance. She walked off, leaving her half-empty plate. After that she avoided the supermarket for a while.

When Anja passes the school building, she can look through the large window into the classroom, but she doesn't recognize any of the children. She walks through the business park. The sky is clouded over. She looks at the display of the domestic appliance store, which is right next to the erotic center. She feels the glances of the men walking in and out, they simultaneously disgust and fascinate her. At the pedestrian crossing, she has to wait for a long time after pressing the button. Trucks are bringing fresh goods; cars have their music turned up so loud, they seem to be throbbing. Behind the main storehouse and the rail tracks is a little creek, along which a footpath leads. Anja looks at the mural on the high wall around the recycling center, it's of a jungle scene. Some things are merely hinted at, green and gray cross-hatched areas, a pale blue sky. Only a few details have been fully executed, crumbling temple ruins, a few enormous trees, a leopard that seems to leap out of the wall at the onlooker. The painter seems to have given up his work long ago, in one or two places the picture has been daubed with graffiti.

The path ends at a railway line. The other side of the line is the soccer field. The humming of the mower blows across, and the damp air carries the smell of freshly mown grass. Anja sits down on the field and watches the passing trains. She lies down and shuts her eyes. She has one more hour before she has to pick up the kids from school.

SHE IS STANDING in front of a staircase that leads straight up. She runs up it, encounters a heavy, battered steel door. She hurls herself against it, the door swings open, and she is standing in a back courtyard. Quickly, but without haste, she walks on. She has never been here before, but it feels familiar, she doesn't hesitate for a moment. The hunter is close behind her, she doesn't turn around, but she can feel his presence, his nearness. It's early in the morning, there's no one out. Only now does it dawn on Anja that she can't hear anything, not a sound, it's as though she were deaf. The road leads through a tangle of alleyways. Eventually Anja comes out on a large square. She walks to the middle of it, then stops and looks around. At this point she sees the hunter. He has emerged from one of the alleys and is standing quite still. Slowly he takes his rifle down from his shoulder, goes down on one knee, and takes aim. His face is rigid with concentration, his eyes expressionless. Even though they must be twenty yards apart, Anja can see his finger slowly curling round the trigger, and then the flash of flame in the muzzle, and at the same instant she feels a great exquisite pain in her breast and a warm dribble of blood—it feels a bit as though she has stepped into a hot bath. Then she is lying on the ground, and the hunter is kneeling at her side. He strokes the hair back from her brow. There are tears in his eyes. He makes to speak, but she shakes her head and smiles. It's all right.

Ice Moon

I T WASN'T UNTIL I locked my bicycle that I registered there was something different from usual. I walked back to the entrance of the industrial park and saw the lowered blinds in the porter's lodge. With the annual Christmas whirl, I had forgotten that Biefer and Sandoz were both retiring at the end of the year. A month before, someone had organized a collection to buy them each a retirement present. I had contributed, signed a couple of cards, and then not given the matter any more thought. Now I felt sorry I hadn't said good-bye to them.

On the glass door of the little porter's house was a map of the premises. Below it was a list of numbers in case of emergency: fire, police, ambulance, and a number for the administration. In a transparent document wallet next to that was a letter from the administrator. He wrote to wish all the tenants a happy holiday, with many happy returns for the New Year. The letter was decorated with an illustration of a fir twig and a candle.

Time was, hundreds of people had worked in the factory, but after production and development had been contracted out abroad, the industrial park emptied, until there were only the two porters left. The manufacturing company had transformed itself into a shell, and moved into offices near the station. The old brick buildings on the lakeshore were left deserted for a while, and then rented out piecemeal. Artists, graphic designers, and architects were now working in the labs. An ex-employee opened a little bar in the weighing room, where we sometimes met at lunchtime, for coffee or a sandwich. A violin maker and a furniture maker set up their workshops in the old production halls. A couple of start-ups that no one knew what they did had leased space. There were rooms that people moved into and then vacated almost immediately.

The lakeside location was nothing short of spectacular, and every couple of months the newspapers would run stories about ambitious redevelopment plans for luxury apartments or a casino or a shopping center. But the necessary investors never came through. We were all on short-term leases, which were regularly extended each time one of these projects went down the tubes. Sometimes the administrator would show up with a bunch of men in dark suits. We'd see them standing around outside, and with sweeping gestures tear down the buildings and run up new ones. Whichever porter happened to be on duty followed them at a distance across the site, and only stepped up when there was a door that needed unlocking. To begin with, these tours had given rise to wild, panicky rumors and speculations, but by now no one seemed to think anything would ever change.

When I got to the office in the morning, one of the porters was always there. Biefer generally sat in the lodge— which was glazed on three sides—smoking his pipe and reading the paper. Sandoz preferred to stand outside— even when it was well below freezing—with his hands in his coat pockets.

Earlier, they had both delivered the mail, but since we now all had mail boxes, all they did was take in occasional parcels or tell the bicycle messengers where our studios were. They took down the numbers of illegally parked cars, and sometimes you could see one or the other of them walking around the site with a huge bunch of keys in one hand and a pointed stick in the other, to scrape the litter away from the disused rails. Mostly, though, they would be at the main entrance, which was now always open, quietly overseeing the comings and goings on the site.

Biefer and Sandoz were never there together. There was a shift change at noon, and they seemed to be at pains never to meet. In the beginning, I couldn't tell them apart, even though they could hardly have been more different. It was only superficially that there were similarities, both of them being short and squat and thinning on top. They wore blue coveralls, and in bad weather Sandoz added a black coat and a leather hat. He came from the French part of Switzerland, and—even though he'd been working here for over thirty years—spoke in heavily accented German. He was a moody fellow, there were days when he'd chatter away, and others when he'd barely get a word out, and would act as though he'd never seen you before when you said hello. Biefer, by contrast, was a local and almost exaggeratedly friendly. Whenever I ran into him, he would ask about my children, whom he'd seen once or twice, no more. We would talk about the weather and football and communal politics—not often about himself or his family. Biefer occasionally referred to his wife, but only once did he tell me about his two sons, who were both living abroad.

One cold foggy morning, maybe two months ago,
Biefer stopped me. From a distance I could make out a
fuzzy outline beside the porter's lodge, and I assumed it
was Sandoz. When I was a lot closer, I saw it was actually
Biefer. I waved to him, but he held up his hand like a traffic policeman. I pulled over in front of him, and he asked
me if I could help him with something. I asked what it
was about. Not here, he said, oddly conspiratorial, and
turned around.

I had never seen inside the porter's lodge. In spite of
the large windows that seemed to bulge outward, the
room was cozy enough. A small oil stove produced a dry
heat, and there was a sweet smell of pipe smoke. Biefer
sat down at his desk and opened a drawer. He pulled out
a worn-looking folder and placed it, closed, in front of
himself. Then he got up and brought, not asking, two
cups of watery coffee. He gave one to me, and pointed to a
plate with cake on his desk.

Gingerbread, he said. If you like that kind of thing.

There was only one chair. Biefer had sat down, and
I stood behind him in the shadow, looking down at his
rather squat head and the strands of gray hair between
which one could see plenty of pinkish scalp. He filled his
pipe but didn't light it. He didn't seem to know where to
begin. He made a couple of false starts, got tangled up,

coughed. Perhaps he was distracted by having to wave to people who were arriving on the site. He said he had once upon a time been a baker, but was forced to switch jobs because he developed an allergy to flour. He had always enjoyed travel, whereas sport held no interest for him. Except for soccer, that is. He said he had married young, which had been the way, back then. He didn't regret anything. He said that several times. He didn't regret anything.

After he had been talking like that for a while, I finally realized what was going on. At the end of the year, when he was due to retire, Biefer was planning to emigrate to Canada and open a bed-and-breakfast there. Why Canada? I asked, but Biefer ignored me. He talked about the visa application he had submitted a few months ago, some points system in which his training and knowledge of French and English all counted in his favor, along with his age and financial status. Then he had got a letter back from the Canadian embassy in Paris, which he didn't understand. He said he hadn't spoken French since school, which was now fifty years ago. For a few months he had been taking English lessons, but he was probably too old to learn a new language. He opened the buff folder, pulled out the top sheet of paper, and hurriedly slammed the folder shut. He handed me the letter.

In fussy legal French, the applicant was required to complete his dossier by supplying an itemized account of his personal wealth, complete with documentary proof, all to be supplied on the same day. When I explained to Biefer what it was about, he seemed relieved. He asked me not to breathe a word of his plans to anyone, and least of all to Sandoz.

I had almost forgotten this when Biefer hailed me the next time, a couple of weeks later. He was looking terribly mysterious, and waved me to follow him into the porter's lodge. It was shortly before Christmas, on the desk was a frail assemblage of fir twigs, two shiny silver Christmas tree ornaments, and a stout candle that hadn't been lit. Beside it was the buff folder. Biefer opened it, pulled out a sheet of paper, and, beaming, handed it to me. His visa application had been approved. He thanked me for my help. I said I hadn't done anything. He hesitated, then he opened the folder again and left it open between us. On top was a red envelope from a photo shop. Biefer pulled out a sheaf of pictures and laid them carefully side by side on the table. The photographs—which were barely distinguishable one from the next—showed forest, low trees and bushes, and sometimes a gravel track in the foreground. Biefer's hands hovered over the prints, he was like a soothsayer trying to predict the future from a deck of cards. This was his land, he said finally, in Nova Scotia. He took some papers out of the folder and spread them out in front of us, a contract of sale, a passport and flight ticket, tourist brochures, and postcards. At the bottom of the folder lay a poor photocopy of a surveyor's map, on which a lumpy-looking lake and a few plots of land were sketched in. One of the plots was carefully marked in red. In the middle were two rectangles in pencil, under them were the smudged traces of earlier outlines that had been rubbed out. This was where he was going to build his house, said Biefer, a blockhouse with ten guest bedrooms and a big day room, and his apartment upstairs. The smaller rectangle was the garage.

I was standing beside him, and I couldn't see the expression on his face while he told me about his project, but his voice sounded enthusiastic and full of energy. He had bought the land some years before, he said, ten thousand square meters for thirty thousand Canadian dollars. He had no direct access to the lake, but then again the land was on the main road, and that was good for trade. At the end of January he would be flying to Halifax. From there it was another two hours by car. He had been to look at it already, last year. The countryside was amazingly beautiful, a bit remote, true, but with bags of potential. A paradise for hunters and fishermen.

I couldn't imagine Biefer in the wilds of Canada. He was
pale and puffy-faced, and didn't strike me as particularly
healthy. But he went on enthusing about his property and
about Nova Scotia. The area was on the same latitude as
Genoa, he said, in summer it got into the nineties. The
winters admittedly were snowy and cold. Building per-
mits were no trouble to get, he said, and gas cost barely
half of what we paid here.

I asked him why he wanted to emigrate in the middle
of winter, wasn't it cold enough for him here? He said that
way he would have time to get everything ready for the
tourist season in summer. First the forest would have to
be cleared, and then the house built. There was a lot to get
done. He said the movers were coming after the holidays.
His whole household would be packed into a single con-
tainer and put on a ship. It would have to remain in stor-
age until such time as the house was built. I asked him
what he was going to do with himself until it was time to
go. He looked at me as though it hadn't occurred to him.
What about your wife? I asked. What does she think of
your plans? He said they weren't plans, they were deci-
sions already taken. Before I left, he asked me again not
to breathe a word of this to anyone.

When I came out of the porter's lodge, I saw Jana,
a young artist who had her studio on the same floor as

me. She rode up on her bike, braked at the very last moment, and squeaked to a halt a few inches from my feet. She grinned, and asked if I was taking over as porter now. Sure, why not, I said. There are worse jobs, it's not too strenuous, and there's a regular paycheck at the end of it. I'll miss those two just the same, she said. Albert especially.

She got off her bike and we walked to the lab building together. She had been one of the first to move to the site. Back then, nothing worked, the heating failed all the time and the electricity most of the time. She saw a lot of the two porters then. Albert had been really helpful. He was an incredibly nice person.

THE EMPTY PORTER'S LODGE had something depressing about it. I couldn't exactly say I missed either Biefer or Sandoz, but I'd always been pleased to see someone there when I got to the office in the morning, someone who unlocked the gate and turned on a few lights, someone to start the day. Now the site seemed dead, the facades of the old buildings were even more austere than usual, and all the windows were dark. Sooner or later it would all be demolished, we were only guests here, our days were numbered, even if we carried on like the new masters.

The violin maker parked his car. I waited for him outside the entrance, and we chatted. He asked me if I felt
good here, and I said it was probably just temporary for
me, and I would probably leave one day. He wanted to stay
here as long as he could. He would probably never find
such a perfect place to work again. We were still talking
when Jana came along with a journalist who had moved in
to a downstairs office just a couple of weeks ago. We talked
about Biefer and Sandoz. The journalist said he'd never
been able to tell them apart. I asked what our retirement
present had been to them. No one seemed to know.

I was meeting a client for lunch. It was about a double
garage, my first proper commission for months. We ate
in a restaurant in the city center. When I got back to the
site at two o'clock, the fog was just beginning to clear. I
went down to the lakeshore and gazed out at the water,
which was smooth and perfectly clear. I suddenly felt
pretty certain that I would never leave, and would stay
until the end of my days, building garages or single-
family homes, and if I was lucky, the odd kindergarten
or tenement building. We all would stay here, the violin
maker, the journalist, Jana, and the rest. Biefer was the
only one who would have managed to get away.

Jana was sitting on her own in the weigh-house bar,
reading the paper. I picked up a coffee and joined her.

She went back a couple of pages, folded the paper in the middle, and passed it to me.

Have you seen this? she asked, pointing to an item on the obituary page.

Gertrud Biefer, I read aloud, dearly beloved wife, mother and grandmother, left us on December 27, after a long illness, borne with patience and fortitude. Family only.

That must be Albert's wife, said Jana. There's his last name. And the two following, I bet those are his sons.

She said it was awful. Just when he could have had a little time to enjoy life. He had often talked about the travels he wanted to go on once he was retired.

He was planning to emigrate to Canada, I said, but didn't pursue it. Jana said she really couldn't imagine that, not with his wife so sick.

It's true, I said. I helped him out with his application. He showed me the letter from the embassy, and pictures of his property in Nova Scotia.

Jana said again, she couldn't imagine that. I said she should call him if she didn't believe me, but she said it wasn't really our business.

Do you know where he lives? Jana shook her head. She said she'd look him up in the phonebook and send him a sympathy card.

The next morning, the weather was so nasty that I left my bicycle at home and walked to work. The fog was thick, as it was almost every morning at this time of year, but from a long way off I could still see a light on in the porter's lodge. The blinds were open, and there at his desk sat Albert Biefer in his blue coveralls. He looked the same as ever, only he wasn't smoking and he wasn't reading the paper. He was looking straight ahead, as though he hadn't seen me. I tapped on the window, but he still didn't react. His eyes were pinched shut, and the corners of his mouth were pulled up. He looked as though he might start grinning or crying at any moment. I waved to him again. When he didn't respond, I left. About an hour later, there was a knock on the door of my office. It was Jana. She asked me if I'd seen Albert.

I tapped on his window, I said. It was as though he couldn't see me.

Jana thought we should call someone, a doctor or the police, or at least the administration. I said I thought it was better to wait. He's lost his wife. I can understand him not wanting to sit around at home.

At lunchtime in the weigh house, Biefer was the only subject. Everyone had seen him and was talking about what to do. The room was full of smoke, but when someone entered or exited, a burst of icy winter air came in.

The man who ran the bar turned the music down, and was talking too. He had known Biefer longer than any of us. He said he tried to open the door of the porter's lodge, but it was locked. It might have to be forced open. I didn't say anything about Biefer's plans to emigrate, and when Jana made to speak, I gestured to her and shook my head. Suddenly someone called out, Hey, there he is, and pointed out the window. Biefer was just going by, shuffling along, eyes straight in front. He had nothing on over his coveralls, his face was white with cold. For a moment there was silence, then the journalist said one of us should go and try to speak to him. Who knows him best? We all looked at each other. In the end, Jana said she would give it a go.

We watched as she walked along beside Biefer, talking to him. He didn't say anything, just looked straight ahead and kept on walking. After a while, Jana returned. She said there was no point. Albert hadn't seemed to even notice she was there. The journalist said there wasn't much we could do. Biefer was a free man. We couldn't force him to talk to us. At the most, we could inform the management. But everyone agreed that that wasn't a good idea. We decided we would wait. Feeling a little chastened, we all went back to our respective jobs.

From then on Biefer was there every day. Most of the time he sat at his usual place, and he walked across the

site once or twice. Jana tried to speak with him a few
more times. Eventually she gave up. She told me her
note of condolence had been returned by the post office, marked No Forwarding Address. We agreed to meet
on one of the following evenings at the violin maker's,
because his workshop had the best view of the porter's
lodge. We wanted to catch Biefer and see where he went.

The violin maker opened a bottle of wine and drank a
glass with us. At seven o'clock he said he was going home
and left us the keys. Jana and I sat by the window, drank
wine, and kept an eye on the porter's lodge. We dimmed
the light so as to see better and not be seen. Even though
we had known each other for quite a long time, we had
never talked all that much. Now Jana started to tell me
about her childhood in an Alpine village, and how she
had left home at sixteen to do her exams. Since that time
she had had almost no contact with her family. She went
back to the village very rarely. Her parents didn't understand her art, and she hadn't even told them that she was
living with a woman. She could imagine how they would
react. I asked what her art was like. She said it was hard
to describe, but I could visit her studio and she would
be happy to show me. We were a bit tipsy by then. Jana
laughed, and said we should ask Albert up for a glass of
wine. Then we stopped talking and just looked out the

window. The moon had risen, it was almost full, and as bright as the snow. Its glow dimmed that of the lights in the deserted factory yard. The snow was marked by a strange tangle of footprints and tire marks. Over in the porter's lodge, the little lamp was still lit.

Did you see his face? asked Jana. He looked miles away. I wonder why he wanted to go to Canada of all places, I said. Having an end in sight is what matters, said Jana.

At eleven, Biefer got up and switched off the light. Then nothing. We waited a while longer, but when he failed to emerge, we finally went home.

JANUARY THAT YEAR was exceptionally cold. On the edge of the lake, ice had formed, which broke up the waves. The wind pushed the layers of ice into tangled sculptures of bewitching beauty. The snow that came shortly after Christmas remained, and grew compact and dirty. In some parts of the site it had melted and refrozen into a thick sheet. The few times Biefer left the porter's lodge, he walked very slowly and barely picked his feet up at all.

Then, one day at the end of the month, he was gone. When I arrived at the office in the morning, there was no light on in the porter's lodge, and the blinds were down. The door was unlocked. I opened it cautiously and went in. The smell of pipe smoke was still there, but the stove was cold. It took me a while to find the light switch. The door to the back room was unlocked as well. It was tiny. There was a thin foam rubber mattress on the floor, but that was the only sign that someone had been staying here overnight. I walked back to the front room, lit the oil stove, and sat down at the desk. I was waiting, but I don't know what for. When a car entered the site, I reflexively raised my hand to wave. Slowly it got warmer and a little brighter, but the sky was still a forbidding gray. A little before ten, Jana arrived. I waved to her, and she parked her bicycle and came over.

Has he gone? she asked.

I've been waiting for you, I said.

She stood behind me, just the way a month ago I had stood behind Albert Biefer. She laid her hand on my shoulder. I turned to her, and she nodded. Only now—it was as though I'd been waiting to have a witness—did I open the drawer. I wasn't surprised to find the buff folder.

Seven Sleepers

MAY HAD HAD the least sunshine since measurements began, about a hundred and fifty years ago, and June didn't look as though it was going to be any better. For the past ten days there had been a batch of lettuce seedlings in the barn that Alfons had been unable to plant on account of the rain, and the next batch was due to arrive in three days. The squash field badly needed hoeing, but the ground was so sodden that the tractor would only have done damage. Even though Alfons had laid protective netting over the beds, blackfly destroyed most of the French beans, and it was too cold to plant new ones. He would have to resow the carrots as well.

When he finally put away his papers with a sigh at midnight, it was raining. At six the next morning, it was still raining. After breakfast he pulled on some rubber boots and went out into the orchard. He stood under the apple trees, feeling depressed. The fruit was already walnut-sized, but the trees were bearing poorly: it had been cold during the flowering season, and the bees hadn't been able to pollinate them except on the odd day. He went to the hives, lifted the lid off one of the wooden boxes, and observed the swarm. Bees were the only animals he kept on the farm, he had no dogs, no cats, nothing.

He walked up to the top field, where last year he had put in a second PVC tunnel. The tomato vines were gray with the stone dust he had powdered them with, but if it carried on so wet, he would have to spray them with copper or he would lose them as well. The bell peppers were at least two weeks in arrears, only the cucumbers were more or less on schedule. He worked for a while with the hoe, even though he had weeded the tunnel only a couple of days ago. At least it was better than sitting around indoors, thinking how everything was going to rack and ruin.

He had already begun to ask himself how he was going to get the lease together in November, twenty thousand for the land and the farm buildings. Every month so far, he was relieved to make the rent on the house. He had exhausted his business credit line with the purchase of the lettuce seedlings and a new seed drill, the bank wasn't about to offer him more. If worse came to worse, he would have to go to his father for a loan, or to Kurt, his brother, who was running the family farm with his father. Alfons could vividly remember their reaction when he told them he had found a farm on the ridge over the lake. As far as they were concerned, someone who grew vegetables wasn't a farmer. A farmer was someone who kept cattle, produced milk, and pastured his animals in the mountains over the summer.

ALFONS NEVER LIKED COWS. As a child he had been afraid of the enormous, cumbersome beasts; later on it was having to shovel their dung, the stink of which seemed to get into everything and stay there. Even the milk smelled of dung, and the butter and the cheese. Nor did he get along with the other animals on his parents' farm: the hens, the rabbits, the pigs. He didn't even like the dog, an aggressive little Appenzeller, who seemed to feel his dislike and return it. All three children helped out in the cow barn, but even his younger sister Verena was a better hand at milking than he was. Whenever he found himself with some free time, he would be in his mother's vegetable patch, where he worked selflessly. He loved the smell of the earth, the dusty savory aroma of the tomato plants and the mint, and the subtle, endlessly varied smells of compost. He managed to get things to grow that otherwise didn't thrive in the rough climate of the Lower Alps, things like peppers and eggplants, which his mother didn't know how to prepare.

After he finished school, he helped his father for another year, while Kurt was at agricultural college. From the outset, it was clear that his brother was going to take over the farm. His parents shrugged their shoulders when Alfons told them he had found a place with a vegetable grower by Lake Constance.

The farm was on a gently sloping northeast incline. Alfons loved the soft hills and the long views. While working, he could see the enormous body of water below him that seemed to look different in different weather. When it was clear, he could see right across to Langenargen on the German side, but what he liked best were days when the lake was hazed over, and seemed perfectly endless. That was how Alfons liked to think of the sea, an infinite expanse, behind which another world began, and a different sort of life. From day one, he felt more at home in this landscape than he ever had at home.

During his time as a trainee he lived on the top floor of the administration center, a plain and functional building that had a couple of bare rooms. He shared the bathroom and shower with a couple of Croats with whom he got on pretty well, but whom he never saw outside of working hours. He made no friends at agricultural college. He was always the outsider in the class. Most of his classmates were local, had grown up on big farms, had cars or motorbikes, and dressed like young townies. They made fun of Alfons's clothes and the way he spoke, until he said no more than he had to. The teachers liked him, he was a good pupil, and on the practical side he was also one of the best.

WHEN HIS APPRENTICESHIP was over, Alfons stayed on for a while. He was still living in the little upstairs room over the offices, even though he could have afforded something better. But he didn't need an apartment, he was saving to fulfill his own dream, a farm of his own, where he could put his ideas into effect.

Perhaps he acquired the farm too soon. He was only twenty-three when he responded to the advertisement. This farm was also on the ridge, but on the side facing away from the lake, on the edge of a small village. There was a small patch of woods that went with it, and twelve hectares of arable land, just enough for him on his own. The property belonged to a rich farmer from the Canton of Zurich, who had bought it for his son, who chose to follow a different calling, and so the farm was on the market. Alfons asked himself why it was that he, out of the twenty interested parties, had got the lease. Maybe the farmer saw a son in him, the young man with dreams, working to make his fortune. Alfons's father helped with the down payment. They signed the lease in the pub and wet it with a glass of wine. Now all you need is a wife to keep the business together, said the man from Zurich. Alfons nodded vaguely and mumbled something.

His parents were always on at him about it as well. Have you got a girlfriend yet? What are the girls like in Thurgau? When can we expect to become grandparents? What do you do all the time? asked his brother. You can't always be sitting around at home. That won't get you anywhere. But Alfons wasn't thinking in terms of weeks or months or years. He thought in days, and every day he said to himself, Not today, I'm tired, I need to make the payments, prepare the sower, check up on the bees. In that way three years passed, imperceptibly, without him taking any steps to find a wife.

Kurt had married a girl he went to school with. Verena had been in a steady relationship for years, and it

was only a matter of time until she tied the knot. Only
Alfons was still single. He was a member of the rifle
club, but that didn't take women. In the gymnastics as-
sociation there was too much drinking and not enough
gymnastics for his liking, and he didn't want to join the
choir, though he enjoyed singing. Once he had gone to a
meeting of the rural young people, but all the others had
known each other forever, and he felt excluded. Some
evenings he went to the local bar, he liked the waitress
there, but he didn't know how to tell her, not under the
eyes of the entire village. And with her looks, becoming
a farmer's wife was probably the last thing on her mind.
He spent most of his evenings at home, doing sums. He
kept precise accounts on each crop he grew, calculated
the returns, compared them to those of last year and with
the averages of the co-op. Every morning and every night
he took note of the temperature, the air pressure, and the
humidity. He made graphs and observed the changes in
the weather. He also kept track of his expenditures on
heating oil, water, and electricity. Whatever could be ex-
pressed in figures, he wrote it down.

At noon the rain stopped, and the gray murk turned
into a layer of small clouds. Alfons picked up the lettuce
seedlings in the barn and tossed them on the compost. It
felt like throwing away money, but he had no choice, it was

pointless to produce more than the market demanded. In the news they said the weather was on the mend. Still, by the time his fields had dried out sufficiently for him to go out on the tractor, another two or three days would be gone.

While he rinsed the plates, he heard engine noise from outside. He wiped his hands and looked out the window. A big truck stood on his neighbor's meadow, the other side of the road, and a couple of young men were rolling up the canvas cover. Then they separated, as though each was searching for something.

Alfons stepped outside and took a few steps closer, then he recognized one of the men, it was Klemens, the carpenter's son, and it dawned on him that these must be the guys from Open Air. The idea had struck in winter, and for weeks the whole village had talked about nothing else. The young people wanted to organize an Open Air Festival for local bands, with a bar and activities for children. In January, Klemens had come by. He had introduced himself as president of the Organizing Committee, told Alfons that the festival would take place in the meadow below his house, and asked if they could take power and water from him. Of course they would install meters, and he would be properly reimbursed. Alfons felt he had little choice but to agree. After that, he had heard nothing more from the organizers, and forgotten all about the whole thing.

He was surprised when his neighbor had part of the pasture mown a couple of days ago, even though the grass wasn't that long. That was where the truck was parked now, and the men were starting to unload timber. Alfons walked down and asked them when the festival was happening. In ten days, said Klemens, the last weekend of June. That Sunday is Seven Sleepers. Klemens asked what that was, and Alfons explained. He had read the story in a farmers' almanac. On Seven Sleepers' Day, according to an old legend, seven Christians were found who in Roman times had been walled into a cave and had slept through two hundred years. From a farmers' rule of thumb, that day predicted the weather for the next seven weeks. Then we can only hope it will have picked up by then, said Klemens, and returned to the planks.

All afternoon Alfons chopped weeds in his celery field. By the time he was finished and came home, at six, the truck was gone, but there were piles of boards and beams in the grass. The young men were busy putting up a large white tent at the bottom of the meadow. They worked until it got dark, then they lit a fire and drank beer. They had a CD player with them, and through his closed window Alfons could hear the distant music and

the men laughing and shouting. It was midnight before
there was quiet.

The next day, a workman came from the utilities company and laid improvised water and power mains from
Alfons's cellar across the road and down into the meadow.
Alfons knew the man from the rifle club. He offered him
a cup of coffee, and they talked about the festival a bit.
The workman said he thought it was good for the young
people to set something up on their own, instead of just
hanging around and doing drugs. Even though Alfons
was younger than some of the committee, he noticed the
workman talked to him as though he was an old man.

THE MEN MUST HAVE got time off from work, because
from now on they came every day and worked from early
morning until late at night. They built a stage, fenced off
the field, and put up a second tent. A portable toilet was
brought along, and fridges and sinks installed. One time,
a truck with a black cover was parked behind the stage,
and a couple of fellows in black T-shirts set up lights and
amplifiers. While Alfons was working after lunch on the
top field by the edge of the woods, he could hear one of
the men going one two, one two, all afternoon, one two,
one two, and then a shrill whistling sound.

Occasionally someone would come up from the field and ask Alfons for a tool, or some bandages, or a wheelbarrow, whatever they happened to be short of. He fetched whatever it happened to be, and said, That's fine. Oskar, his neighbor, turned up on the meadow almost every day, to keep an eye on things. He parked his Subaru on the grass and watched the workmen, kidded around with them, and lent a hand when asked.

The weather was cool that whole week, but sunny. At last, Alfons was able to put his French beans in and go out on the fields with his machines. At night he was tired, he just quickly filled in his weather chart and went to bed early. Then he heard the music and the voices of the men sitting around the fire after their day. The noise really didn't bother him; on the contrary, he had the feeling of being part of the village for the first time.

On Friday morning the rain returned. Alfons worked all day in the tunnel, with a short break for lunch at home. He saw three men and a woman unloading instruments from a white minivan and carrying them onto the stage. When he finished work in the evening, there were already a few little tents up in the bottom of the meadow, and the first visitors were standing around on the festival site, mostly in rain ponchos, a few under umbrellas. From a temporary parking lot on the edge of the village, others walked up in dribs and drabs. The big feeding tent was lit up, even though it hadn't gotten dark yet. The trestle tables were half full. Alfons wondered about going down there himself, but he had been outside all day, so he fixed himself something and ate it at home.   ·

THE MUSIC STARTED a little after six. Alfons was listening to the evening news, then it was suddenly there, so loud it was as though the musicians were in his living room. He looked out the window. In spite of the rain, there was a decent crowd in front of the stage. From where he was, he couldn't see the players. He sat down by the window, opened it a crack, and listened. Even though the music was very loud, the falling rain was clearly audible. It got a little quieter during the pause between sets, and Alfons sat down at his desk and did a few calculations, but as soon as the next band struck up, he couldn't concentrate, and returned to his place by the window. In the meantime, even more people had turned up, the meadow was pretty full. Five hundred, reckoned Alfons, and he multiplied it by the entrance price. The bar must have a good turnover, and then there were the T-shirts with the festival logo on them. He had no idea what the bands were paid to perform, or what the equipment cost to rent. The building materials had presumably been provided free of charge by Klemens's father, but if you threw in all the work the men had put in, there was probably not much left by the end.

There was another break, and a third band started to play, even louder than the two before. It had got dark by now, and there were colored lights flashing over the stage. A few people were dancing at the front. The crowd farther back was more slow-moving, swaying back and forth, as though trying to keep its balance on shifting ground. Right at the edge of the crowd, people were coming and going. A few sat on the grass, in spite of the rain.

Alfons was in bed by the time the music stopped on the dot of one. There was a fiercely strummed guitar chord, one last crash of the cymbals, and then some applause, followed by total silence. Alfons got up one more time and looked out of his bedroom window. Two spotlights under the roof of the stage were playing over the crowd. People dispersed, visitors drifted to their tents or to the parking lot. A sort of haze seemed to come off the people, and Alfons was put in mind of his father's cows, standing steaming on the grass in the rain or fog.

There were two long lines outside the toilets, and in the campsite he could make out the uncertain beams of many flashlights. On the road a truck was parked, with motor running and lights on. Alfons watched the band climb into the truck and drive away. He was glad of his warm bed, and not to have to spend the night out of doors.

ALTHOUGH HE HAD got to sleep so late, and it was a Saturday, he was up at six. He had breakfast, got the details from the weather station, and ambled down to the festival site. It was no longer raining, but the sky was clouded over, it could begin again at any moment. There was no one on the doors. The meadow had been turned into a swamp, there was hardly a blade of grass left near the stage. There was litter everywhere, empty bottles and cigarette packs. Everyone seemed to be asleep, except in the food tent a couple of women were already at work. They said hello to Alfons, and he asked if there was coffee yet. In five minutes, said the younger of the two, and rolls should be here any moment as well. Aren't you Klemens's girlfriend? asked Alfons, and they shook hands. Jasmine, she said. Her father owned the farm machine store in the village, where Alfons had bought his seed drill.

Didn't the music keep you up last night? asked Jasmine.

Alfons shrugged his shoulders. If you carry on like this, Oskar can start a potato patch here on Monday. She laughed. How many people did you get last night? he asked. Five hundred?

I don't know exactly, we sold six hundred weekend passes in advance, but some of those people will only show up today. Or not at all, if the weather doesn't improve.

Wouldn't some straw help, for the meadow?

Oskar promised to put some down, said Jasmine. It would be nice if he got around to it before everyone gets up.

Klemens came across the meadow, clutching four paper bags. He said hello to Alfons and put the bags of rolls on the bar. Then he pulled a white plastic armband out of his pocket and handed it to him. I wanted to give you this, just in case you fancy coming on down. Although come to think of it, you've got a box seat up where you are. Or do you prefer folk?

I don't listen to music, said Alfons, and once again he felt like an outsider.

Appenzeller bluegrass, said Klemens, and laughed.

The other woman came along with a coffee urn and filled four plastic cups. She gave one to Alfons and said, I'm Lydia. He thanked her. Conversation ceased while everyone drank their coffee and looked in different directions. Finally, Alfons asked Lydia if she lived in the village too. The question struck him as embarrassing in front of the other two. Klemens clutched at his forehead and said he had a headache, he must have overdone it last night. He sat down on one of the window seats. Jasmine went over and started stroking his head.

I'm a teacher, said Lydia, and when Alfons looked at her blankly, I live in Weinfelden, but I work here. I'm the new teacher.

Did Herr Tobler retire then? asked Alfons.

Lydia nodded. Do you run the farm up there?

Yes, he said, I'm not from here either.

She laughed and said, Yes, I can hear that.

I grow vegetables, organic vegetables.

All the veg I buy is organic, she said, pretty much.

Well, if you got it from the agricultural co-op, then you'll have eaten something of mine, said Alfons. Lydia smiled. He didn't know what else to say. Finally he asked what he owed.

It's on the house, she said, and he said thank you again and left.

Alfons did the shopping, then he paid bills and checked on things in the tunnel and in the beehives. He kept having to think of Lydia. She was no beauty, she was small and stoutish, her hair was cut very short, and she had bad acne on her face. But she had a nice way with her, and her voice was beautiful and warm.

At lunchtime he went down again. It was still cloudy, and muggily warm. He showed the man at the gate his white plastic armband. The guy said he had to wear it, and they argued about that for a while. Finally, Alfons gave in. Onstage the band was playing a sort of mixture of folk and rock. It was much quieter than it had been last night, and Alfons stood for a while in the sparse crowd. Then he went to the food tent and got himself a helping of macaroni with tomato sauce. He looked around to see if he could see Lydia, but she wasn't there. He ate his lunch and went back up to the farm.

IN THE AFTERNOON, he was fooling around with his machinery when suddenly he heard Lydia's voice. Is there anyone there? Alfons pulled himself up and saw her standing in the doorway of the barn. Here I am, he said, and approached her. His hands were coated with grease, and he put on an apologetic expression. Lydia squeezed his forearm, shook it, and said, Hello, I was just coming by and thought I'd look in on you. Alfons asked, Can I treat you to a coffee back? Sure, she said, but did he have anything else?

Alfons scrubbed his hands in the trough, then he showed Lydia into the house and poured two glasses of his home-pressed apple juice. How come you're not working? he asked.

I was on the early shift, she said. Of course. Alfons nodded. They all prefer the late shift, she said, and smiled. But I'm used to getting up early.

I'm an early riser too, he said.

I thought only dairy farmers have to turn out early.

My father has cows. Once you're used to it, it's a hard habit to break. He poured them some more juice and they drank it silently. Would you like to have a look around the farm?

Very much, said Lydia.

Alfons was surprised how much Lydia knew. When they were with the bees, she asked him if he had had trouble as well, she had read that lots of bee colonies were ailing.

I was lucky, he said, I only lost one hive, and that wasn't because of illness. The queen must have been old. They got a new one in, in the fall, but presumably it was too late. I don't think there were any drones left to fertilize her. In spring the hive was empty.

A few odd bees buzzed around their heads, Lydia ducked, and Alfons shooed them away with his hand. Thank you, she said, and smiled.

He was surprised how much he had to say, while he showed her around. He showed her the fruit orchard and the vegetable fields, talked about organic fertilizers and pest control. The farmers in the valley can water their fields with groundwater, or they pump it out of the Thur, he said, but up here I have no water. Just out of the mains, and that's too expensive.

All along, the music had been quietly audible, a song-writer was singing for the children, a comedian did his show, and later an acoustic group played traditional ballads. There were long pauses between sets, while a DJ played records. It started raining again. Lydia asked Alfons if he felt like wandering down and eating something. We can always sit in the tent.

WHILE THEY WERE LOOKING for space at one of the long tables, the music suddenly kicked in again, and people leaped up and ran in the direction of the stage. As they ate, Alfons and Lydia exchanged few words, and those were shouted so that they could be heard. It's so amazing, shouted Lydia, down in the village you can't hear anything at all. Do you know who's playing? Alfons shouted back. She shook her head and slid a program to him across the table. He hadn't heard of a single one of the bands. She pointed to one of the names with her finger, and said right in his ear, They're the ones I really want

to see. He read the name of the band, Gallowbirds, and
shrugged his shoulders. Never heard of 'em.

When they had finished eating, Lydia wanted to go over
to the stage, and Alfons went with her. They snaked their
way through the crowd, which still wasn't all that dense,
to the front. He kept in her wake. The band was playing a
South American–inflected number, and Lydia began to
dance. First she started to sway her shoulders and turn her
head this way and that, as if she were looking for someone,
then she started to move her hands about, and her arms,
and she made circling motions with her pelvis like a belly
dancer. Not many people were dancing, but that didn't
seem to bother Lydia. Her movements were fluent; they
seemed natural and unaffected. It was as though she managed to infect the others, because after a while everyone
around Alfons was dancing, only he stood there, feeling
increasingly ill at ease. He was glad when the band played
their last song and left the stage to applause. Lydia took his
hand and pulled him out of the crowd. Her face and hair
were shining from the rain and the exertion. Where the
crowd was not so bunched together, she let go of his hand
and they walked together to the food tent. I'm thirsty, she
said, wiping the sweat from her brow. It still felt warm.

No sooner had the next band started playing than Lydia
wanted to go back to the front. She pointed to Alfons's

boots and said, No wonder you can't dance in those. She herself wore a pair of ancient, muddied flip-flops. He hesitated briefly, then he pulled off his boots and socks, stood them next to the bar, and followed her. He looked around uncertainly, but everyone was preoccupied with themselves, and no one seemed to notice him. Lydia started dancing again right away. The crowd in front of the stage was thicker now, and people were bumping into Alfons the whole time. Finally he began to move himself, at first in a spirit of evasion, then later in a sort of dance, staggering back and forth to the music. Perhaps it was the beer that had relaxed him, perhaps the falling darkness. He didn't care that he could see Klemens and Jasmine nearby, also dancing, and he shut his eyes, and raised his face to the heavens, and felt the fine raindrops and the deep mud into which his feet sank.

During the next break they remained in front of the stage without talking much. Next up was the group Lydia wanted to hear, four men of around fifty. It must be ten years since they last played together, said Lydia, one of them works in television now, that guy over there. It wasn't really dance music, but plenty of people in the crowd seemed to know the songs, sang along, and danced in a vague sort of way. Alfons stood right behind Lydia. During one ballad she leaned against him and he put his hands around her waist and felt her moving. *You can always stay,* sang the men, *I'm not going anywhere.* When Alfons looked around he saw Jasmine, who smiled at him and nodded, and he smiled back.

They stayed until the end. Then they went to the bar and had another beer. All around, people were standing and chatting and laughing. Alfons found his boots where he had left them, and he carried them when he left the festival site with Lydia. There was no one standing at the gate now, and he ripped off his white plastic armband. He looked down at the ground, which was covered with rubbish, and put the armband in his pocket. Are you not camping, then? he asked, once they had reached the road at the top. From the parking lot farther down, they could hear doors being slammed and the sound of car engines getting quieter, then disappearing altogether.

No, said Lydia. I thought about it, but the forecast was so rotten, I didn't feel like it.

So now you have to drive home? Are you good to drive?

I probably shouldn't have drunk that last beer, said Lydia, and smiled at him. They both said nothing. Well then, she said finally, and put her hand on his upper arm.

And then he finally managed to get out what he had had on his mind all evening. If you like, you could stay at my house. I've got plenty of room. Lydia said yes right away, and took his arm, and they walked up to the house together.

They washed their feet in the trough outside the house, Lydia holding on to Alfons. I'm a bit drunk, she said, so it's good I'm not driving anywhere. Tomorrow is Seven Sleepers' Day, he said. If it rains then, it means it's going to rain for the next seven weeks. Didn't the seven sleepers wake up long ago? asked Lydia. It's just a farmers' superstition, said Alfons, but it's been proved right two-thirds of the time. It has something to do with the Gulf Stream. Then let's just hope tomorrow's a nice day, she said, squeezing his arm.

ALFONS STOOD IN FRONT of his bedroom closet, pulling out fresh sheets and a towel. When he turned around, Lydia was standing just behind him. Don't go to any trouble, please, she said, taking the things from him. I don't have to have my own bed. He wasn't sure what she meant by that. He pushed past her and led her to the guest bedroom, which had almost never been used by guests, and had become a sort of spare office for him. I hope the computer doesn't bother you. He began to make up the bed. Lydia helped him, and smiled at him again.

Alfons showed her the bathroom, and asked her if she needed a toothbrush or anything. Would you happen to have a clean T-shirt for me? she asked, my things are all so sweaty. While she was in the shower, he sat down at the computer and checked his emails. He wasn't expecting any news, but the idea of being in Lydia's room gave him a little thrill. Suddenly there she was behind him, laying a hand on his shoulder and asking him for a T-shirt again. She was wrapped in a towel. Alfons led the way to his bedroom, opened the closet, and said, Here, help yourself. She rummaged around in his things, pulled out T-shirts, held them to herself, and made funny faces. She even took out a pair of his neatly folded boxer shorts and made some remark. Alfons took them out of her hand, folded them up, and put them back. In the end, Lydia settled on a white T-shirt with TRUST A CARPENTER written on it. Dropping the towel, she spun around and stood naked in front of him. He looked at her back and shoulders, which still had a couple of drops of water on them. He had his hand raised to brush them away when Lydia pulled the T-shirt over her head and simultaneously turned to face him again. He caught a flash of her breasts, which were smaller than he had imagined. He was put in mind of the time Kurt had taught him about milking. He had shown him how to massage the udder before hooking it up to the milking machine. Not so hesitant, he said, imagine they're a woman's breasts. Alfons had been ten or twelve at the time, the tip hadn't helped him an awful lot, rather confused him more. Aren't you going to have a shower yourself? asked Lydia. Yes, sure, he said, even though he usually showered in the morning.

Lydia's clothes were all over the bathroom floor. Alfons picked them up and ran his hands over the fine, slightly damp material. Then he folded them and put them down on the toilet seat. After he had showered, he got into his pajamas and came out of the bathroom. Lydia was standing on the landing, as though she'd been waiting for him, with a bottle of beer in her hand. I helped myself, she said, and held out the bottle. He took a big swig and handed the bottle back. Don't suppose you've got anything to smoke here? she asked. I don't smoke, he said, sorry. I thought you grew things, said Lydia with a laugh. Had he not heard of the farmer who had a little patch of hemp in the middle of his cornfield? The police stumbled on it with the help of some aerial photographs. It was quite near here too. I don't do drugs, said Alfons. He suddenly wished he hadn't asked Lydia back. Nor do I, she replied, a little miffed. She emptied the bottle in a couple of swallows, passed it back to Alfons, and said she'd changed her mind, she would go home after all, she wasn't tired, and at this time there wouldn't be any traffic cops around. She took off his T-shirt, tossed it on the floor, and went to the bathroom. He followed her and watched as she got dressed. When she was done, she looked at him, and he saw that her eyes were moist. Then he went up to her, wiped the tears away with his thumb, and kissed her, first on the forehead, then on the mouth. Don't go, he whispered, I don't want you to go.

The Last Romantic

ICHAEL HAD BEEN distracted the whole class. Sara told herself it was on account of the heat or the upcoming summer vacation. When he made the same mistake for the fifth time, she suppressed her irritation and said, There's no use, in your head you're already at the beach. Then he looked at her with big round eyes that seemed to be on the point of bursting into tears. It'll come, said Sara, patting him on the shoulder and standing up. Michael lowered his gaze and muttered that he wouldn't be having any more piano lessons after the vacation. There's no reason to give up, said Sara, even the great maestros had to practice.

That's not the reason, said Michael. His parents had told him he couldn't carry on swimming *and* playing the piano, otherwise his classwork would suffer. He stood by the piano, shoulders slumped. I'm sorry.

All this is about one hour a week? said Sara. How often do you have swim training?

Four or five times, said Michael. It's the practicing.

Sara made a face. But you don't practice, admit it.

You're right, said Michael.

Maybe Clementi isn't the right thing for you. Perhaps you'd rather be playing something rockier. Or do you like jazz?

Michael lowered his head, and for a moment they stood silently facing each other, then the boy packed up his notes and held out his hand to the piano teacher. Goodbye, Frau Wenger, and have a good holiday.

I'm going to phone your parents, said Sara.

He was her last pupil that afternoon. Sara didn't show him out onto the landing as she usually did. She sat down at the piano and waited for the apartment door to close behind him. Then she started to play—the first movement of Rachmaninoff's Second Piano Concerto, which she had been working on for two years now. The eight chords of the opening were like blows, the louder and more violent, the more Sara's fury was dispelled. It was as though she were dissolved in the music, were transformed into music. Then the strings came in and carried her away. She saw herself on the stage of the concert hall, and the music streamed through her to the audience, which was raptly listening. Halfway through a bar, she broke off. She sat there breathing heavily, not thinking of anything at all. After she calmed down, she went out on to the landing and phoned Michael at home. No one picked up.

BUT HE'S NOT the first pupil of yours to give up, said Victor, gathering up his scores. He's my best, though, said Sara. He's really talented. But if he prefers sports, said Victor. Music isn't very cool. The word sounded strange, coming from a sixty-year-old. He's keen enough, said Sara, but his parents won't let him. I'll try it once more. She rang the number for probably the tenth time that afternoon. When Michael's father answered, she didn't know what to say. He listened to her patiently, then in a friendly tone of voice said he was sorry, but Michael needed to concentrate on just one hobby. You can't just take him out of lessons like that, said Sara vehemently, at the very least you'll have to pay for next term's lessons. Michael's father said he had talked to the school office, and everything was settled. Music isn't a hobby, said Sara. She avoided looking at Victor, who was shaking his head and lowering his hands placatingly. Any fool can swim. Frau Wenger, Michael's father broke in, we are grateful to you for all you've done, but the decision has been made.

Sara dropped the telephone and stared at Victor in consternation. He hung up on me. Come on, said Victor, have a glass of wine. He went on ahead into the kitchen and took an open bottle of wine out of the fridge and a couple of glasses, as though he were at home here. Swimming! said Sara, shaking her head in incomprehension. They shave their body hair. Victor smiled and took a sip of wine. Probably not if they're kids. He hasn't heard the last of this, said Sara, I'm not going to stand for it. Probably to distract her, Victor asked how she was getting on with the Rachmaninoff. I'm working on it, she said, but it's bloody hard. Did you ask at the Academy? She shook her head. They want big names, someone like me wouldn't stand a chance. You should at least try them, said Victor, we've just renewed our sponsorship deal, and I happened to drop your name. And? asked Sara. The conductor said you should get in touch with him. Say hello to him from me. Victor laid his hand on her shoulder. She liked these friendly little gestures and stroked the sleeve of his jacket in return. When are you leaving? Day after tomorrow, he said, his hand still on her shoulder. I'm exhausted, said Sara. Look after yourself. Victor emptied his glass and wished her a happy vacation. Sara said nothing back. They kissed each other good-bye on the cheek.

THE AIR IN THE PIANO ROOM was stale, the yellow curtains half drawn, and it was dusk. Sara watered the philodendron that was growing along the ceiling and sprayed its leaves with leafshine. She had taken over the plant some years back from a pupil who was emigrating to America with her parents. Philodendrons purify the air, the girl claimed, they absorb formaldehyde and other poisons. The shapeless plant with its air roots dangling in space struck Sara as an emblem of her own life, in her slow growth she put out one leaf after another, without the prospect of ever leaving this room.

In the afternoon she called the school office and demanded to speak to the director. She put him in the picture, and complained at the way Michael had simply been allowed to quit. The director said he wasn't familiar with the particular case, but if the boy wasn't motivated, there was no sense in forcing him to take lessons. You have enough pupils, he said. That's not the point. Michael is gifted, it would be a pity if he stopped now. Don't get so worked up, said the director. We have no leverage, as you very well know.

Sara called Michael's teacher. He was still more curt
with her than the director had been. When she asked what
Michael's grades were like, the teacher said he was not
at liberty to divulge such information to her, she should
ask his parents. What a pupil did in his or her spare time
didn't matter to him, so long as he did it willingly.

Furiously, Sara leafed through the phone book as if
there was anyone there who could help her.

ALL HER FRIENDS seemed to have left town, and so for
the next few weeks Sara was mostly at home, practicing
the Rachmaninoff or reading. She didn't feel like going
out alone, besides it was too hot. One day she got a postcard from Michael. He had never written to her before,
and she took it as a cry for help, even though it was just
a few banal sentences on a card. She drafted letters to
his parents, furious, factual, imploring, and threw them
all away. On the Internet she found the training times
of Michael's swimming club. That afternoon she went
to the pool. She hadn't been there in ages. At school she
hadn't been a good swimmer. Once or twice during her
time at the conservatory, she had gone to the lake with
her fellow students, but she hadn't seen the attraction of
prancing around half-naked in public. The actual water
was always too cold for her anyway.

She looked at herself in the changing room mirror. Her one-piece bathing suit was hopelessly out of fashion, the fabric cracked and dry, the colors faded. She wrapped a towel around her waist so as not to look quite so conspicuous. Then she stepped out uncertainly into the dazzling sun. The big pool was full of people, but there were no lanes. Sara turned to the attendant standing at the edge of the pool. The swimming club trains indoors, he said, not looking at her, and he blew his whistle to call a couple of youngsters to order.

Indoors it was even hotter, but quieter. The chlorine took Sara straight back to her school days and her gym teacher, a sadist who poked fun at the kids who were frightened of water. She had hated swimming lessons so much that she got a stomachache each time. Eventually, her mother had grasped what was happening—but still sent her. Only a couple of lanes of the pool were being used, in which half a dozen kids were swimming laps. A man in shorts and a T-shirt was writing figures and letters on a slate—it seemed to be a sort of code. Sara asked him if he was Michael Bernold's swimming coach. Yes, he said, and held out his hand. He's on vacation. I'm . . . I used to be . . . his piano teacher, said Sara, shaking hands with the man. She felt naked, and looked down at her body. In the neon-lit hall, her skin looked greenish, and she noticed a nasty-looking pimple in her cleavage.

Does he play the piano, then? asked the coach. He's very talented, said Sara, but he's giving up, because swimming takes up too much of his time. Too much, the coach repeated, tonelessly. That's my view, said Sara. I hate the word talent, said the coach. In the end, success comes to whoever trains hardest. That's what I've told him all along. Sara smiled. What is success, in your view? Just a minute, said the coach. He went up to the board, wiped away the letters and numbers, and wrote down some new ones. The children who had been waiting at one end of the pool set off. It looked as though they were being pulled along on ropes, that's how effortlessly and quickly they were moving. The coach went back to Sara, and pointed to one girl who was just swimming past them. Take Lea. She has an amazing feel for water. Look at her moving. But if she doesn't train for three or four days, it'll all be gone, and I can start over. How do you define success? repeated Sara. The main thing is they enjoy themselves, said the coach. Michael has a winner's instincts. He trains hard. If he didn't train quite so hard, he'd have time to play the piano, said Sara. Couldn't you have a word with him? The trainer smiled absently and shook his head. No. Look, I've got to work now. Sara remained where she was for a moment and watched the swimmers. Then she circled the pool, took off her towel, and climbed down the steps until the water reached up to her belly. She glanced over at the trainer, but he wasn't looking.

SARA FELT RELIEVED when the weather finally broke, and it cooled down. Every day she resolved to talk to the chief conductor and make an appointment, but she ended up putting it off, telling herself either he was on holiday or she needed to get a better grip on this or that passage. Victor sent her regular emails from Madeira, attaching photographs of red cliffs and exotic tropical plants. He seemed to be bored in his fancy hotel. Some of the emails, Sara could tell, he had written while drunk, they were so full of typos. She answered briskly, saying there was nothing much happening, the weather was bad, she was practicing hard. After two weeks something changed in the tone of Victor's emails, he still wrote regularly, but it sounded as though he was just doing it out of a sense of duty. Perhaps he's met someone, thought Sara. The idea incensed her. Strangely, she had never felt jealous of his wife, and even after his divorce, she had never wanted more from him than their weekly meetings, conversations, and his friendship. But it hurt her to imagine that he might have a lover, a woman who enjoyed more rights and privileges than she did.

The second-to-last holiday weekend, Sara finally called the sponsorship office of the orchestra. She told the man on the other end what it was about. He tried to dissuade her, told her they worked exclusively with agencies and artists of an international reputation. Couldn't I come along after a rehearsal and play for the conductor for ten minutes? she suggested. Ten minutes isn't asking a whole lot. He's terribly busy, said the man on the phone. Finally, Sara had no option but to make use of her connections and drop Victor's name. The man at the other end was silent for a minute, then he said in an offended tone of voice that he would have a word with the chief conductor and call back.

For the next few days, Sara practiced more than ever. Sometimes she played the same few bars over and over again for an hour, until her fingers hurt. On Thursday the man from the orchestra called. Once again she missed his name, and didn't trust herself to ask. He was short with her, and said that the conductor could fit her in tomorrow after rehearsals, at half past twelve, and she should try to be punctual.

That afternoon she played through the whole concerto. For the first time she noticed that her playing was entirely lacking in brilliance and expression. She needed all her strength and concentration to master the

technical difficulties, and even then she wasn't successful. She made mistakes, many mistakes. How deluded
she had been for all those years. Even when she'd been a
conservatory student she hadn't been allowed to take the
concert diploma, because she hadn't been good enough,
and she hadn't got any better since. Perhaps the swimming coach was right, and talent didn't matter, but nor
did she have sufficient enthusiasm to carry her through,
the energy, the thing he'd called the winning instinct.

Left to herself, Sara wouldn't have turned up to the audition at all, but she couldn't do that to Victor. Perhaps
she was too self-critical. That too was part of the makeup
of a proper artist, that restlessness, that dissatisfaction.
In the evening she drank a couple of glasses of wine, and
suddenly she felt confident again.

SARA WAS AT THE CONCERT HALL far too early. The side
entrance was locked, so she waited outside the front door.
Even though it was a cool day, she was wearing a skirt. She
had spent a long time thinking about what to wear, she had
even briefly pulled out the rather garish dress she had worn
to her sister's wedding. In the end she settled on a knee-
length tartan wraparound skirt paired with a cream silk
blouse. She felt cold and clenched her hands, which were

PETER STAMM

slowly turning clammy. At last the door opened and a mob of chatting, laughing musicians came pouring out, some of them with instrument cases. Sara recognized an oboist who was her contemporary at the conservatory, but the woman ignored her greeting. Sara walked into the lobby, where a few musicians stood around and looked at her.

She recognized the conductor at once, even though he was in a cardigan and some baggy old cords. He walked very confidently toward her and held out his hand, without saying his name. Sara was amazed by his youthful appearance, he seemed younger than she was. He led her to the soloists' room, a small space that, apart from a grand piano and a music stand, contained only a small side table and a hideous black-and-white designer couch that reminded her of the chair at the gynecologist's. The blinds were down and two neon tubes spread a cool, diffuse light.

The conductor sat down on the couch and stretched his legs; the attitude had something a little obscene about it. While Sara took the score from her bag and adjusted the piano stool, he asked her what sort of piano she played at home. Just an upright, said Sara. Better a good upright than a poor grand, said the conductor. What was the last concert you've been to? Sara thought about it. She had heard Britten's *Ceremony of Carols*, but that was years ago. I don't get to listen to as many concerts as I'd like, she said, I have to teach on some of my evenings. The conductor furrowed his brow and asked what her connection to Victor was. He takes lessons from me, she said, has done for years. We're friends. I'm sure I don't need to tell you how extremely grateful we are to his company for their generous support, said the conductor, but of course that mustn't play any part in the decision here . . . Well, whenever you're ready. He looked at his watch.

IT WENT BETTER than I expected, said Sara.

And what did he say? asked Victor. The phone connection was poor, his words sounded chopped up and kept being interrupted by brief moments of stillness.

He said he would be in touch, said Sara, and then, louder, He'll be in touch, he said.

I can hardly hear you, said Victor, but we'll see each other in another week. Bye.

Sara hadn't managed to tell Victor the truth. That the conductor had ended the audition after a few minutes by saying there was no point. He had walked up to the piano, taken her score, and flipped through it, as though to check for himself what she had been playing.

Then he passed it back to her and gave a little lecture on
Rachmaninoff, whom he called the last romantic. His
kindliness and patience with her were perhaps the most
hurtful of all; he talked to her as to a child that needed to
be comforted. He said she had picked an extremely difficult piece, which was simply beyond her. She ought to try
something simpler. And as far as public performances
went, he could imagine that an old age home or care facility would provide a grateful public. Though best steer
clear of Rachmaninoff, he added, laughing, otherwise all
the old folks will get coronaries. Sara smiled dutifully
and allowed the conductor to usher her to the door and
wish her all the best.

At home she sat at the piano for certainly an hour,
shaken with crying jags, until her throat felt sore. She
drank a glass of tap water in the kitchen. She dropped the
score in the recycling.

TEN DAYS LATER Victor came for his lesson. Sara said
the audition hadn't worked out. He seemed to sense that
she didn't want to talk about it, and started speaking of
his holidays. When the lesson was over, they sat in her
kitchen, and Victor showed her his holiday snaps of Madeira. They had to put their heads together to make out

anything on the little display of his digital camera. Victor had laid his arm around Sara's shoulder. And did you have your holiday fling? she asked. He moved away, looked at her in surprise, and asked, How can you think of something like that? So you did. Look, he said, I have my life and you have yours. We may be friends, but that doesn't mean I have to tell you everything. Sara could feel the tears running down her cheeks. You're so obtuse, she said, you're so bloody obtuse. Victor stroked her shoulders and talked soothingly to her, but she stood up and coldly told him to go. Find some other woman you can exploit. He tried to placate her, but it only made matters worse.

After he had gone, Sara remained sitting at the piano for a while. She struck a couple of notes at random, but they sounded wrong, and no tune was forthcoming. Finally, she pushed the piano stool back against the wall, climbed up on it, and carefully started to unpick the raffia knots that held up the philodendron. It took a long time before she had undone every one, and the plant was a crumpled heap next to the piano. When she cut it into little pieces with her pruning shears, she felt like a murderess, but after she had stuffed it into garbage bags and stood them on the edge of the sidewalk, she felt oddly relieved.

The Suitcase

N O SOONER DOES Hermann put the list down on the unmade bed than he picks it up again. He has already forgotten everything on it. Toiletries. He goes to the bathroom and gathers up Rosmarie's things: the olive oil soap she bought last year in the south of France, her hairbrush, toothbrush and toothpaste, her deodorant. He's not sure which of the many shampoos is current, and packs one, hoping it's the right one. What else? Nail scissors. He puts back the nail polish, after briefly hesitating. He goes into the bedroom, pulls the small suitcase down from the top of the wardrobe, and puts the sponge bag in it. Then he checks the list again. Several changes of underwear. He stands in front of the open wardrobe, roots around in Rosmarie's underthings, fluffy tangles of white that remind him of peony blossoms in the garden. He has the feeling he is doing something inappropriate. How many do they want? He doesn't know how long Rosmarie will be kept in for, he'll be glad if she's allowed back at all. Pajamas or nightie. He prowls through the apartment looking for her slippers. Then he remembers seeing them when Rosmarie was on the stretcher, being carried out by the paramedics. They were on her feet like two hooks. He had even wondered for a moment about maybe putting her shoes on. She wouldn't even have gone out to the mailbox in her slippers. Stout trainers, in case physiotherapy is indicated. He doesn't know what the doctors have in mind for Rosmarie. The very notion of her in trainers makes him smile in spite of himself. For the moment, there's little prospect of such therapy. The doctors have put her in an artificial coma and cooled her temperature down to a constant ninety-two degrees. They're refrigerating her, he keeps thinking.

He looks at his watch. She is under the knife right now. A swollen blood vessel in her brain, one of the doctors said after hours of tests, and explained what they were trying to do. Then the doctor gave him some hospital literature and packed him off home. Have a rest. The literature includes a message from the chief surgeon, a map of the layout, a train schedule, and various other information. At the very end, Hermann found the checklist. Please bring the following items with you on the day you are booked in.

No one was able to tell him what would happen next, no one seems to have any idea. Hermann looks at the list. Personal supports, such as glasses or hearing aid (incl. batteries). Rosmarie doesn't need any support. If anyone needs help, it's him. It's decades since he last packed a suitcase. Even his army kitbag, in the time he was doing national service, was always packed by Rosmarie, and that was thirty years ago. Each time he arrived in the barracks and unpacked his bag, he always found a bar of chocolate she had smuggled in among his things. He goes into the kitchen but he can't find any chocolate. Ever since he became diabetic, Rosmarie's kept all the candy out of sight. Reading matter, letter paper, writing things. On the night table are three library books. He reads the titles and the names of the authors—none of them means anything to him. He's not a reader. Rosmarie's reading glasses are on top of them. He packs everything. Because he can't find the spectacle case, he wraps the glasses in a handkerchief and stuffs it in her sponge bag. The suitcase is about half full. Hermann throws in a cardigan and a couple of magazines he finds in the living room, and he carefully closes the suitcase.

In the cafe opposite the entrance are patients and their visitors. Some are wearing dressing gowns, walking sticks are leaning against the tables, one trundles an IV along with him on a stand. Hermann hasn't seen inside a hospital for years, but the smell takes him back immediately. There is a little kiosk behind the cafe, where he buys a bar of chocolate, even though he knows Rosmarie isn't a great one for chocolate. It's the only thing he can do to prove his love, flowers are too ostentatious. You give flowers when there's a baby on the way, and everyone knows. He remembers seeing bouquets on hospital corridors, looking like trophies in their vases. Rosmarie will be able to keep the chocolate in her bedside table. She will think of him as of something clandestine, here, where everything is out in the open, in the bright light of the fluorescent tubes. Hermann opens the catch of the suitcase, to slip the chocolate in between Rosmarie's things, but the lid flies open and everything spills out on the polished stone floor. He kneels down, grabs the things, and stuffs them back in as quickly as he can. He looks around—it's as though he were doing something forbidden. The man on the drip looks his way, without expression. The clothes Hermann went to so much trouble to fold together are all crumpled.

The porter tells him how to get to the intensive care ward. The wards are all color-coded, to ease orientation.

Intensive care is blue, yellow is the children's ward, urology and gynecology are green, surgery is purple. Hermann tries to find some rationale for the pairings, but he can't do it. Only the red of the cardiology ward makes sense to him.

He is standing by Rosmarie's bedside. Her head is bandaged and her body is connected up to machines, she is breathing artificially, she has a stomach probe and a catheter. Drugs are being fed into her bloodstream via tubes. Her arms and legs are being kept cool, so as to keep her body temperature down. She is naked except for a sort of white loincloth open at the sides, which can barely cover her. There is a strangely flaccid quality to her features. Hermann stands at her bedside, staring at her, he doesn't even want to put his hand on her forehead, that's how strange she looks to him. Only her hands with the painted nails look familiar. From time to time he hears the beep of an alarm from the corridor. It sounds like the hour being struck on a grandfather clock.

A doctor says they will need to perform another operation, create a bypass. His expression is serious, but he also says Rosmarie has been lucky. If she had been brought in just half an hour later . . . He doesn't finish his sentence. Hermann imagines what he might have gone on to say. We're hoping for the best, says the doctor. Do you have any questions? No. Hermann shakes his head. He has the feeling that all of this has nothing to do with him or Rosmarie. The doctor nods to him and leaves with a look that is probably intended to be encouraging. The sister says Frau Lehmann didn't need anything, she would rather he took the suitcase back with him, then at least nothing would go astray. He should bring her things once his wife was able to leave intensive care. She gives him a form about the patient's habits and personal preferences. Your answers will help us to look after her, she says; she gives him a pencil and conducts him to a waiting room. He reads through the questions. Does the patient belong to any religion? What form does worship take? Does the patient like music? If so, what? Which smells does the patient like? He thinks of the olive oil soap. Which does she not like? What is her favorite color? Does she have a set ritual at bedtime? Where does she like to be touched?

He walks down several corridors, past reception and the cafe and out into the cold winter afternoon. The stop is between the hospital and the lake. Hermann sees a streetcar leave. The next one won't be for another half an hour. He could walk home, it wouldn't be more than an hour or so, but he's already bought the return ticket and he's tired, he barely slept last night. He presses the button for STOP ON DEMAND and sits down on the narrow bench.

The suitcase is on the ground beside him. He looks at the lake. About a hundred yards from shore, the color of the water abruptly changes from pale blue to deep green. A couple of walkers pass down the shore promenade. They stop at a marker and look back. By the time the streetcar comes, Hermann is frozen through.

HE HASN'T BEEN to the library very often. On rare occasions he has accompanied Rosmarie, or he's taken books back for her when he's had to be in town. Even so, the librarian greets him by name. She takes the books from him and asks whether Rosmarie enjoyed them. Hermann is bemused by her referring to his wife by her first name. Yes, he says, I believe she did. I've set aside the new Donna Leon thriller for her, says the librarian, and she picks it up from a little rolling shelf next to her desk. I promised her first dibs at it. She stamps the date on the borrowing slip at the back of the book. Only then does she seem to become aware of Hermann's suitcase, and she asks him if he's on his way somewhere. Yes, he says. He's not in the mood to answer questions. The librarian says she could hang on to the book if he didn't want to take it with him right now. I'm not going away for long, he says, and he grabs the book with a quick movement of his hand. *Through a Glass Darkly*. The librarian makes some remark about an active retirement and laughs. Hermann thanks her and leaves.

Darkness is falling outside. He turns once more when he notices the librarian watching him through the glass doors, then he heads off in the direction of the station. On the way he runs into a neighbor. The family only moved there two years ago, the man works for an insurance company, the woman stays at home, looking after the two children. Hermann sees her in the garden sometimes. She once complimented him on his peonies and asked him for tips. She said they had lived in a condo before, and she had little experience with plants. The most important thing is to find the right place for each plant, he said. It needs to feel at home there, and then it'll thrive by itself.

Off on holiday, then? asks the man. Hermann mutters something and the man goes on to wish him a good holiday. Same to you, says Hermann, not thinking. The neighbors seem not to have heard the ambulance yesterday.

HE TAKES THE NEXT TRAIN. When the conductor comes along, Hermann asks him where the train is going and buys a ticket to the final destination. Most of the time he just stares out of the window into the dark. Gradually the train fills up, then, after Zurich, empties again, the names of the stops get less familiar. An elderly woman—roughly in Rosmarie's years—sits across from him in the compartment and stares at him so brazenly, he ends up moving. At the end of three hours the loudspeaker announcer says the train has now reached its final station stop, *gare terminus*. The announcement is in two languages, as the city where Hermann finds himself is bilingual. He can't remember having been here before, but perhaps he has. He is on a narrow street that follows a canal. He comes to a park and then a lake. A long pier leads far out into the lake. Hermann walks along the curving, wood-planked jetty, which is lit by little lamps, till he gets to a small triangular concreted area, way out in the lake. He stands there for a long time, the suitcase beside him, like a traveler at a bus stop. It feels as though the old suitcase contains everything that's left of Rosmarie. The objects have more to do with her than the cold body he saw lying on a metal bed in the hospital a few hours back, reduced to its vital functions. He stoops and picks up the suitcase and walks back down the jetty. Only now does he see, on the side away from the port, a sandbank, with a little fir tree on it, presumably a Christmas tree dumped in the canal after Christmas and now washed up here. He walks through the park, along the canal, and back into the inner city.

The night porter gives Hermann a funny look when he asks for a double room and pays cash, but he asks no questions, only whether he needed a parking spot or a wake-up call. Breakfast was on the sixth floor, from seven o'clock to half past nine. Over the rooftops of the city, he volunteers.

Hermann sits on the bed in his room. He hasn't even taken his shoes off, he feels a little nauseated by the worn carpet and the coverlet that God knows who has sat on before him. The room is small, and the only light is from a dim economy bulb that isn't enough to dispel the darkness. There's a draft, the aluminum windows don't seal properly. Hermann could have gone to a better hotel, but that didn't seem appropriate. Church bells ring nearby. He counts the chimes. Ten. Then eleven. He must have dropped off. Only now does it occur to him that no one knows where he is. He has forgotten his medication, and has had nothing to eat since lunchtime. At least he's filled in the registration form for the porter. If something happened to him, they would be able to trace him. He wonders about calling the hospital and asking about Rosmarie's condition, but he doesn't do it. Presumably

they don't release information over the phone anyway. He
takes off his shoes but not his socks. He hangs his clothes
over the back of a chair. Then he lies down in the bed. The
suitcase is on the pillow next to him, in Rosmarie's place.
He leaves the light on.

WHEN HERMANN WAKES UP the next morning, it's still
dark. Before he gets up, he opens the suitcase and takes
the things out, one after the other, looking at each item
for a long time. He puts on Rosmarie's cardigan, eats the
chocolate bar, reads the blurb on the book jacket. Was
there a family argument between the factory owner and
his son-in-law? Or did the night watchman of the glass-
works pay the price for being such a devoted reader? Hermann turns a few pages and finds an epigraph from Don
Giovanni:

What strange fear
Assails my spirits!
Where do they come from,
Those horrible whirlwinds of flame?

The book is full of Italian words in italics: *maestro,*
canna, servente, l'uomo di notte. Hermann can't imagine

what Rosmarie saw in such nonsense. He puts the book away and takes the underwear out of the suitcase, counts the items, the way you might count days, with a brief lurch of memory.

That morning he washes his hair with Rosmarie's shampoo, he uses the olive oil soap and cleans his teeth with her toothbrush. He doesn't eat any breakfast, he feels a little sick from the chocolate. He is terribly thirsty and drinks three glasses of tap water.

On the train he puts the suitcase on the seat next to him. A lot of people get on in Olten. A young man asks Hermann whether the seat next to him is free. Yes, he says, and he puts the suitcase on his knee. Would you like me to put that on the luggage rack for you? asks the young man. No, says Hermann, more roughly than he intended. He clutches the suitcase for the whole journey, as though someone was going to come and try to take it away from him. He takes it with him when he goes to the bathroom.

IT'S THE HOSPITAL that Hermann was born in, where his children were born. At that time there was only the old building. The long brick building next to it must be from the seventies or early eighties. Hermann walks past the porter, he thinks he can remember the way to intensive care, but then he gets lost and needs to ask a nurse for directions. She asks him if he's feeling all right, and insists on escorting him to the ward. There is no news for him there. The doctor was just in a meeting and would be out in a moment. Did Herr Lehmann want to see his wife? He asks for a glass of water and sits down. A nurse gives him the form he didn't fill out yesterday. It's very important.

Hermann sits in the waiting room, going through a brochure on the early detection of heart attacks, and then he looks at some women's magazines. Franz Beckenbauer is praying for the seriously ill Monica Lierhaus, a TV sports show host Hermann has never heard of. He is not interested in sports, but he reads the article all the same. The woman had a blood clot in her brain, underwent an operation, there were complications, she was put in an artificial coma. Her life is hanging by a thread, the article ends, her closest relatives fear the worst. Why her? it says under the picture of a beautiful young woman with chestnut hair. Hermann feels tears coming on. He clears his throat and tears the page out of the magazine, folds it, and puts it in his pocket. Then he goes with the suitcase into Rosmarie's room. He looks around, there is no one around. He hides the suitcase under the stand with medical equipment, and, without looking back at Rosmarie, leaves the room.

Sweet Dreams

I should have known
I'd never wear your ring
—REBA MCENTIRE

THE CORKSCREW WAS made in the shape of a girl in
a pleated frock of the sort Lara knew from girlhood
pictures of her mother, a short light green summer
dress. Only the red collar didn't really fit, it should have
been embroidered tulle, and white. Lara could see the pictures, big family get-togethers in a garden in the north
of Italy, pictures full of people she didn't know, even her
mother didn't know some of the names. That man was a
neighbor, what was his name again? And aren't those my
mother's cousin Alberto's children, Graziella, Alfina, and
what was the little one called? Antonio? Tonino? The colors were bleached, which made them somehow more garish. It was as though the pictures had caught the sun, the

sun of childhood, pale and ever-present. Thereafter the family had fallen apart, people had gone their separate ways. When Lara had visited Italy with her parents, there hadn't been any more big reunions, only visits in darkened homes with old people who smelled funny and served dry cookies and big plastic bottles of lukewarm Fanta.

The grip on the corkscrew was the girl's head. She had a pageboy cut and a fixed smile. Lara looked at the price tag. They already had a corkscrew, and they hardly ever drank wine. She hesitated for a long while, the shop woman was already eyeing her doubtfully, then she pulled herself together and took it to the register. Is it for a present? asked the woman, unpicking the price tag and dabbing it on the back of her hand. No, Lara shook her head, no need to wrap it, I'll take it like that. She looked at her watch. The bus wasn't due for another half an hour.

Lara worked at the Raiffeisen Bank, and she got off work before Simon, but she liked to wait for him so they could travel home together. Generally, she would sit in the bus shelter, smoke a cigarette, and browse through the free paper. Suddenly she was aware of someone in front of her. She looked up and saw Simon standing there smiling. She jumped up and kissed him on the lips, and he made a remark about her awful habit, sometimes he meant it, at others he was just being flippant. The last few days it had been so cold, she skipped her cherished after-work cigarette and piled into the bus, which was usually standing there when she got to the station. Simon worked in a hi-fi store. After it closed, he needed to tidy things away, and when the boss wasn't there, to do the register. The bus drivers knew him and they waited when they saw him running around the corner. I had to stay and do the till, he would say breathlessly, drop onto the seat, and kiss Lara on the lips. Have you been smoking again? They were sitting right at the back, the row with the three seats together was their favorite. There wasn't much light there, and the noise of the engine muffled their whispering.

Lara hadn't taken off her coat, but still she felt Simon's shoulder against hers. He told her about his day, picky customers and new equipment and an argument with the owner. Lara loved these rides with him, especially in winter, when it was already dark outside, the half hour up and over the ridge through little villages, past meadows with old apple orchards and plowland. The radio was playing a country music song. That was "Sweet Dreams," said the presenter, by Reba McEntire, to whom we are devoting the whole of our show today. Lara kissed Simon and laid her head on his shoulder.

They had been living together for just over four months in a little one-bedroom apartment over the station restaurant not far from the lake. It wasn't ideal, but Simon had wanted to remain in the village he had grown up in, and even though there wasn't much going on in the place, it proved difficult to find anywhere at all. The building was old and run down, the staircase was a mess, with an old freezer unit in the way, and stacks of white plastic chairs for the beer garden, empty cardboard boxes, and lots of other junk. On the second floor there were a couple of rooms for guests, which were rarely taken, and up on the third was their little apartment and a couple of studios. One of these was empty, in the other lived Danica, a young Serbian girl who waited tables in the restaurant. When Lara and Simon first went to look at the apartment, Lara hadn't been able to envisage them living there at all. But after they'd been to look at a couple of other places, all much more expensive, they went back to it. Before they moved in, they repainted all the rooms: the landlady chipped in with paints and brushes and left them a free hand with the decoration. They spent whole evenings talking about various color schemes, but in the end they just painted everything white. The rooms looked cozier right away, and Lara was happy. It was the right time to leave home, even though she got on well with her parents. She was ready to decide her life for herself, buy things, move out.

Lara was twenty-one, Simon three years older. He'd had one girlfriend before Lara, but they hadn't lived together. It wasn't anything serious, he would say if Lara asked. He had lived with his parents so far, and still needed to get used to the fact that clothes didn't wash themselves and the fridge wasn't automatically kept full. But he too seemed to get a kick out of going shopping together on the weekends, and wondering what they would cook today and tomorrow and the next day. Do we need milk? You know, the coffee's almost finished. We're out of garbage bags. Sentences like that had an unexpected charm, and a full shopping cart was like an emblem of the fulfilled life that lay before them. When Simon wheeled it into the underground parking garage, with Lara at his side, she felt a deep pride and a curious satisfaction at being grown up and independent.

They had been to IKEA a couple of times, and bought a mattress and a box spring and various bits and pieces for bathroom and kitchen, lamps and tablecloths and silverware. Simon's parents had given them an old table and four chairs. For a wardrobe they had a set of cheap shelving for which Lara had sewn a curtain of red material. She loved these little tasks, sewing cushion covers, fitting a new toilet seat and a showerhead, putting up posters. Simon would watch her and enjoy it with her. The electrical things were his department.

Every week there would be something new, a barely used coffee machine that Lara found on eBay, a wooden crate for their shoes, a whole stack of yellow bath towels that were on sale. Simon hardly got involved, at most he would say, Do we really need this? Or, How much did you pay for that? It's a mistake to economize on quality, these towels will last us forever. Forever is a long time, answered Simon.

He hadn't brought much into their household, the rented van they had driven first to his parents', then hers, was barely a quarter full of his boxes of clothes, CDs, and old schoolbooks. Most room was taken up by his stereo equipment, the gigantic loudspeakers, and the computer. They bought a TV on the never-never, an ex-showroom model Simon's boss had given them a good price for.

How do you like it? asked Lara, producing the corkscrew from the bag she had next to her on the empty seat. Simon picked it up and played with it, saying nothing. He furrowed his brow, pulled on the screw, and the girl raised her arms. A ballet dancer, he said. No, said Lara, just a girl. Do we even have any wine? That bottle from your parents, said Simon. He was still playing with the thing, pulling the handle up and down, causing the girl to wave her hands, as though cheering or calling for help. Was it expensive? We drank that when Hanni and Martin came, said Lara, don't you remember?

The restaurant downstairs was a bit seedy. Lara and Simon never went there, even though the manageress was their landlady. If they went out anywhere, it was to a place a hundred yards up the road, which did stuffed chicken breasts. They didn't go to the lakeside disco much anymore where they met. During the week they went to bed early, and if they felt like going out dancing on the weekend, they would go to the city, where there were better clubs and where not everyone knew them.

THE BUS STOPPED outside the station, and the driver wished everyone a nice evening over the p.a. and turned off the engine. The passengers got off, said a word or two in parting, and went their separate ways. Lara knew most of them fleetingly, there was only one man she hadn't seen before. He had turned once or twice during the trip and looked at her. When the driver said the next stop was their final destination, he had got up right away and gone to the door, even though the bus was stopping anyway. While the bus took its last few corners, the man stood directly in front of Lara. He held on tight and pressed the Stop button again. He had to be about forty, and with his long black coat didn't seem to really fit in. While she was

studying him, their eyes met. The man seemed quiet, almost indifferent, but in his eyes Lara saw an attentive-
ness and a kind of hunger that were a little disagreeable,
but at the same time provoked her. She turned to Simon,
kissed him, and asked, Will you come to the market with
me tomorrow during your lunch break? She could feel
how her voice sounded artificial and even a bit loud, but
she felt she had to say something. The man in the black
coat was the first to get off the bus. Lara saw him go back
in the direction of the main street. After a few steps he
turned around quickly, as though to see whether she was
following him, and their eyes met once again. Do you
know him? Simon asked. Lara shook her head. The face
looks familiar to me for some reason.

When Lara locked the door after her, she read, as she
did every evening, the handwritten sign that hung there.
PLEASE DON'T THROW BREAD AWAY. Beside the door was
an old cardboard box filled to the top with stale bread.
Lara asked herself what her landlady planned to do with
it. From downstairs came music and the sound of loud
laughter. When folk groups played there on Fridays, they
could hear the racket up in their apartment. Even worse
were the toilet smells in the passage and the smoke that
wended its way up the stairs. Simon had been down to
complain a couple of times, but the landlady just said if

they were that bothered by the smell, they should open a few windows.

Are you hungry? Lara asked. I wouldn't mind a hot bath before dinner, I'm chilled to the bone. The half hour in the bus hadn't been enough to warm her up. I bought some fresh ravioli, they only take three minutes. I had a late lunch, said Simon, I'm not hungry yet. They were standing together in the kitchen, and Lara was putting the shopping away. She held up the corkscrew. Do you like the color? Green, said Simon, and Lara thought about the bleached colors of the Italian photos again. It was forty-five francs, she said. Do you think that's too much? Simon shrugged. You could always get a bottle of wine from the restaurant while I'm in the bath, said Lara, and then we can initiate the corkscrew.

She went to the bathroom, filled the tub, and got undressed. The mirror misted over with condensation, and the smell of pine needles filled the air. She turned off the water, and the apartment suddenly seemed very quiet. Then she heard footsteps and Simon's voice through the half-open door. He said, I'm just going downstairs for the bottle of wine. I thought you'd gone already, said Lara, and she poked her head through the crack, and he kissed her on the lips and tried to barge the door open, but she held it shut. They kissed again. See you in a minute, said

Lara. It was odd, she still felt a little ashamed in front of him. When they went to bed, she would get changed in the bathroom and slip under the sheets next to him in her nightie. She would wait impatiently for him to slide across to her, but she would never dream of taking the initiative.

Before they moved in together, it had all been pretty complicated. She introduced Simon to her parents fairly early on in the game, and they liked him, but he never spent the night under her roof. Lara would have felt ashamed of sleeping with him in her childhood bedroom, she would have been scared of her parents walking in on them, or hearing them, even though they weren't noisy in bed. The times they had slept together were at Simon's. Lara had always felt tense, and jumped at the smallest sound. In the summer, they had done it in the forest a couple of times, but that was uncomfortable, and Lara had felt just as nervous. She had yet to get used to the new freedom. Even now, she was still scared someone would see them or hear them. Sometimes, when Simon was lying on top of her, she pulled the covers up over his head. When he tried to pull them down, she held on to them and said, I'll get cold.

She basked in the warm water, and thought about what still had to be done in the apartment, what they were still missing. She would have liked a bedside table, but that didn't make much sense, as they didn't even have a bed frame. They had seen a colonial-style bed in the furniture store, a sort of four-poster in poplar, with white tulle curtains. A dream, said the salesman, who had approached them and was looking expectantly at them both. That bed came with fitted tables, and a wardrobe as well. But for the moment it was more than they could afford, and Lara wasn't sure if Simon liked it, or if it wasn't a bit girly for him. When they went to see the beds at IKEA, Simon's only question each time had been, Is it strong? Will it hold up? He probably didn't mean it like that, but Lara still felt embarrassed in front of the salesman. We don't need to buy everything at once, she said. So now they had a mattress and box spring on the floor.

After twenty minutes she got out of the bath and pulled the plug. She dried herself on one of the big yellow bath towels. It wasn't actually a color she liked, that slighty off-, mustardy yellow. But you couldn't argue about the quality, the quality was excellent. She had put them through the wash a couple of times, and they still felt brand new. Lara had to think about what Simon said: Forever is a long time. Presumably the towels would outlast their relationship, she thought, and that gave her a shock. She loved Simon, and he loved her, but was there any guarantee that he would still love her in five or ten years' time? Her notions of the future were both very precise and very vague. She wanted children, and a home, and she wanted to go on working part-time once the children were there. In a few years she would get her promotion, and maybe one day she would become branch manager. But all that seemed very far off, a different life. Sometimes she would ask herself if Simon had the same sort of dreams as she did. It made her suspicious when he said, Let's just see, *que sera sera*, we're still young. In fact he felt as strange to her as this apartment that was only slowly turning into home. She never knew exactly what he wanted, he didn't talk much about himself, it was only when he was together with his friends that he seemed perfectly natural and relaxed.

She wrapped the towel around her, rinsed her hair in the sink, and put it up. Suddenly she felt a longing for Simon, she wanted to throw her arms around him, lie in bed with him, and press herself against him. She went to the kitchen, but he wasn't there. Simon, she called, and went into the living room and then the bedroom. Simon? He must still be down in the restaurant, he was sure to be back any moment. She sat at the table, leafed through the free paper she had picked up at the bus station. One ex–Miss Switzerland wanted to climb Kilimanjaro to raise money for a children's cancer hospital, Prince William had worn a toupee for a portrait photographer, or so at least the newspaper claimed, an American was put to death for a murder he had committed twenty-five years ago. Under the headline Gruesome Find on Lake, there was a story about a trout fisherman who had stumbled upon a dead body in the water just offshore. The policemen who pulled the body in were quoted as saying that the dead man had been missing for a couple of months. Presumably it was suicide, though accidental death was also a possibility. The water temperature wasn't above thirty-eight or forty degrees, if you fell in you wouldn't last more than a few minutes.

A drop of water fell from Lara's hair to the picture of the yachting marina where the body had been found. With a shudder she pushed the newspaper away. She had to think about that man being found in the water no more than a few hundred yards away, while she and Simon were getting moved in, or eating their supper, or making love. She felt cold in her towel. There was only a gas heater in the apartment, and the windows were not exactly insulated. Lara went into the kitchen and put on the water for ravioli. She took two plates from the cupboard and a couple of forks off the draining board, and scrubbed at a stain on one of the units, but it wouldn't budge. The kitchen was from the seventies, and you could scrub away at it as much as you liked, it never got completely clean. Lara went to the bathroom, blow-dried her hair, and put on some clothes.

SHE SNEAKED DOWN the creaking staircase. She didn't turn on the landing light, she didn't want to be seen. The music had stopped, and the voices had quieted down too. She had almost reached the bottom when the door to the bar opened, and she saw the backlit silhouette of an enormous man. At the same moment, the light went on. The man had a flushed complexion, he pulled the door shut behind him, and passed her without a word on his way to the gents, as though he hadn't seen her. The voice of the landlady was loud and distinct. He didn't recognize him right away, she was saying, because the man was lying face down. In summer he would probably have bobbed up sooner. Lara pushed open the door to the bar and stepped inside.

There were half a dozen men at the bar and at one or two tables, and Lara was alarmed because they were all looking at her; but then she realized their attention was on the landlady, behind the bar. She was talking about something else now. They ought to poison that son of a bitch, she said, to teach him what it feels like. Those poor dogs. Lara had seen the tabloid headline: ANIMAL HATER STRIKES AGAIN. She saw Simon standing on one of the benches along the wall, his head obscured by an enormous TV mounted on the ceiling. Right behind him and looking up at him stood Danica, the waitress. Even though they were neighbors, Lara had only run into her once or twice on the stairs. Sometimes she heard her footsteps on the landing late at night, but there was never any sound from the studio. Danica had come to Switzerland from Serbia with her parents when she was little, she told Lara and Simon the first time they met. She hadn't managed to find an apprenticeship, even though she had good grades. Do you think she's attractive? Lara had asked Simon later. Other women don't interest me, he replied. But surely you've got an opinion? I don't know, he said. I think she's got bedroom eyes, said Lara, and Simon laughed and kissed her.

Simon seemed to be doing something with the TV. After a while, he jumped off the bench and said something to Danica. She smiled and switched the TV on, and together they looked at the screen, which was showing a grainy picture of a downhill skier. Simon spotted Lara and went over to her. A faulty connection, he said, and when she looked at him in bemusement, the TV's on the blink. He turned to the landlady and said the antenna wire's bent, he could bring her a new one tomorrow. Isn't it practical having a workman in the house? said the landlady. What will you have to drink? A glass of red? I was going to buy a bottle of wine, said Simon. It's on the house, said the landlady. And the young lady? Simon looked at Lara, and then he said I'd rather have a beer, and to Lara, Are you hungry? Sit down the pair of you, said the landlady, dunking a glass in murky dishwater and pouring a large beer.

There wasn't a free table, so Simon sat down opposite an old man who seemed to have had a few already. Lara slid in on the bench next to him. She asked me if I would take a look at the TV, he said half apologetically. A faulty connection. I thought you weren't coming back, said Lara. She sounded reproachful, which she didn't mean to be. She had promised herself that she wouldn't be clingy with Simon. He had just wanted to help out. She was sorry she'd come down. If she'd stayed upstairs, he would surely not have accepted the landlady's offer, and would have returned right away. Danica stepped up to the table, bringing Simon's beer and a glass of wine for Lara. The landlady and the men were still talking about the poisoned dogs, and what the authorities should do to the guilty party if they caught him. The drunk at their table said under his breath that he could think of a couple of dogs he wouldn't mind poisoning. Lara wasn't sure it was for their hearing, and she didn't reply. She felt her hair, which was still a little bit damp.

For no obvious reason, the drunk started talking about a cruise he'd gone on almost twenty years ago, on the Black Sea. It was dull, those cruises were pretty un-eventful. I've been in the Crimea, in Sebastopol, where the Russians have a navy base and submarines. That was an experience, that was worth it. Simon didn't seem to be listening, he drank his beer and looked up at the TV set, where a different skier was on the piste. From the loud-speaker came the sound of cowbells and the rhythmic shouts of supporters. Lara wasn't sure where the Black Sea was.

Danica appeared at their table, and filled up Lara's glass before she was able to say no thank you. Now she was sitting there foolishly with her hand over the full glass. She hadn't had anything to eat since lunchtime, and she could feel the alcohol going to her head. Will you have another beer? Danica asked. Simon glanced quickly up at Lara, as though he needed her permission. Then he said, Yes, sure, and half got up. Will you excuse me, I'll be back in a moment. Lara let him out. No sooner had she sat down again than the drunk asked if she was from hereabouts, he hadn't seen her before. She felt ill at ease in the bar, threatened by the loud landlady and the drunken men who were ogling her. I grew up in Kreuzlingen, she said. The man held out his hand and said Manfred was his name. She shook it and said Lara. *Dr. Zhivago*, he said. That was a nice film. With Omar Sharif, and . . . who was she again? Julie Christie, said Lara. In the streetcar. The drunk smiled. I have a sister in Kreuzlingen. Have you ever been to Russia? No, said Lara.

She wanted to say something else, it would make her feel safer if she was talking, but she couldn't think of anything. Where is the Black Sea again? she asked finally. If you're coming from the Mediterranean, you pass Istanbul and go through the Bosporus, then you're in the Black Sea. The south shore is Turkey, and in the north are Bulgaria, Romania, Ukraine, and Russia. Have you been to all those places? asked Lara. I went on that cruise, said Manfred, that's where I met my wife. She's Ukrainian. She was working on the ship. But that didn't work out. Danica came back and asked if they wanted anything. Both shook their heads. When she was gone, Manfred said in a whisper, I tell you, those women from the East, and then he laid his finger across his lips.

Lara was relieved when Simon finally returned. She thought he might have gone to the bathroom, but he was holding a dirty white cable in one hand. He had a brief word with the landlady, and then he climbed up on the bench once more and switched the cables. For a moment, there was just a streaky gray on the screen, then the picture suddenly came clear, and the sound seemed even louder than before to Lara. Simon punched through a few channels on the remote, probably to check that the reception was uniformly good. There was a brief glimpse of two men sitting facing each other. Lara was almost sure that one of them was the man in the black coat, on the bus. But the scene disappeared immediately, to be replaced by a woman arguing with a little girl, and then a group of soldiers sneaking through a forest, and then back to the skiing. Simon returned to the table. I just remembered I had an old cable lying around, he said, and smiled in satisfaction. Shall we go? said Lara, getting to her feet.

The landlady didn't want any money for the bottle of wine. It's in return for the cable, she said, giving Lara and Simon her hand, which felt soft and a bit soapy from the washing up. Don't do anything I wouldn't do, one of the men called after them as they left the bar, and everyone laughed.

THE WATER WAS BOILING violently, half of it had evaporated already, leaving a white chalky line at the top of the saucepan. Lara quickly turned off the gas. Never ever leave the stove on when you go out, not even for a second, said Simon. As if Lara didn't know that. It's not my fault, she said, I thought you'd be back right away. She felt like crying. I didn't mean it like that, said Simon, and kissed her. Nothing happened. Lara turned away and picked up the corkscrew. Simon watched alertly as she took the plastic seal off the bottle. She had to overcome her own resistance to place her thumb over the girl's face and apply enough strength to insert the screw into the cork. She looked Simon in the eye, let him see how furious she was. I'm sorry, he said, I know, it's my fault. She set down the bottle and said, as if in conciliation, You do it. Simon put on a rather ceremonious expression, as though God knows what surprise was in store, and slowly pushed down on the girl's arms. With a bright popping sound, the cork came out of the bottle.

Simon looked at Lara with a grin. She threw her arms around him and started to kiss him, went on repeatedly kissing him, and tried to undo the buttons on his shirt. Simon, not looking where he was putting it, laid aside the corkscrew, and with their mouths glued together they undressed each other and let their clothes drop to the floor. Simon almost fell over as he wriggled out of his tight jeans, he was only just able to catch himself on Lara, who was impatiently tugging at the hooks on her bra. When they were both naked, Lara lay down on the coconut matting they had bought at IKEA, and Simon knelt between her legs. He tried to enter her, but couldn't. Wouldn't you rather go on the bed? he asked. Wait, said Lara, and she disappeared into the living room and came back with one of the sofa cushions. She lay down again and pushed the cushion under her bum. The matting was rough, and Lara could feel it scratching her back, but she didn't care. Soon Simon rolled off her and lay next to her, and she understood he had come.

She was still aroused, and stroked him until he was hard again. This time she sat on top of him. Simon didn't seem to be really focused, but she didn't care. She rode him till she could no longer feel the burning in her knees, and sensed the blood rushing to her face. She shut her eyes and moved more and more vigorously, it was as though it was all happening inside her head, as though all her sensations were merging into one overwhelming feeling. Then she heard herself scream loudly, and dropped panting onto Simon, her head beside his, not daring to look him in the eye. For a while she lay like that, then her breathing came more evenly, and she could feel her body again, the pain in her knees and the chill against her back. She sat up. Simon looked at her in astonishment, and asked with a smile, Did the earth move for you, then? She laid a finger across his mouth. Her face grew very earnest, and she said, If you stop loving me ever, I want you to promise to tell me. But I do love you, protested Simon. I mean, because you never know what will happen, Lara said. And now I have to put something on, or I'll catch cold.

In the bathroom, she saw that the pattern of the coconut matting was imprinted across her back, and that her knees were scraped open and sore. She thought of taking a shower, but for now she just put on a fresh pair of panties and pulled on her dressing gown. When she went back to the kitchen, Simon had got dressed, put on fresh water, and laid the table. He poured two glasses of wine and passed her one, and they toasted each other. Here's to us. The wine was awful.

Lara didn't sit facing Simon as she usually did, but beside him, and she kept touching him during the meal, grazing his arm or stroking his neck and back. After it was over, they stayed sitting for a long time and talking. Lara was bubbly, she spoke more quickly and volubly than usual. I think I must be a bit drunk, she said. I'd better look out then, hadn't I, said Simon with a smile. Shall we go to bed?

Simon went to the bathroom and came back in pajamas. Lara didn't feel like brushing her teeth. She just pulled

off her dressing gown and slid into bed with Simon. He
lay on his back and she pressed herself against him,
pushing her hand in under his pajama top and stroking
his chest. Are you tired? she asked. Yes, said Simon, and
with that he turned onto his side and soon his breathing was calm and even. Lara didn't feel at all tired. After
lying there awake for a time, she got up and made herself
a cup of tea in the kitchen. Then she went to the living
room and turned on the TV. She zapped her way through
the programs. It was mostly films and talk shows. Lara
stopped for a while at one station with phone-sex ads, and
watched the women rubbing their breasts and moaning
Call me, call me. For once, she didn't feel disgusted, on
the contrary she felt a kind of sympathy or solidarity with
the women, which surprised her. She clicked onward,
and suddenly there was the man from the bus again. It
was the local channel, which recycled all its programs
every hour. The studio was in the old town, not far away.
Lara knew the host by sight, he used to be a teacher,
Simon had gone to his school.

She listened for a while before it dawned on her that
the guest on the show had to be a writer. She'd never
heard his name before. The host's questions were often
longer than the man's short, factual replies. Again, Lara
was caught by his alert look, which had got her attention

on the bus. Asked where he got the ideas for his stories, he said he found them on the street. Only today, on the bus to the studio, there was this young couple, two perfectly ordinary young people, sitting together and talking terribly earnestly. They reminded me of my youth, a woman I wanted to marry and have kids with. Then something got in the way. But I never felt so sure of anything as I did then, before I really knew the first thing about living.

He imagined the couple had only just moved in together, they were furnishing their apartment and buying things for it, and maybe with slight astonishment contemplating all the years that lay ahead of them, asking themselves whether their relationship would last. It's that blissful but slightly anxious moment of starting out that interests me, said the writer, maybe I'll write a story about it. And how will the story end? asked the host. The writer shrugged. I'll only know that when I've finished it.

He said young couples sometimes resembled very old couples, perhaps because they both had to deal with uncertainty. The host asked if it wasn't tricky writing from life. The writer shook his head. He wasn't painting a portrait of these two individuals. They had given him an idea for something, but they had nothing to do with the people he might write about in his story. In actual fact they weren't a couple at all, he said. They got off at two different stops and kissed each other on the cheek.

Lara heard the last train pull in. Quarter to one. She went up to the window and saw the train standing there, with no one getting on or off. After a while, it silently pulled away. The writer would have gone home long ago, even while he continued to speak on the TV. For a month they would keep replaying the conversation with him in an endless loop, until he himself had become just as much an imaginary figure as Lara and Simon.

Coney Island

TEAR OFF THE cardboard match in the matchbook, turn it around without looking at it. Your thumb knows the way. It recognizes the under edge of the flap, and then stops on the head of the match, and presses it against the emery board. A rasp, and the thumb jerks back, allows the match head some air to burst into flame. Carry the flame, hidden in the hollow of your hand, to the tip of your cigarette. A quick first drag, not inhaling. The flame lengthens in the air current, and quickly collapses in on itself, grows darker, having moved on to the fibrous cardboard. Then it goes out in the wind.

Sit on a lump of granite. Your legs drawn up, your arms around your knees. The cigarette in your right hand, between index and middle finger. The left hand first laid over the right, holding on to it, then it relaxes its grip, dangles down toward your knee, and stops there, hanging. The tips of your fingers not resting on your knee, so much as merely brushing against it. The cigarette hand approaches your mouth and turns through ninety degrees. As soon as the cigarette is gripped between your lips, the fingers let go. The hand stays where it is, the head turns away. By a slight forward movement of the lower jaw, the cigarette is ever so slightly raised. The head returns, the fingers lock, take back the cigarette, which detaches itself first from the lower then the top lip. The arm slowly falls back. The hands join again. Smoke flows out of the mouth, and while the right thumb flicks the cigarette filter and then lets it go, and the cigarette bounces and loose ash is dislodged from the burning cone of tobacco, the lower lip half pushes over the upper lip and wipes away the sensation left there by the touch of the cigarette.

The ash falls onto the rock, a few flakes of it break away, tumble down over the rock, driven by the wind and the unevenness of the granite, and fall over an edge and out of sight. The wind, coming off the land, has picked up. The few people walking on the beach are all heading toward me, as though we had arranged to meet here, only subtly changing direction when they have almost reached me, and walking past me. The flat waves make a feeble splash as they crest and spread out. In the distance there's the wail of a siren. One man flies a kite, another walks over the beach with a metal detector. He walks slowly to and fro, following some system that only he knows. It's twenty to three on October 21, 2002.

The granite block is one of several that have been dropped into the sea every couple of hundred yards or so. A Spanish-speaking family has stopped near me, a man, a woman, and two little girls. They laugh, talk, feed the gulls, which are squawking greedily and fighting for pieces of bread with jagged motions.

Down by the sea, two young women have been taking pictures of each other. Then they draw nearer. One walks past me, the other asks if she can take my picture. Her companion stops to watch. Her eyes are staring and the corners of her mouth are turned down with impatience or dismay. Her face looks like a skull.

The one taking the picture stands with feet apart. The camera masks her face. She doesn't take forever framing the image, just squeezes the release, once, and again. I ask, Do you want me to smile? She shakes her head. No, she says. Just the way you are. That's perfect.

Also available from Granta Books
www.grantabooks.com

SEVEN YEARS

Peter Stamm
Translated by Michael Hofmann

'*Seven Years* is a novel to make you doubt your own dogma.
What more can a novel do than that?' Zadie Smith

Alex is caught between two very different women. Sonia, his
wife, is intelligent, beautiful, charming, and ambitious. Together
they have established a prestigious architecture firm and a life
of luxury. But long hours and failed attempts at starting a
family bring about the seven-year itch, and soon Alex begins an
affair with dull, passive Ivona, with devastating consequences.

'A quietly shattering meditation on the depths of desire'
The Times

'I love this novel . . . It has the makings of an existential classic'
Sunday Telegraph

'Cool and immensely accomplished' Adam Mars-Jones, *Observer*

'Quietly spectacular' *New Yorker*

Also available from Granta Books
www.grantabooks.com

ALL DAYS ARE NIGHT

Peter Stamm
Translated by Michael Hofmann

Gillian seems to have it all – she is beautiful, successful, and
securely married. But one night, after an argument with her
husband, their car crashes on a wet road, and everything is lost.
When she wakes in the hospital, she is a widow with a ruined
face, and no way back to the person she thought she was. It is
only when she begins to piece together the painful shards of
her present existence and revisit a relationship from her past
that she is able to glimpse the freedom that might come
with her loss.

From the master of unadorned storytelling, *All Days Are Night* is
a quietly disquieting exploration of identity, inside and out.

Keep in touch with
Granta Books:

Visit grantabooks.com to discover more.

GRANTA